TRUTH OR DARE

VOLUME 1

LEE BRAZIL

TRUTH OR DARE

VOLUME 1

LEE BRAZIL

Includes

-KEEPING HOUSE-

-TELLLING THE TRUTH-

-GIVING UP-

This is a work of fiction. Names, characters, places, and incidents are products of the author's imagination or are used fictitiously and are not to be construed as real. Any resemblance to actual events, locales, organizations, or persons, living or dead, is entirely coincidental.

Truth or Dare
Copyright© 2011 Lee Brazil

ISBN: 978-1-77101-034-4

Printed in the United States of America

Breathless Press
www.breathlesspress.com

CONTENTS

DEDICATED AS ALWAYS TO E, FOR
GIVING ME THE OPPORTUNITY
TO FULFILL MY DREAMS.

KEEPING HOUSE

Poker Night at the Blakes'

The door slamming behind Mischa Blake drew all his brothers' attention to him. He sauntered slowly into the room, resisting the urge to run his hand over the hair he knew damn well still stood in four-inch spikes down the center of his head to the nape of his neck. He met each pair of familiar green eyes defiantly, refusing to look away.

"Hey," Mischa offered, hoping his voice wouldn't squeak.

"Damn it, Mischa!" Terry, Chief Financial Officer of the family-owned production studio that employed every member of the Blake family—except Mischa—immediately leaned away as Mischa took the seat at the green baize game table right next to him. "You stink! Where the hell have you been?"

Dan, the creative brother, studio scriptwriter, the brother most like Mischa in personality—though even that was a stretch—leaned in and sniffed appraisingly. "Somewhere that beer and pot are readily had in great quantities, judging by the smell."

Brandon, eldest brother, CEO of the studio, and all-around royal pain in Mischa's ass, frowned in disapproval. "Are you hanging out in those clubs again? Damn—the fucking paparazzi would love to catch you in some club. I can see the headlines now. 'Blake's Youngest Son—Underage Alcoholic and Drug Addict—Caught in Gay Sex Club Scandal'."

Mischa scowled in return, clicking the stud in his tongue against his front teeth, just because he knew it annoyed Terry. "Fuck you all. Are we playing poker or not?"

Wednesday night poker games among the Blake brothers were a long-standing tradition. With all the other traditions Mischa rebelled against, he couldn't fathom why he'd rather die than miss this weekly game with his brothers. Not that he'd let them know that, though. He made it a habit of either showing up late or insisting on leaving early—as though they were an added burden he could scarcely make time for in his busy life.

He reached to his back pocket for his wallet and realized almost immediately that he must have left it behind. Instead he reached for Terry's wallet on the table to his right and rifled through it for cash to buy in.

"What the hell?" Terry demanded. "Are you broke already? I just deposited money in your account yesterday!"

"No. I'm good, for a while anyway. Just forgot my wallet. And you wouldn't have to deposit money in my account all the time if you'd just loosen up the controls there and give me direct access to my money." Millions of dollars in a trust fund and he had to beg for cash from his brothers before he could make a purchase, at least until he was thirty-five—fifteen long years from now. He pulled a wad of hundred dollar bills from the leather wallet and tossed them on the table.

Terry grabbed the wallet back, muttering dire insults under his breath. "You're paying that back."

Mischa smirked and loudly clicked his piercing. "You'll end up owing it to me in a few hours anyway!"

Brandon, Dan, and Terry did the older brother thing. Their gazes met in a circle around the table that excluded Mischa, and he flushed.

"Want to put your money where your mouth is, kid?" That was Brandon, pushing his buttons as only an older sibling can. He hated being reminded he was so much younger than his brothers.

"I'm not a kid. I'm an adult, a licensed driver, and a registered voter." He forced the words out, trying not to scream them. He'd made the same protest so many times before.

"When you support yourself and don't live off a trust fund, you're an adult. Until then, you're another rich kid with too much money and time on your hands."

"Hey! You guys all have trust funds too! If having one makes me a kid, then you're kids." He fucking knew he wasn't going to win this one; he never did.

"We also have careers with futures. You have nothing but a trust fund." That was Terry, putting in his two cents. Fuck that. Terry knew the value of a dollar—probably figured his two cents was actually worth two dollars.

"I'm an artist." That was the answer he gave his mother every time she asked, and it always resulted in an indulgent smile. She and his father had taken it into their heads to retire in the French Riviera last year, but they had traveled and been on set so much during his childhood that Brandon had really stood in more of a parental role than his parents.

"Bull shit." Brandon spoke again.

Mischa glared at Dan who was busily shuffling cards and had been for the past five minutes. "Fucking deal already so these assholes have something to think about besides my life and how they can ruin it."

Dan cleared his throat and swiftly dealt the cards around the table. "You guys up for a little side bet?"

Mischa peeked at his cards then turned to Dan, who's face was impassive, but there was no denying he was up to something.

Terry chimed in, equally impassive. "Money means nothing to us as the kid has pointed out, so how about we play for Truth or Dare?"

Brandon was nodding before Terry had even finished speaking. "Yeah, last hand of the night. Winner's choice. Loser pays a penalty to each of the players if he chickens out."

It was a plot. Somehow, they were all in it together, and he was going to come out on the bottom of this. While he considered his options, he picked absently at the loose threads in the rips of the five-hundred dollar black jeans he'd bought, cut, and pinned back together. He had to make some move to salvage the situation, because protesting the game would mean he really was just a kid. The rules had to be established at the beginning and he had to find a way to slant them in his favor.

"And if the loser follows through, he gets to claim a boon from each of the other players." It was the best he could do, and he knew exactly what boon he'd ask for too, because he was damn sure his brothers were going to manipulate him into losing. No way could his brothers come up with a dare he wouldn't fulfill. He'd do anything. There was no truth he wasn't willing to tell. This could definitely be worked to his advantage either way the chips fell. And if the cards fell in his favor tonight, his brothers better look because he had some pretty good dares he could lay on his superior older brothers.

Two hours later, his chances of being the big winner of the night looked good. Despite losing the last hand, he'd turned Terry's thousand dollars into twelve thousand and was easily way ahead of his brothers for the night.

Terry shoved his chair back from the table. "Okay, guys, I'm done. That was the last hand."

Brandon and Dan made agreeing noises and Mischa stiffened in shock. Fuck. He was screwed.

"Wait a minute... You guys usually play a lot later than this. I mean, it's only eleven o'clock!"

"Nope." Brandon shook his head. "You usually leave around this time, and we always quit when you leave."

If that was the last hand, which he'd lost, that meant he'd *really* lost.

Dan nodded in agreement. "And I make Brandon out as the winner of that hand, and you as the loser, squirt. So what'll it be, Brandon, truth or dare?"

It was so fake. So fucking staged, it was obvious. He'd been set up. The first hand he lost was destined to be the last hand they played no matter how many it took or how few.

Brandon was a terrible actor. He smiled as he spoke lines that had probably been written by Dan expressly for the occasion. "Well, brother, I'm going to have to say dare. But we should name the penalties before I tell him the dare, don't you think?"

"Oh, yeah," Terry was outwardly smirking now. "If you welsh on the dare, you owe one penalty per player, kid. Then I get to give you a complete makeover, new clothes, new hair, whole new style."

Surveying his brother's style —navy-blue Brooks Brothers suit, crisp white cotton shirt, Italian silk tie, and neatly trimmed blond hair—Mischa shuddered. He turned to Brandon, next brother seated at the round table, and quirked a pierced left brow in what he hoped was a sardonic Spock-like inquiry and not a laughable dumb, younger brother affectation.

Brandon smoothly responded with an elevated right brow and cough into his fist. "If you welsh, you take the assistant producer's job I've been holding open for you since you graduated high school. Join the family business and make yourself useful."

Damn. That was even worse. He held his breath momentarily before turning to Dan. Dan could swing either way. He was the brother who understood Mischa best, but he was also the cleverest, most devious, and creative of the brothers. No doubt he was the mastermind behind this whole plot.

Dan smiled broadly, tapping the playing cards against his chin gently, as he considered his youngest brother. "If you welsh, brother, you attend the college of my choice for a full four years—or until you attain a degree, whichever comes first."

"That's a bit harsh!" Mischa protested. "Because I lost a single hand of cards, you guys expect to run my life to suit yourselves for an infinite amount of time?"

"Oh, no," Brandon interjected smoothly. "We expect you to honor your debts, brother. Are you saying that you aren't up to the dare? You don't even know what it is yet."

Good point. Given the penalties though, Mischa was pretty sure the dare was going to be something he would really hate.

"Okay. What's the dare?"

They did it again, the older brother, silent communication thing. This time Dan broke the silence.

"We dare you to get a job and support yourself without relying on your trust fund for a whole year."

Mischa's mouth fell open. "That's all I have to do? Get a job?"

Terry shook his head. "No. You have to support yourself. No more sending your bills to me to pay. No more monthly deposits into your account. Take care of yourself."

If Terry had deposited his usual allowance into his account yesterday, that meant he had fifty thousand, plus the twelve on the table in front of him, to get through the next year. "What if I can't find a job? I mean, I'll make every effort to find one, but what if I don't get one?"

"Nope. Have to get a job." Brandon was insistent.

"But I have plenty of money to get through a year... even if I don't find a job."

Terry shook his head again. "No. You don't. You don't have any idea how much your lifestyle costs, do you? The money I put in your account this morning won't last you a month at the rate you normally spend it. When the money you have now is gone, that's it. If you don't find a job, you'll be living a very different lifestyle next month, with a new hairstyle and a new wardrobe to match."

No freaking way. He'd find a way to beat his brothers at their own game.

CHAPTER ONE

Getting a Job

Donovan Holloway flung the heavy oak front door of his new dream home open with a *thud*. He peered at the extremely tardy final interviewee for the position of housekeeper and groaned inwardly.

"Yes?" He didn't have time for neighborhood boys selling magazines, cookies, or candy bars, even if they were sexy as hell. The kid at the door might, *might*, have been seventeen. He should just shut the door and hope the kid went away. Shutting the door on temptation incarnate seemed like a damn good idea.

Wearing a tight, black T-shirt, black skinny jeans, and black skate shoes, his visitor carried a skateboard under one arm and a black backpack hung off the other. His head was shaved on both sides, leaving an ink black strip down the center that, despite the rain, stood in four-inch porcupine spikes. He was pale, his eyes red-rimmed, and he was drenched. Damn. That wet look sure looked good on him. Pervert! *Note to self—get out of the office and get laid this weekend.*

Donovan stepped back, prepared to slam the door, but

something sad in those green eyes gave him pause. "Hey, are you alright? Do you need help?" He scanned the quiet neighborhood, looking for a reason the kid might be knocking on his door, envisioning gangs of hoodlums stalking the as-yet-silent boy through the upscale neighborhood.

He shuddered, and then swallowed audibly before speaking. "I'm Mischa Blake."

Donovan stared, uncomprehending.

"Mikhail?" Deep green eyes stared at Donovan expectantly. When no response was forthcoming, he added, "Michael? Blake? I have an interview?"

Donovan shoved his hand into the pocket of his trousers and pulled out a pink phone slip from his secretary. M. Blake was his sixth scheduled interview for the position of housekeeper-cook-gardener.

The first applicant, a beady-eyed battle-ax, had taken one look around his yard and at the clutter in his house yet to be unpacked, and announced that she most emphatically did not work for pigs.

He knew the place was a mess. He'd found his ranch-style house on the market at the right price and decided to celebrate his recent promotion to vice president of the advertising agency he'd worked for, for the past twenty years. He moved out of the tiny apartment he'd lived in for years and into a real home. It was the house he'd imagined owning so often as a kid, with a large yard, open floor plan, huge kitchen, four bedrooms, three bathrooms, gorgeous picture windows, and vaulted ceilings.

Of course, in his childhood fantasies, the house had been occupied by him and a beautiful wife—a golden-haired, blue-eyed, petite Florence Henderson look-alike—and a bevy of beautiful, intelligent children. He'd suffered a minor setback at seventeen when he discovered he was gay, but after due consideration, he replaced Florence with Phillip Henderson and had been instantly back in business.

The housekeeping candidate hadn't cared about his dream-turned-nightmare. She'd flounced out before he could even give her the job description. The second applicant had sat sipping coffee in his office, murmuring noncommittally in response to his job description for several moments. He nurtured high hopes for the middle-aged lady, until she abruptly interrupted him to demand: "Are you one of them? Because I'm looking at you, and I'm guessing, Myrtle, he's one of them. You're a *gay man,* aren't you?"

He'd sat in stunned silence, mouth hanging open a bit too long as she began to spout fire and brimstone and call upon God to wreak his vengeance on all sodomites. She'd still been spewing vitriol as he clasped her elbow and hustled her from his home office to the front door and out onto the sidewalk.

"I'm looking for someone to cook a few meals and scrub the toilets, not validate my existence!" He called after her and then slammed the door.

The third applicant hadn't spoken a word of English, and since he had zero chance of learning to speak Hmong, he'd nodded, shaken his head, and hustled her out the door as quickly as he could as well. The fourth applicant had been a no-show. It was depressing. He'd really screwed up his chances of fulfilling his lifelong dream by purchasing the house before he'd found the Phillip Henderson to manage it!

Hiring a housekeeper to manage his home life, much as his secretary managed his business life, was a brilliant option. The housekeeper could handle the dream house that had become a nightmare, and he could concentrate on finding that Phillip Henderson after he got his work life sorted out again.

Instead, the only candidate he would even consider hiring had been the fifth. She'd been a perfectly wonderful grandmotherly type who'd labeled him adorable and patted him on the cheek like he was a six-year-old boy instead of a forty-year-old businessman. He'd fallen more than a little in love with her the moment her soft, wrinkled hand patted his cheek so sweetly. Unfortunately, she looked to be about ninety-six, and delicate—as though her spun sugar, white hair would melt in the rain. He'd have felt guilty as hell asking her to clean up after him. He'd kept her number, just in case he could come up with a reason to invite her back over after his house was in order. She'd be the perfect grandmother figure for the children he had yet to adopt. *Phillip Henderson, where are you?*

Sighing, he looked up from the scrap of paper. "You're applying to be my housekeeper?"

Mischa/Mikhail/Michael nodded, shook his head, and then with a deep breath visibly forced himself to be still. "More like a butler and/or personal assistant, sir."

Butler? What the hell? Who had butlers in today's world? Whatever. Could he just get rid of the kid? An underage temptation walking around his house wouldn't be a good idea.

"I'll be honest with you, kid. I'm looking for someone a little more mature."

"I'm older than I look." The boy wasn't taking a hint.

"Okay. Why don't you come on back to the kitchen?" He'd conducted the other interviews in his office, but couldn't see the drenched kid sitting in his leather chairs or dripping on his plush new white carpet.

"Oh, yeah." Mischa dropped his battered skateboard on the porch next to the door and stepped over the threshold.

Donovan gestured for this latest applicant to precede him down the hall and closed the door behind them. He walked carefully, skirting the unpacked boxes and observing the layers of dust. Donovan strolled behind him, taking in the view as he went. Tight butt, slim legs, straight back, nice swimmer's build. Mischa might well have been Phillip, if it weren't for the Goth garb, piercings, green eyes, and black Mohawk, that is.

Seated at the breakfast bar in the kitchen, he studied his prospective employee. First things first. "How old are you?"

Mischa shrugged. "I'm twenty. Is there an age requirement for this job?"

Donovan started to say yes, that would be the easy way out, but the words of the personnel director he'd spent many hours with since his promotion taunted him. *Equal opportunity is the law, not a choice, Mr. Holloway.* He hummed under his breath instead.

"So, tell me why you want to work for me." That should give him pause.

"I don't. My brothers dared me to get a job, and it's been a lot harder than I expected. I just came from a McDonalds where the manager had a guy with a BS cleaning the toilets and an MBA flipping burgers. The economy sucks." Mischa sounded dejected.

"Ahh." He wanted a job on a dare? What the hell? Who told a prospective employer they didn't want to work for them? "Let me tell you a little about the parameters of the job."

Mischa gazed at him quietly, waiting. Maybe the daunting aspects of the task would send the kid the way of the first applicant. "You'll be responsible for preparing meals. I eat breakfast at six, daily, take a boxed lunch to work, and expect a minimum of a three-course dinner. Sometimes I have guests, and occasionally dinner parties." He didn't really, but threw out the possibility anyway. For a moment, he was distracted by the amusing vision of a room full of elegantly clad clients and coworkers staring in horror as a Goth-garbed Mischa, hair spiked and piercings glittering in the candlelight, announced that dinner was served.

"Got it. Cooking. I can do that." Mischa seemed to be trying to convince himself, as much as Donovan, of that fact.

"You'll have to do the shopping. I don't have time for things like that. Then there's the cleaning. I expect the house to be spotless at all times." He assiduously ignored the fact that the house was currently anything but clean.

Mischa wasn't inclined to be so kind, though. He glanced pointedly around the kitchen, at the stack of dirty dishes in the sink, the debris from several takeout meals on the counter tops, and the unpacked boxes of kitchenware. "Okay. Clean. I can do that."

"I need the house put together too. The boxes," he waved around, "unpacked and stuff put away. The walls painted, furniture ordered and assembled and put in place."

Mischa looked shocked. "You trust me to decorate your house?"

"No. I have the plans here." He thumped the red, leather-bound album on the marble counter that held the dream house drawings he'd labored on over the years. "I need my housekeeper to coordinate the workmen, decorators, deliveries and so on."

More nods. "I can do that."

Donovan stared helplessly at the kid. *Stop calling him kid. It's too pervy.* What else? "References? Do you have references?"

Mischa bent over and the tight black T-shirt rode up as the skinny jeans inched down. Damn. All that creamy, white flesh—hairless and smooth—tempted him to reach out and touch, to examine the texture and resiliency. He wondered if there were any more shiny piercings hidden under that severe, black garb.

"Hey," Mischa was waving a handful of papers in front of his face, and Donovan flushed slightly. Could Mischa tell he'd been staring inappropriately at his exposed skin?

"I'll, ahh, I'll keep these. I need to call on them later." He searched desperately for something, anything, to turn the kid-man off the idea of working for him. Recalling the indignation and vitriol of the second applicant, he took a shot in the dark and threw it out there. "I'm gay."

No response.

"I said I'm gay, a homosexual, a flamer."

No response. Just inquiring green gaze locked on his face. Someone must have told the kid–man that eye contact was important.

"I sleep with other men?" Shit now he was turning statements as questions.

The pierced brow rose slightly in an enigmatic gesture, but no response was forthcoming.

"This is a live-in position. You don't mind working for and living with a gay man?"

Finally, Mischa smiled. Donovan's heart lurched at the sexy sweetness of that gesture. The tiny, silver hoop in his lower lip glinted seductively. Wonder how that piercing would feel when he pressed his lips to Mischa's? It certainly drew attention to the swollen plumpness of the full, red lower lip. Yeah—he really needed to get laid this weekend.

"No. I don't mind working for a gay man, as long as you don't mind hiring one." Mischa's smile was now a broad grin, and he settled back more comfortably on the barstool, as though he were suddenly making himself at home.

Sudden sympathy overrode Donovan's concerns. Why not give the kid a chance? If Martin Weston hadn't hired him to work in the copy room at his company all those years ago, despite his being an underage, gay hippie, he wouldn't be where he was today. He'd probably regret this, but it looked like the skater-Goth-boy/man had talked himself into a job. And the corporate, advertising executive was sentencing himself to a series of cold showers.

He sighed. Such melodrama wouldn't go over well in an advertising campaign. His active imagination might just become a potent enemy in the coming months. *Go for it. Let the kid–man try the job, and when he quits, ask him out.*

"All right, here's how it works. I provide you with a debit card for household expenses. You maintain a spreadsheet for expenditures and put it on my desk on Fridays. I'll give you the list of contractors and people I'm using for the house. You call them then get them in and out as quickly as possible. You get paid on the fifteenth of every month. Anything outside the normal household budget needs prior approval. Do you have a car?" It might be pretty tough to do the shopping on a skateboard.

"My brother has my Porsche." The kid-man managed to say it with a straight face, but Donovan couldn't see how. *Wiseass.*

"Right, well, the keys to my old Toyota are on the hook in the garage. Gas counts as a household expense, keep it filled up. You can use it only for household errands. Got it?"

"I need Wednesday nights off."

That was pretty demanding for someone who a moment earlier was pretty much willing to be walked over to get a job.

"I planned to give you Sundays off." He paused as the other man shook his head firmly. "Okay, you'll have Wednesday nights and Sundays off. When can you move in?"

"I'll be back tonight with my stuff. I can start tomorrow. You have wireless access?"

Now he was getting picky about the Internet service? Jesus, this had mistake written all over it. "Yeah, but you'll have to provide your own computer."

He led Mischa, his new housekeeper, back down the tiled walkway to the front door. As he opened it, something occurred to him, and he stuck out his hand a bit awkwardly. "I'm Donovan Holloway, by the way. You might want to know who you're working for."

Fascinated, he took in the lovely pink flush that spread over the other man's face. Mischa reached forward awkwardly, hampered by the backpack hanging off his wrist, and took Donovan's hand. "Thank you. I really appreciate the opportunity, Mr. Holloway." His husky, sexy voice nearly succeeded in pulling Donovan's attention from the impact of the small, warm hand grasping his own. The tingling awareness of that simple touch sent little signals to various parts of his brain and body that his cock refused to be distracted from. *Oh, fuck, this was looking like a really, really, big mistake.*

CHAPTER TWO

MISCHA MOVES IN

Mischa pulled the clunky, awkward U-Haul truck into the dead-leaf-laden path that he hoped marked Donovan Holloway's driveway. Shutting off the engine, he let out a shaky sigh and tried to relax his posture. He sure, fucking missed that Porsche. Turning to face his companions on the bench seat of the boxy vehicle, he announced, "Here it is."

Belladonna patted his hand gently. In her soft, soothing voice, she whispered, "It's so ... nice."

Nice? He peered at the house. Yep. He was in the right place. All the charming aspects he'd noted this morning were still there: mud pit front yard, dead plants in the flower beds, overgrown shrubbery around the small front porch. He nodded dubiously, looking past Bella to where the twins sat huddled together, whispering in each other's ears.

Dex shifted to meet his glance and spoke for both of them. "We're ready."

They'd exited the truck and opened the back cargo door with admittedly quite a bit of noise when a pricking of awareness indicated Donovan's presence. He breathed deeply a few times, hoping to still his racing heart and keep his voice from betraying the instant lust that surged through him at the awareness of the handsome, older man.

Calmer, Mischa turned and immediately caught sight of Donovan leaning against the post of the front porch. He was sex personified in soft flannel sleep-pants, chest bare, and hair sticking up in messy disarray. The tumbled-out-of-bed image went straight to Mischa's cock, and he groaned. Damn skinny jeans.

"Sorry to wake you, Mr. Holloway," he called, grateful that his voice came out sounding masculine instead of squeaky. Knowing there was nothing he could do to disguise his erection in his tight clothes, he turned quickly back to survey the jumbled interior of the small van.

He heard Donovan's approaching footsteps squelching in the soggy leaves and looked down to see the man's long, elegant feet in flip-flops parked next to his own combat boots. Fuck. He even had sexy feet? There really was no justice in the world. If there were, the man would have some visible flaw to counteract his gorgeousness. *Maybe he's got a tiny cock, and that's God's little joke, or he prefers to bottom too. In that case, even if I got him into bed, neither of us would know what the fuck to do with the other.*

Coughing, he turned to his friends. "Mr. Holloway, these are my friends, who were kind enough to help me move." Actually, he'd quite recently discovered that they were his only real friends, but Donovan didn't need to know that the hundreds of hangers-on who'd been happy to party with him when he was flush had disappeared when the money had gone. He pulled Bella forward from where she tried to hide behind him. "This is Bella and that's Dex and Trick." He waved in the direction of the twins, hoping their behavior at the moment was discreet enough not to turn Donovan off the idea of letting them in his house.

Donovan murmured greetings to the others before hoisting himself quickly into the U-Haul. He assessed the contents of the van quickly then began issuing orders that everyone else immediately and unquestioningly followed. Mischa marveled as in moments Donovan had effortlessly taken control and organized the unloading. He had Bella carrying boxes into a large room off the kitchen while the twins carried Mischa's antique secretary-style desk. He and Donovan struggled with the awkward weight and angles of his day bed.

They paused in the hallway when he dropped his end of the bed to answer his cell phone. He smiled apologetically. Donovan rolled his eyes in acknowledgement of the delay. Donovan put his end of the bed down and leaned back against the wall. He crossed his arms over his broad chest. Mischa licked his lips, toying with the little hoop in the bottom lip. He studied the other man's firmly muscled chest while he snapped into the phone, "Terry, what the fuck do you want?"

Donovan's brows rose, but he pointedly looked down the hallway toward Mischa's new room.

"Yes, I am well aware that I am being evicted." He ignored Terry's offer to come and pick him up. "No. I am not giving up and moving back home."

He could tell from Donovan's intent stillness that he was absorbing every word he could hear, even though he stubbornly refused to look back at Mischa . No matter, that half-naked, athletic body had his full attention since Donovan stepped through the front door earlier. "No, as a matter of fact, I did find a job that includes a place to live. No. I have no idea how much it pays. Don't call me, dickhead. Yeah. I love you too. I'll see you Wednesday."

He shoved the phone into his pocket and cleared his throat to let Donovan know it was okay to look at him again. Jesus. Talk about willpower.

Donovan swung back toward him and the expression on his face could only be described as stormy. "Problems?" he asked icily.

"No, at least it's not a new problem, anyway." Fuck if he was going to admit his dumbass brothers were checking up on him.

An hour later, the room was laid out perfectly. His daybed, dressed impeccably in fine black Egyptian cotton sheets and comforter, fit snuggly against one wall. His grandmother's antique Chippendale table was graced with the stained glass Tiffany lamp he'd purchased at Sotheby's last year. The petrified wood coffee table shone darkly from its place in front of the bed, and his La-Z-Boy recliner beckoned from nearby.

Dex and Trick were across the room, gently petting each other and sneaking little kisses while they worked to hang the fifty-inch plasma screen TV on the wall opposite the daybed. Bella, having arranged the jewel-toned throw pillows and cushions on the black comforter to her satisfaction, crossed to his glass-fronted bookcase and opened one of the several boxes of books stacked on the floor.

Satisfied that his room was coming along nicely, Mischa turned back to check the truck for more boxes. He collided immediately with Donovan who stood in the doorway holding two boxes in his muscular arms and staring at Dex and Trick.

"Shit!" Mischa grabbed for the box on top as it slid away.

Donovan's warm, brown gaze jerked from the twins to Mischa before he cleared his throat. Donovan's Adam's apple bobbed under Mischa's fascinated gaze.

"Where do you want these?" Donovan asked. Together they added the boxes to a pile growing against the wall.

Mischa urged Donovan to precede him down the hall as they went to check the truck for any last boxes. He had to return it to the rental place first thing in the morning. Once they were outside, Donovan turned to him with a slightly troubled expression.

"I had the idea that those two were brothers."

Mischa calmly met the inquiring brown eyes. "They are. They're just... close. Really close," he added.

He studied Donovan's handsome face, looking for signs of disgust or anger, but couldn't see anything except a vague concern. The warm brown of the man's eyes melted into a golden glow. Mischa whimpered in response as his own heart raced, and a tingling heat began spreading throughout his body. He fell forward into those passionate eyes as though he were drowning in honey.

Unable to stop himself, he reached out a trembling hand and touched Donovan's firm lower lip. Slowly, cautiously, he moved up on tiptoe and leaned forward to press his lips where his finger had been. Donovan's mouth opened immediately, and Mischa mewled in sensuous approval. He slid his tongue into the warm cavern, eager to learn the taste and textures of this man.

He was completely shocked when Donovan pushed him aside with a muffled curse. He looked up in protest and saw that Donovan's gaze was on something over his shoulder. Turning slightly, he snorted to see that the object of Donovan's lust was the twins entwined in an embrace on the front porch. Dex had backed Trick into the porch railing and was licking his neck while grinding his pelvis against the other man's jean-clad thigh.

Damn. Guess that passionate, lust-filled look was for the scenery and not for him.

Donovan made a visible effort to bring his head back around to face Mischa. "That's it then. All the boxes are inside. I'm, uh… I'm heading to the shower and back to bed."

Mournfully watching the muscular buttocks flex under the soft sleep-pants as Donovan rapidly entered the house, Mischa sighed. He followed slowly, hoping to keep the man's gorgeous body in view a little longer. As he passed the twins on the porch, they broke apart and followed him into the house.

Donovan was up the stairs and out of sight by the time they made it through the entryway. Mischa strained his ears in the late night quiet to catch any sounds of Donovan stirring upstairs and then shrugged. Donovan was attracted to him, he could tell. Just because he was distracted during their first kiss by Dex and Trick's impromptu private porno display didn't mean a thing.

A sense of pride and homecoming crept into his heart as he took in his room from the doorway. Bella had arranged a few of his books on the shelves and some of his art on the walls. Other items were waiting to be put away, but the pretty little black-haired girl had curled up on his daybed with a leather-bound copy of the *Iliad*. Poor Bella, beautiful Bella, was as straight as they came, but absolutely terrified of men. Straight men that was, because she was openly affectionate and cuddly with her gay friends. She smiled in greeting and the three men moved as one across to her.

Strange.

Bella curled into his lap while Dex and Trick coiled together next to them on the smooth black comforter. The huge loft all this stuff had barely filled had always seemed so un-homelike. It was the place of his rebellion. A place he'd rented in spite of Terry's protests—well, to be honest, maybe *because of Terry's protests*. Despite living there for two years, aggressively making it scream with his own personality, wants, and desires, he hadn't regretted leaving it behind. Eviction had actually been a blessing.

A polished ebony-and-bone antique box on the table caught his eye and with a grin, he leaned forward. His movements disturbed the tangle of limbs around him and the others straightened as well. He flicked open the lid of the box and Bella's slim, white hand dipped in, coming back with a delicate blown glass pipe. Trick selected a small ski shaped incense burner and set it down on the polished surface of the petrified wood table. Dex added a scented incense stick to the burner and Trick lit it smoothly with the solid gold Zippo lighter Dan had given Mischa last Christmas.

Mischa untied the silken rope around the neck of a velvet bag, opened the plastic baggie inside, and extracted a generous pinch of the fragrant contents. He tamped the herb down into the bowl of the glass pipe and Bella leaned forward for Trick to light it. After inhaling deeply, she pressed the pipe into Mischa's hand and curled back into his lap. With a sigh of contentment, Mischa rested one hand on her silky black hair and brought the pipe to his lips with the other.

Almost instantly, the tension and stress of the day drifted away. He held in his breath as long as he could before gently letting it out and passing the pipe along. Dex quickly inhaled then turned to press his lips to Trick's, exhaling into his brother's mouth in a long, steady stream. Mischa's eyes drifted shut, and he smiled contentedly, shifting slightly in the cozy nest of pillows, blankets, and warm bodies.

CHAPTER THREE

How Hard Can It Be?

Tiny chirping noises from the onyx face of his wristwatch dragged Mischa from a cocoon of warmth. He struggled to pull his arm closer to his face and peered at the dial. Yeah. It was four in the morning, time to make the coffee and get Donovan's breakfast ready.

He carefully extricated himself from the tangle of arms and legs and anxiously checked to see that he hadn't wakened his friends as they lay coiled together in a heap like puppies on his daybed. He met Dex's clear blue eyes as they blinked sleepily open, pressed a finger to the other man's lips, and backed away from the bed. It was so very tempting to crawl back into that warm haven, but Mischa was determined to meet every one of Donovan's demands and prove to him and his brothers that he was capable of doing something.

He grabbed a change of clothing from a box on the floor near the closet door and his laptop from the coffee table then left the room tiptoeing quietly so as not to wake anyone. Halfway down the hall, he stopped. What the fuck was he doing? Who was he going to wake up? Donovan was upstairs, and after the night they'd had, the others would sleep like the dead until noon. It was four o'clock in the fucking morning. The last time he'd seen this time of day he'd been crawling into bed not out of it.

He slipped into the bathroom to brush his teeth and scramble quickly into the clean clothes before heading back to the kitchen. Setting up his laptop on the marble breakfast bar, he turned to survey the mess. Clearly, with cooking comprising a large part of his duties, this was the place to start. First thing, though, he needed to find the coffee pot.

On the counter near the sink, he found it. Unfortunately, it looked as though Donovan had been conducting some kind of science experiment in the thing. Murky brown liquid, that retained only the faintest remnants of the smell of coffee, half filled the glass carafe, and little quarter sized islands of mold floated across the top. *Disgusting.* Wrinkling his nose in distaste, Mischa picked up the carafe and carried it the few steps to the sink. There he was momentarily stymied by the fact that both stainless steel basins were full of dirty dishes. No time to waste. He shrugged and dumped the contents of the pot over the dishes in one sink. He returned to the coffee pot and accidentally discovered the flip-top lid revealing the filter.

That was even more disgusting than the contents of the carafe itself. A soggy, white paper filter packed full of moldy, soggy grounds gave off an unpleasant odor. *Gross.* Gingerly, he reached in, pinched the damp edges of the filter together, and lifted it out. He held the offensive object as far away from his body as he could while he searched for the trash can. Spying it, he moved quickly across the room to the where the trash can stood by the back door to unload it as soon as possible. Midway across the kitchen, a soft soggy thump failed to capture his attention soon enough, and he slid a few feet across the floor as he stepped into the mess of soggy coffee grounds that had broken through the wet filter.

"Fuck!" he swore under his breath, remembering at the last moment to keep his voice low. He slammed the remains of the disgusting mess into the ridiculously overfull trash can before turning back to his laptop.

As long as he had the Internet, there wasn't a chore Donovan could throw his way that he couldn't handle. He might barf while doing it, but he could handle it. He typed into the Google search box—*How do you make a pot of coffee?* Six million plus results. Wow. Surely not. How many ways could there possibly be to make coffee? He randomly clicked on a likely link and turned back to the coffee pot. If the coffee pot was on the counter there, logic dictated that coffee beans, cups, and stuff must be nearby.

Naturally, they weren't. Apparently all the coffee cups were in the sinks, and who knew where the coffee itself was.

Skimming the first article proved helpful, as he'd hoped. He discovered that many people store their coffee beans in the refrigerator to help keep them fresh. A search of the huge three-door refrigerator revealed a few more science experiments and not much else. A fluttery panic began edging into his consciousness. He did not want to fail his first task on his new job. The panic increased when he heard the unmistakable sounds of Donovan stirring upstairs.

"Fuck it." Whirling about, he dashed through the laundry room into the garage and searched frantically for the keys to the Toyota Donovan had said he could drive. A quick trip to the nearest Starbucks and breakfast would be taken care of. A little calmer with a plan in place, he snagged the keys off the hook by the door only to come to complete stop at the sight of the car he was expected to drive.

"You've got to be fucking kidding me." This was Donovan's old Toyota? A vision of his beautiful black Porsche brought tears to his eyes as he approached the monstrosity parked in the garage. The little Toyota was painted a puke green color and liberally decorated with large, white peace signs and purple daisies. It was an offense against God, nature and the engineers who designed the vehicle. Not even the most flaming homosexual would be caught dead driving that car. "Fuck you, Terry! I want my damn Porsche back!"

Cursing brothers, coffee pots and working for a living all at once, he slammed into the vehicle and pealed out of the garage.

As he puttered down the streets in the hippie car, missing the smooth handling and quiet purr of his Porsche, he figured the amount of money he had left in his account and added to that the contents of his pockets. It would be impossible to pay what he owed on the Porsche even if Donovan advanced him six months' salary. Resigned, he ignored the mocking stares he was sure he was receiving from the other drivers on the road and pulled into the Starbucks's drive-through lane.

When Donovan strolled into the kitchen at six o'clock on the dot, Mischa had managed to unearth a clean place setting and silverware from one of the boxes. The breakfast tray he'd bought at the coffee shop had contained a croissant, cut fruit and a yogurt cup, so he'd arranged the items on the plate. The gallon of coffee he'd purchased sat in an insulated carton on the table along with packets of sweeteners and creamers.

Mischa couldn't take his eyes off the fine figure of a man in his navy-blue suit and crisp, white dress shirt. Why did the same outfit on Terry make him want to rail against conformity? On Donovan the effect was just plain hot.

"Do I smell coffee? I wasn't expecting breakfast this morning, because I know you didn't have the chance to shop yesterday."

Mischa noticed that not expecting breakfast didn't stop Donovan from seating himself at the table and pouring a cup of coffee. He surveyed the food on his plate and picked up his fork to start eating. "Have a seat." He gestured Mischa to the adjoining chair. "Aren't you eating?"

Mischa couldn't hold back the shudder that racked his thin frame. "Eat at this time of the morning? No. Thanks. I'll eat later. Right now, the whole idea of eating in here makes me nauseous."

Donovan nodded understandingly. "I see what you mean. This place is kind of unappetizing, isn't it? That's why I need you. I can't keep up with it and the new job."

"But it doesn't bother you?" Mischa asked, wondering if that was too rude for his first day of work.

"I grew up eating meals in places that would make this look like a castle, so, no, it doesn't bother me. Anyway, here's the debit card I told you about. Your first priority should be buying cleaning supplies and food. Don't worry," he added, "I don't expect miracles. I know it'll take a few days for you to get this place together."

Mischa accepted the debit card dubiously. Closer inspection revealed that it resembled the credit cards he had turned over to Terry as part of the dare to live within his means. He'd honestly never used one before. "Okay."

He'd learned during his first few interviews that when you don't know what the fuck you're talking about, it was better to keep quiet. Bella, Dex, or Trick could tell him how to use this thing, no doubt.

Donovan was speaking again, tapping the card. He produced a white business card from the breast pocket of his suit jacket and handed it over as well. "My cell number, the house phone number, and the pin number for the debit card are on the back, but call the office number first if you have any questions. Probably my secretary can help you with most of what might come up."

Donovan was up and out the door before Mischa had assimilated all the information the man had crammed onto one flimsy business card.

Daunted and unsure where to start, Mischa surveyed the mess in the kitchen. Unpack first, he decided, then shop, then clean, then cook. Rising, he peered into the first box and grimaced. A few minutes at the computer had soothing jazz music playing in the background, and the tension once again eased from his body. He dragged all the boxes into a row on the side of the room opposite the cabinets and cut them all open with a grimy knife he'd found near the sink. Once the contents of all the boxes were visible, he studied the layout of the cabinets and appliances. Plan in place, he dove into the first box and began, item by item, to organize the kitchen.

He'd made quite a bit of progress when the others slipped out of his room and joined him. It lightened his heart that they didn't even ask if he needed help, just took in what he was doing, and pitched in immediately. Soon the boxes were empty and all of them were hungry.

"Let's go. I have to get cleaning supplies and I'm starved."

Dex, Trick and Bella swung as one to face him. Of course they knew he no longer had the Porsche. A twinge of momentary concern made him pause. Would his friends mock the Toyota? He pulled the keys to the monster out of his pocket and jingled them in his hand. "Donovan left me the keys to his other car."

Quietly they trooped after him through the laundry room and into the garage. That newly familiar warmth spread through his chest again as Bella whispered, "Cool," and Trick's seldom heard mellow giggle was muffled by Dex. None of them protested or disdained to ride in the humble vehicle, and Mischa smiled. If asked a month ago who his best friends were, these wouldn't have been the three he'd have named, but here they were now, helping him hold his head above the water and openly accepting everything about him. Including the fugly car he was driving them around in.

By the time Bella had explained the purpose of the necessary cleaning supplies to him and he'd made his purchases, including a few sacks of foodstuffs that she promised him would be easy to prepare, it was too late to get home in time to prepare a meal for Donovan by six.

When he dropped his three friends off at Bella's apartment, Trick leaned in his open window. The fugly car had no air-conditioning, a factor he hadn't noticed at six in the morning that was now unmistakable at three in the afternoon.

"Stop at Boston Market," Trick suggested shyly. "Get a family meal and reheat it when he comes home. We do it all the time."

"Thanks, Trick. That's a great idea." Tingling tremors of shock and pleasure zipped through him as Trick leaned closer and pressed a light kiss to his cheek. His gaze jerked up the sidewalk, seeking Dex. As he suspected Dex had halted on the path and was looking back at the car, waiting for his brother to rejoin him. His blue eyes glinted with approval and he lifted his hand in a silent farewell as Trick jogged up the path.

CHAPTER FOUR

Finding Phillip Henderson

In the late evening light, Donovan passed the welcoming glow of his neighbors' homes, porch lights on and windows glowing. Shadowy figures moved about inside. The tight muscles at the back of his neck loosened a bit, and a niggling smile pushed at his mouth. Tonight, he'd be coming home to a lit house with figures moving about inside, a home instead of a house.

The smile became full-blown when his mind turned to that someone he was coming home to. Mischa. *Damn. The sexiest housekeeper on the block!* Remembering the aborted kiss from the night before, for the hundredth time, he kicked his own mental ass for pushing the man away.

Pulling into the drive with a sense of letdown, he noticed all the windows were dark and no welcoming figure moved around in the house. On the plus side, the porch light glowed and the trash cans sat at the curb. The U-Haul was missing, and a momentary disquiet crept through his soul as he wondered if it had departed jammed full of his own hard-earned possessions. Recalling the amazing collection of antique furniture, fine art, and expensive electronics he had helped Mischa and his friends move into the housekeeper's room last night, he highly doubted that any of his belongings equaled his housekeeper's in fiscal value.

Unsure what to expect, Donovan unlocked the door and entered his home. The faint notes of a light jazzy instrumental drifted from the kitchen and soothed his troubled emotions. He smiled as he stepped into his office to drop off his leather briefcase before seeking his errant housekeeper.

There wasn't much difference in the front of the house that he could see. The packing boxes still lined the walls, furniture was jumbled in any which way. The light from the kitchen and the soothing jazz beckoned, and he wandered on down to the kitchen where he found exactly what Mischa had been doing all day. The room smelled enticingly of cinnamon and apples with a faint underlying odor of bleach and lemon. Every surface gleamed and the packing boxes had disappeared.

Unlike this morning, the small kitchen table was set with service for two, and Mischa sat in one chair, his laptop open in front of him. The jazz came from the laptop, and Mischa hummed along in spots as he worked diligently typing something. Yesterday Donovan had found the young man to be physically appealing, edgy, and intriguing. Tonight, there was soft vulnerability in the tired eyes and the troubled frown. Mischa in skinny jeans and a tight black T-shirt had sent his heart racing and his blood pumping. Mischa in black, silk pajama pants and a gauzy, white peasant style shirt melted his heart into a puddle of goo. An unexpected desire to embrace, soothe, and cuddle the younger man rippled through him.

"Hi." Damn. That was scintillating conversation at its best. So seductive, sexy, and appealing was the image before him that his brain reverted to yesterday's inability to come up with a single topic of conversation. "So, I see you cleaned the kitchen?" *Argh, again with question-statements.*

"Yeah, when do you want to eat?" Mischa met his intent gaze wearily.

"Umm, is now good?" Wow. At least this time the question was an actual question.

"Yeah, it's all ready, just keeping warm in the oven." Mischa rose and retrieved a tray from the oven with covered serving dishes on it.

When the covers were removed, Donovan, long accustomed to take-out cuisine, recognized the smell of Boston Market roast chicken and stifled his smile. "It looks great, Mischa." Would the kid have the integrity to admit that he'd bought the food, or would he claim to have made it himself? Donovan began serving himself as he waited for Mischa to comment.

Mischa sat indecisively for moment and then shrugged. "It was Trick's suggestion. I didn't have time to prepare a meal, so I picked up Boston Market after doing the shopping."

And if that wasn't just the cutest thing. Mischa's cheeks flushed and he looked down at his plate as he put a spoonful of green beans on the white china.

Mischa's good looks and integrity drew him to the boy even more than before.

"I need to talk to you about this job." Mischa had recovered from whatever embarrassment had created the flush and was meeting his gaze challengingly.

"Yes? What about it?" Donovan wondered if he was going to give up and quit so soon. He was surprised by the degree of disappointment the notion of Mischa leaving his home created. Leaving your employ. *You are surprised that he wants to quit working for you, not that he won't be living with you.* His disappointment today almost matched his reluctance to hire the boy yesterday.

"You need to hold off on scheduling the decorators and all until after I get the house cleaned up. This kitchen took me all day, and that's without preparing any meals, or doing any laundry. I'm going to need at least three weeks to get the unpacking and organizing done. The yard has to wait until the house is habitable, and I don't want to do the yard while people are traipsing all over the place building and painting and such. They'd just tear up anything I put in."

Chewing his chicken carefully, Donovan nodded. His relief that his new housekeeper planned to stay and actually had a sensible grasp on what needed to be done seemed a bit out of proportion. He wouldn't complain as long as he got what he wanted. Apparently his heart and his cock were outvoting his head on the issue of Mischa.

"Just tell me when it's ready. Anything else?" *Please let there not be anything else.* He prayed to a God whom prior to Mischa's advent into his life he'd never suspected of having a sense of humor. Mischa licked the chicken grease from his lips. Donovan found his gaze focused on the tip of that pink tongue as it traced the full lower lip and then paused to toy with the little silver ring there. When the plump, pink curve dropped and more tongue became visible, he shifted awkwardly on his chair for a moment. He'd suspected that Mischa had more piercings than were immediately visible, and that suspicion had just been confirmed. If he'd accepted Mischa's kiss the night before, it would have been an experience he hadn't had in a long time.

The boy had pierced his tongue. Shuddering, he jerked his gaze higher with effort and met knowing green eyes.

"I'd also like to buy a Crock-Pot and some pans. You have crap to cook with in this kitchen." Wicked laughter twinkled in the boy's eyes and he no longer seemed so tired or innocent as he had before dinner.

"Uh, sure, little things like that you don't need to ask about."

"You said to get large purchases preapproved, and the pans you need are going to cost over a thousand for a basic set." Mischa's eyes were sparkling with excitement now, and he reached across for his computer, turning it to show Donovan a website.

Donovan noted absently that the laptop was a top of the line Mac. He took in the displayed pictures of shiny copper pots and heavy-looking pans. His eyes widened slightly at the figure in the bottom corner.

"I need those? Why? Do they do the cooking and shopping for you?" Jesus, those pans cost more than the entire contents of his kitchen—including the appliances! Fascinated, he stared as the boy straightened and drew in a deep breath before words tumbled out pell-mell in what appeared to be a single breath.

"These pans are the highest rated in customer satisfaction for use, durability, and functionality. Nothing sticks, they're easy to clean, and they have like a hundred year warrantee. Also, they are nice to look at and would look great hanging from a rack over your stove or work island."

Work island? He had a work island? Swift glances around the kitchen revealed no island, but he let it pass. "But thousands of dollars for pans?" A childhood of deprivation made the idea ludicrous. He'd cooked meals for himself and his parents in the tiny kitchen of a converted school bus using two pans, one pot, and large skillet. The items he had on hand in his kitchen today put that existence to shame. He shook his head doubtfully. "I—"

"They would be heirlooms." Mischa interrupted him, face already tinged with disappointment. "Hundreds of years from now, these pans will be used by your descendants."

Heirloom treasures that he could pass on to his children and grandchildren. Items like Mischa's cherry-wood secretary and the Chippendale table his grandmother had once owned. He liked the idea. His parents hadn't passed anything on to him. If they ever owned anything of value or beauty, it had been hocked to pay for drugs or some grand social justice scheme long before he was old enough to know about it.

Making a snap decision, he reached for the computer. They were beautiful pans. Mischa leaned over the small table to point out the pans' many valuable benefits, and instantly Donovan was distracted by the proximity of the other man. Warmth seeped through the thin layers of gauzy shirt and silk pants, and a tingle of sensual awareness bled into his body with the heat.

"I don't want to buy something like this online. Can you get them locally?" *Concentrate!* Seductive employees were not a new experience in Donovan's life. He'd once hired a personal assistant, before Margo, his omnipotent secretary, who had no concept of personal space and the two of them had functioned just fine. Of course, that personal assistant had more the physique of a body builder on steroids and really wasn't his type anyway. Mischa, however, was perfect with the possible exception of the black Mohawk and piercings. Every inch of the lean, firm, white flesh fulfilled his fantasies. The overall effect was so sexy, he was eager to amend his fantasy to include the piercings.

Without further thought, he twisted sideways in his chair and pulled the younger man into his arms. Mischa met his seeking lips with an open-mouthed caress of his own. Grateful for the access, Donovan slipped his tongue into the waiting heat. Mmm, the vaguest hint of mint and a seductive, dark sweetness teased his taste buds and he eagerly probed the moist interior, seeking more of the intoxicating flavor. He gasped into Mischa's mouth as the other man's tongue joined his in playing. The tiny silver ball, which pierced Mischa's tongue, rubbed against his own, then clicked gently over his teeth, before stroking the roof of Donovan's own mouth.

The clicking sound brought Donovan abruptly back to his senses. Reluctantly, he pulled away. Gazing down into Mischa's passion-glazed, green eyes, he pressed a finger to the temptingly pouting lower lip. "We can't do this." He carefully lowered his hand and backed away. "I'll transfer enough into the household account to buy the pans and whatever else you need for the kitchen, just please buy them locally and not online."

Certain he'd doomed himself to another cold shower and a night of restless dreams, Donovan regretfully headed down the hall to his office.

CHAPTER FIVE

DREAMING OF PHILLIP HENDERSON

Donovan threw the pen he'd been doodling with across the room at his whiteboard when he realized that, for the third time in as many minutes, his mock-up of a print ad for a local Mexican restaurant chain featured a character sketch of a heavily pierced, Mohawk-wearing man eating a taco instead of a sombrero and poncho clad bandito. Visions of Mischa and memories of that kiss kept getting between him and his creative side.

Sighing, he decided to call it a night and head to bed. Aware that Mischa had finished in the kitchen and retired to his own room, Donovan resisted the urge to creep to the boy's room and check on him. Avoiding temptation was the better part of valor in this case, and he didn't have the fortitude to pull away from another kiss like the last one. Yesterday it had been hard enough, but now that he knew the taste and texture of Mischa's mouth, it would be fucking impossible to resist.

Trudging up the stairs, he made a mental note to ask Mischa to do some laundry the next day. Clothing littered his room, and he was running out of towels in the bathroom. Shivering as a delicious tremor spread through his body, he stepped under the warm spray of the shower and raised his face to the water. Mischa was back in his mind, and in this setting, Donovan could indulge his imagination.

His soapy hand running over his body switched from business-like to lingering caresses. His hands became Mischa's smooth white hands, stroking the hard muscles of his chest, pinching at his nipples until they hardened into tiny nubs.

"Oh, yeah," he groaned, confident the rumbling patter of the water covered any sound he might make. He'd always been vocal in bed and wondered if Mischa would be as well. The very thought of Mischa's piercing rubbing over his nipples and trailing down the grooves of his chest had his cock throbbing hungrily, eager to experience that slick silver ball working over the rim and fucking the slit at the top.

Moaning loudly, Donovan grasped his cock with one hand. He traced soap-slick fingers down his body starting at his throat and Adam's apple with the other. Pressing against his flesh with the tips of his fingernails, he raked gently, trying to re-create the sensation of a pierced tongue assaulting his flesh. His blood rushed and his skin prickled with awareness as his balls drew up tight against his body.

"Oh, fuck, Mischa, harder, baby. Suck me." His imagination fired by the sensations, his hand moved in rapid jerking motions up and down the length of his cock, relentlessly, building the pleasure, increasing the pressure of his strokes. He brought his other hand down and tapped the tip of his cock with the blunt nail of his index finger, moaning again.

The burst of cum came with a vision of Mischa's smiling eyes, and Donovan collapsed, gasping and whimpering against the wall of the shower. Shaking drops of water from his hair, he reached with a trembling hand to shut off the flow. He was in so much fucking trouble with this relationship. He'd had less powerful orgasms with fully active, real life partners. Genuine sex with Mischa might well kill him.

Wrapping a towel around his hips, he hastily brushed his teeth and flicked off the light before stumbling down the wide hallway to his bedroom. He considered climbing into bed without bothering with pajamas, but perhaps it would be safer to put on his flannel sleep pants just in case Mischa's friends showed up in the middle of the night again. The memory of the twins wrapped around each other on his front porch in full sight of the neighbors made him groan again. His cock gave a valiant stir, but he quelled it with an image of the police arresting him for public indecency and the image of the homophobic, second applicant for Mischa's job. Indulging his creative side was one thing, being ruled by his cock, quite another.

He snapped the waistband of the white, flannel pants into place for emphasis, and then crawled under the soft, blue sheets. Stretched out with his head on the pile of feather pillows, his mind turned once again to Mischa.

"Damn it!" He rolled over and squeezed his eyes shut. *Get out of my head!* Grimly he began counting by threes, focusing his attention away from Mischa lying in the bedroom downstairs, sprawled in the black sheets and jewel-toned pillows of his cozy daybed.

Eventually he drifted off to a restless sleep, plagued with vague, disconnected dreams. In his dreams, he ate a dinner from Boston Market with Florence Henderson while the Thompson Twins made out in the background. Mischa popped into the room with a Cheshire cat grin and demanded, "Aren't you gay?" The dream scene vanished and he stood in a desert, stumbling about and looking for something he couldn't find, but needed desperately. In the distance something moved closer to him, stirring up huge clouds of dust. Thank God. He flung up a hand to stop the rapidly moving vehicle, shocked to note that it was the converted school bus he'd been raised in. The wildly painted vehicle stopped directly in front of him, and he backed away. Instead of his hippie parents climbing out the open doors to greet him with their over-effusive hugs and offers to hook him up, Mischa climbed out again asking, "Which way is the right way?"

Before he could find an answer to that, a whirling sandstorm rose up around them, and he, the bus, and Mischa were swept into a whirling spiral that flung them high above the desert then abruptly ceased. He had a Wile E. Coyote moment of stillness before his mouth opened in a silent scream, and he accelerated rapidly toward the earth far below.

Crashing into wakefulness, still reeling from the vertigo as though he'd really fallen, Donovan realized that it was four thirty in the morning and he'd have to be getting up soon anyway.

Shaking his head at the crazy dreams, he pushed himself upright amid the tangle of sheets and rubbed at his eyes. He'd gotten six hours sleep, but no rest. He forced his achy body from the bed, slipping into a pair of flip-flops from the floor as he listened for sounds of Mischa moving around down stairs. He smiled in amused memory. Maybe Mischa was already out at Starbucks scrounging up breakfast again.

Whistling, he headed off to his bathroom to shower, shave, and brush his teeth before heading down to the kitchen to see Mischa.

The aroma of delicious spiced coffee reached him immediately as he exited his bedroom. Mmm, heavenly—that definitely didn't smell like Starbucks. He tromped loudly down the stairs, lighthearted with anticipation at seeing Mischa, and wondering what breakfast might bring today in addition to what smelled like an amazing cup of coffee.

Mischa sat at the breakfast bar with his laptop open in front of him again, and a mug of coffee sat next to him. Donovan inhaled deeply, taking in the delicious aroma of the coffee and the essence of the man across from him as he sat on his own stool.

Mischa looked up and met his eyes with a smile. To Donovan's surprise, his own gaze skittered immediately away from that clear, green gaze. *What the fuck?* He forced his gaze back to Mischa's and realized the source of the problem when his cock stirred eagerly. The sight of Mischa's sparkling eyes brought back the erotic memory of his self-induced orgasm from the night before. His cheeks heated and he worried that his masturbatory fantasy might show in his own eyes. He glanced desperately around the kitchen for a source of distraction.

Spying the pot of coffee on the counter behind Mischa, he hurried over to pour himself a cup. Mmm, he closed his eyes in blissful anticipation but they popped back open immediately as the image of Mischa on his knees flicking his pierced tongue against Donovan's cock seared into his eyelids.

He poured his coffee with shaking hands and turned back to the breakfast bar. To save himself the tease of looking directly at the man who starred in his fantasies, he sat on the bar stool next to Mischa and pulled the covered breakfast plate across the marble counter. Uncovering the plate, he surveyed a meal similar to yesterdays, but with the unmistakable look of home preparation. A bowl of Greek yogurt drizzled with golden honey and sprinkled with chopped nuts sat next to a plate of mixed berries and a few triangles of toast. It wasn't bacon and eggs, but it was a simple, elegant breakfast, probably more nutritious than what he would have picked. Not very filling though; he'd have to get a midmorning snack at work.

Shrugging, he turned to thank Mischa for the meal. A hint of fragrance clung to Mischa, an earthy undertone to his usual scent of warm spice. Some vague familiarity about the fragrance nudged at his consciousness, but he shoved it aside.

"This looks great. Could you make time to do some laundry today? I need towels for my bathroom upstairs. And I'm sorry to say I don't have time to bring my stuff down from my room, but maybe you could make that your priority for the day." The last words had scarcely left his mouth before the source of that familiar odor hit him. He knew that smell—had been raised in a broken down bus on hippie commune in the desert a hundred miles from here surrounded by that smell. *Fuck.*

He ate in silence for a few moments, nodded without comprehension to what he could only assume was Mischa agreeing to do his laundry today, and wondered if he should say anything. Was it his business? Fuck yeah, it was. Everything he allowed to happen in his house was his business. How would Mischa react to a confrontation over his smoking pot in Donovan's home? Did it matter? If he objected, then he'd have to go. No way was Donovan living through the drug-infused nightmare of his childhood with another person he loved.

Oh, fuck. He loved Mischa? Since fucking when did he fall in love on twenty-four hour's notice? His heart shrugged, his dick applauded, and his brain shriveled up and ran for a darker corner. That made his choice all the clearer, didn't it?

"Mischa." He spoke softly, trying to keep any anger out of his voice. "Maybe I should have told you a little more about me before you agreed to work here."

Mischa met his gaze curiously. "You said you were gay. That's about it. But I already know you're a slob and a kindhearted man. And family means a lot to you."

Family? Oh, the pots-and-pans-heirlooms conversation. "Well, I should maybe have mentioned that I grew up in a commune about a hundred miles from here. My parents and I lived in a converted school bus. It was a pretty stark existence. They were always so high, I spent more time taking care of them than myself. Any money they had went first for drugs and then for food."

He met Mischa's stunned gaze directly, pouring all the emotion he could into that connection. "Mischa, I lost both my parents as a result of their dependency on drugs, and I can't go through losing another loved one like that. I'd really prefer that drugs not be brought into my home. That's a deal breaker for me, sorry."

Hoping he'd struck the right balance, said enough but not too much, he slipped off the stool and headed through the laundry room to the garage and out to his car. Mischa still sat silently at the breakfast bar behind him.

CHAPTER SIX

LEARNING NEW THINGS

Try as he might, Mischa couldn't shake the image of a little brown-haired, brown-eyed boy struggling to care for two aging hippies addicted to drugs and living in a school bus. *That's not going to happen to you.* He thought of the black, ebony, and bone box on his coffee table. It probably held a couple of hundred dollars worth of pot and paraphernalia, sure. But the box itself had cost him more, as had the table it sat on.

I'm not addicted to that shit. It's just fun and relaxing, something to do with my friends. He pushed the thought aside and gathered up the breakfast dishes. As he rinsed the plates and bowls in hot running water, he remembered the intensity of Donovan's brown eyes as he made the statement, "I can't go through losing another loved one like that."

What did that mean? Was Donovan claiming that he was in love with Mischa after only a day of knowing him? He carefully placed the rinsed dishes in the machine with last night's dinner dishes and added detergent. No, that would be impossible. Mischa found Donovan highly attractive, and most likely Donovan reciprocated the attraction, but love?

The machine slammed shut and, with a twist of the dial, purred smoothly in the background.

Next issue—laundry.

Sitting at the breakfast bar, he Googled laundry and began skimming articles. Most of them agreed on several key issues that made sense, but many just pimped their own favorite laundry products. As he flipped from article to article, making sure he'd got the basics down, an inner voice nagged at him.

So if I'm not an addict, why not give it up? Donovan doesn't like it, doesn't want it in his house, and if it means nothing to me anyway, why not indulge him?

He slammed the lid of his computer down with more force than necessary—maybe more than was healthy for the machine, which he could not afford to replace any longer. He paused and patted it remorsefully.

I have the right to do as I please. I'm not hurting anyone by smoking up a bit with my friends. He marched up the stairs, pausing in the wide hallway. *Hmmm, this space had potential.* He could picture it as a Grecian lounge with column styled plant stands and mahogany bookcases, a divan or Roman couch or two. Four doors led off the hallway, and he could tell the open one led to Donovan's room because clothing covered every inch of floor visible through the doorway.

Sighing, he moved over to the room. Somehow, knowing the perfect specimen of manhood who'd left here an hour ago looking all *GQ* and sexy was in reality a slob, who apparently would rather buy new clothes than launder his old ones, melted his heart a little more. Scooping up piles and walking back and forth and up and down the stairs, he wondered if those new plans for the modifications to the house included the addition of a laundry chute upstairs.

Having dragged everything downstairs, he began working on what all the websites agreed was the most important factor in correctly doing laundry. He sorted it into piles by color and weight of fabric. A large pile of colored T-shirts and sleep pants made the first load, and he added carefully measured laundry detergent and fabric softener in the appropriate places.

While the machine whirred and thumped away, he headed back upstairs and gathered up a large quantity of suit jackets, dress pants, white, and blue dress shirts. No way was he going to wash these. These things were going to a dry cleaner to get the professional treatment.

He placed the dry cleaning in the back seat of the Toyota and shut the door. Staring at the fugly paint job on the car, he realized that Donovan really had come a long way from hippie commune to upscale neighborhood. He had to respect the other man's accomplishments and his home.

A bit lighter of heart, he headed back into the house to his room. He swiped up the ebony and bone box from the table and hurried out to the car. There he shoved the box under the front seat. Issue satisfactorily resolved. He'd take the box over to Bella's and only indulge while visiting his friends.

As he moved the T-shirts and sleep pants to the dryer, he realized he'd only smoked in the first place because it would piss Terry off to smell it on him every Wednesday night. Sacrificing this act of rebellion for Donovan's peace of mind didn't bother him a bit. How odd was that?

He straightened, tossed a dryer sheet in the dryer, and started the machine. Turning back to the mountain of laundry left to be washed, he sighed. He would be careful to keep on top of this chore in the future. He threw in a load of whites this time, added the bleach to the running water and detergent, and waited a while for the two to mix before adding piles of white towels and T-shirts.

In the kitchen, he closed the laundry sites on his computer and pulled up some recipe sites he'd bookmarked previously. Dinner tonight was going to be all his own work, not necessarily gourmet, but definitely homemade.

Washing, peeling and dicing vegetables was a little more difficult than the how-to video made it seem, but once he got the hang of the strange device for scraping the skins off the veggies, it went faster. Didn't say much for his knife skills that it took him an hour to prepare a diced cucumber, bell pepper, and pineapple salad. To be completely fair, though, a good portion of that time had been spent on an onion. He'd become teary eyed before he'd progressed very far on the thing, and crying had made it even more difficult to make the precise cuts he wanted for the salad.

Crying had brought back to mind the little boy Donovan had been, raised in poverty by hippie drug addicts on a school bus in the desert, and before he knew it, he cried for Donovan, the little boy he had been, and the man he'd grown into.

Eventually, he'd calmed down enough to toss some gorgonzola cheese crumbles in the salad, add the juice of a lemon, and a handful of mint leaves. With the salad in the refrigerator, thankfully cleared of moldy science experiments, it was time to check the laundry.

He shifted the first load onto the counter to fold, and headed back to the laundry room to move the whites over, before washing a load of Donovan's jeans.

When he opened the washer and peered in, he gasped in shock. Somehow, despite all his research, something had gone wrong. He pulled out a T-shirt and held it up to the light. Yep. It was pink, so were the towels, sleep pants, and underwear in the load. The whole load was a dainty seashell pink. How the hell had that happened?

Fuck. Donovan was so going to fire him. He couldn't fucking believe this. Everything had been going so well too. He dropped to the floor and thumped his head against the washer. Why? Why? Why? The urge to run out to the garage and calm himself with a little smoke sobered him up quickly. Shit. Maybe he was worse off than he thought.

No. No smoking. He stood shakily and turned resolutely from the temptation in the garage. *Figure out what made it happen, then figure out how to undo it.* He began removing articles from the washer one by one and eventually found it, a slightly faded shirt that he clearly remembered putting in with the first load of laundry. Somehow, he'd left it in the machine when he'd loaded the whites. He tossed it aside and reloaded the whites, now pinks.

A quick visit to Google and he decided to try running the load of laundry through again. Hopefully since he hadn't dried it, the dye would wash out. If not, all he could do was confess the accident and offer to replace the items from his paycheck.

By six that evening, the dry cleaning had been dropped off, the black box resided in its new home at Bella's place, and the rest of the laundry had been washed, folded and put away as best he could manage. Fortunately, running the whites through the wash again with bleach had resolved the coloring issue.

He'd cleaned the bathroom, stripped and remade Donovan's bed, and finished the simple dinner preparations. Steaks marinated on the counter, waiting to be thrown on the grill as soon as Donovan was ready to eat, and baked potatoes sat waiting in the warm oven.

Mischa paced back and forth, anxiously assessing and reassessing the table setting. He added a centerpiece of fall leaves and scented candles to the table, and then worried that it created too romantic an atmosphere, and took it away again. He'd made the same series of actions three times before the rumble of the garage door announced Donovan's presence.

He snapped to attention and dropped the centerpiece back into the middle of the table. The *snick* of the door opening behind him drew his attention like a magnet to Donovan's sexy presence. Something inside him calmed at that moment. Donovan was home, and the rest of it really didn't matter. Laundry, cleaning, cooking, learning new things at a rapid pace, and giving up his recreational drug of choice were all worthwhile to see the warm delight of Donovan's smile as he met Mischa's eyes.

"I quit." He blurted it out, wanting to get it out before Donovan could speak.

The devastation on Donovan's face confused him. So did the man's fumbling words. "You don't have to. I was wrong. Really, I can live with it. I need you to be here."

Light dawned, and with it came a burst of pleasure. "No. I don't mean I quit working for you. I mean I quit smoking, today. I gave it up. It's important to you, and I respect that."

He'd scarcely finished speaking before Donovan swept him into an embrace and the man's lips crushed down on his own, tongue demanding entrance. *Wow. That was more than nice.* Eagerly he opened up and thrust his tongue into Donovan's mouth in response, hungrily seeking the sensitive places inside. He rubbed his piercing against Donovan's tongue and shivered in delight at the groans of desire. Donovan reached down with one hand and pulled him close, urging him against the hard muscles of his taut thighs and flat stomach.

Mischa whimpered in pleasure as his cock swelled and thrust against the zipper of his jeans in an eager bid to capture some of Donovan's attention for itself. Kissing Donovan was unlike any kiss he'd ever shared, and he owed some of that delicious pleasure to the fact that he could be one-hundred percent certain that Donovan wanted him, Mischa, unlike past lovers who enjoyed the perks of dating and fucking a wealthy man.

Mischa couldn't really claim to be surprised when Donovan pushed him gently away, having endured the same ending to Donovan's passionate kisses twice before. Panting heavily, Donovan bent and rested his forehead against Mischa's. He traced a slow path from the nape of Mischa's neck down the knobs of his spine to the waist of his jeans and back up again. Mischa held still, hoping that if he didn't call Donovan's attention to his actions, the other man wouldn't notice.

Slowly Donovan's breathing returned to normal. He straightened and his hands dropped to cup Mischa's buttocks and squeeze gently before falling back to his own sides.

"What's for dinner?" The conversation said back to business, but a latent, molten heat threatened to turn his brown eyes to liquid honey again any moment, so Mischa smiled and stepped back. Let Donovan have his space. There would be time for them.

"Steak, baked potato, and salad, just a simple meal, but I managed it all on my own, without the help of Boston Market, so I hope you like it." Proud of his accomplishment, Mischa didn't mind hinting that a little approval and appreciation would be welcome.

CHAPTER SEVEN

POKER NIGHT WITH THE BLAKE BOYS

The new ringtone he'd programmed into his phone for Terry blared out during the middle of dinner Wednesday night. Donovan stopped speaking and looked at him curiously. The meal he prepared had been a success, candied sweet potatoes— from the Crock-Pot he'd finally purchased—a juicy pork loin roast, and garlic green beans.

"Sorry," he muttered, as the notes of Dire Straits' "Money for Nothing" continued to blare. "I have to take this."

Donovan nodded understandingly and continued eating his dinner.

"Hi, Terry, what's up?" Cursing Terry for interrupting his dinner with Donovan, Mischa smiled at the gorgeous man eating across the table from him.

"I'm leaving the studio now and heading to the house for the poker game. I can pick you up on my way, since you don't have a car right now."

Terry was nothing if not relentless in his need to poke into his brother's business. "That's all right. I think I can get access to a car. You don't need to pick me up."

Fulminating silence met his declaration, and he noticed he had Donovan's attention now too. He smiled reassuringly at the other man and gestured for him to continue eating. "I know what you're up to, Terry. I'm not giving you my address so you can come over here and check up on me. I'll see you at the poker game in an hour. I love you, dickhead." He hung up without giving Terry the opportunity to protest or respond.

"So, I'm, um, off tonight, and I need to go to a game over on the other side of town. Do you think I could borrow the car?" His brothers would die laughing when they saw the Toyota. Knowing now that it showed where Donovan had come from, he didn't mind the fugly paint job and found something gallant in the ancient beast's continued existence.

Donavan's disappointed expression tugged at his heart, but he had told the man that he had to have Wednesday evening off when he was hired. Failing to show up for the weekly poker game on the first week after starting his job would bring the wrath of the Blakes down on his head with a fury that would put the hounds of hell to shame. He couldn't do that to Donovan, really he couldn't, better to leave the man he'd come so quickly to love to his own devices for an evening than witness the bloodshed if his brothers had to come looking for him.

"Yeah, sure, you can borrow the car." Donovan's face had gone distant, and he resumed eating mechanically.

Guiltily, Mischa added, "Umm, could I get a cash advance on my wages? I wouldn't ask, but I used the last of mine to pick up your dry cleaning this morning and I need a cash stake for the game."

Startled, Donovan met his gaze again, a considering look in his own. "Okay. I have some cash. How much do you need to buy in?"

"Usually it's a thousand."

Donovan's nostrils flared and his eyes widened in shock. Damn, the Blakes really did live a different lifestyle than other people.

Donovan reached into his back pocket and pulled out his wallet. He rifled through it and removed a handful of bills. "This is all I have, if you put the receipt for the dry cleaning and any other expenses you've paid cash for on my desk with the accounts on Friday, I'll reimburse you for them with your pay check. Have a nice night."

Dropping the bills on the table, he pushed his plate away and stalked off down the hall to his office. Troubled, Mischa kept glancing at the money on the table as he cleared the table, rinsed the dishes, and loaded the dishwasher. He left it there as he packaged the leftovers, making a boxed lunch for Donovan to take to work the next day and storing the rest for his own lunch the next day. Something was wrong with Donovan, but he couldn't decide what. Should he go down and tell him he was leaving? A single glance told him the office door, normally left open, had been shut. Shaking his head, he scooped up the cash and put it in his wallet. He'd talk to Donovan and clear the air when he got back from the game.

An hour later, he pulled the hippie car into his usual parking place in the twelve car garage on the family estate, still worried that he'd made the wrong choice. Maybe he should have gone to Donovan's office and cleared the air, at the very least claimed a kiss before he left for the night. His brothers' cars were already in their places in the garage, but his own Porsche was missing. What the fuck had happened to his car? Terry was supposed to have rescued it from repossession and stored it here on the property.

Temper boiling, on edge from the uncertainty of not knowing where he stood with Donovan, he slammed aggressively through the house to the game room and dropped into his seat. He stared defiantly into each brother's familiar green eyes one by one. Terry cleared his throat and shoved a handful of hundred dollar bills across to Mischa from his stack.

"Fuck you, Terry." He pushed the money back and pulled the handful of cash Donovan had given him from his own wallet. Lip curling, he turned to Dan. "Deal."

Brandon started to speak, but Mischa glared him down, and the other man shut his mouth with a click of teeth snapping together. They played a few hands in testy silence. Slowly Mischa relaxed. The others, sensing his more even keel, began the ribbing and teasing that usually accompanied their games.

Brandon never could leave well enough alone. He paused in discarding a card to address Mischa. "So, you found a job?"

Wary, Mischa rearranged his cards and nodded. "I found a job."

"Well, are you going to tell us about it?" Terry chimed in.

Mischa slammed his hand of cards down on the table. Fucking assholes couldn't let anything go. "I got a job as a housekeeper for a busy executive."

The shocked looks on his brothers' faces drained the anger from him and he laughed aloud. The trio of handsome men gaping like trout made the admission worthwhile. He had the distinct impression they wouldn't have been more shocked if he'd told them he'd become a pole dancer in a fetish club.

"You're a housekeeper?" Terry seemed to be recovering more slowly than the other two. "You—*you*—actually cook and clean?"

Laughing again, Mischa picked up his cards. "I do. I cook, clean, do laundry and am working on the gardens. You're up."

Brandon seemed bewildered. "Seriously? You'd rather slave away doing housework than work at the studio? Be elbows deep in dirty dishes rather than go to college and make something of yourself? I don't understand you, brother, I really don't."

"Then again, Brandon, you never have understood me." Mischa looked around the table; his brothers were great people, each in his own way, but none of them really understood Mischa's wants and desires. They all had their own ideas about what he should do and how he should live his life. He sighed. "I'm out. And I need to get back home." He scooped up his winnings, pleased to see he had more than enough to pay back Donovan for staking him to the game and turned to leave, ignoring his brothers' protests.

Outside the door, he paused to put the cash in his wallet and caught his name.

"Mischa's different. Something about him, it wasn't the same." That was Brandon, nitpicking and criticizing as usual.

"I can tell you one thing that's different," Terry drawled. "He didn't stink of booze and pot for a change. That's a difference I can get behind and support one-hundred percent."

"And he didn't borrow money, or ask for money," Dan noted.

"Still, keeping house is no career for a Blake! What the hell are we going to do with that kid?" Brandon, still pushing his control issues.

Fuck Brandon. He was going home to a man who appreciated him as he was.

"Oh, please. He'll get bored with that gig long before...."

On that note he headed off. He had no desire to listen to his brothers analyze his personality and plan his future. He was pretty damn certain that he loved Donovan and would never get bored with taking care of the man.

Pulling into the drive and seeing the lights on in the living area of the house, he decided to enter through the front door. He was deeply pleased that Donovan had chosen to use the living room he'd unpacked and arranged just that morning.

He strolled over and dropped onto the leather sofa near Donovan. Donovan turned toward him, face troubled.

"Mischa, I don't know how to say this, so please, don't get angry with me, okay?"

Fuck. What the hell had happened while he'd been gone? Things had been awkward, but this went beyond awkward to *holy shit* serious. "Okay. What's the problem?"

"I'm worried about this money issue. I can tell you're used to having money, and I'm worried that you're just a gold digger interested in being with me only because I have money." The intent look in the other man's eyes as he stared at Mischa told him how serious this was.

It made Mischa uncomfortable, to say the least, that he probably spent more money last year than Donovan had made. "Donovan, I am used to having money, but wanting money isn't why I'm with you. If all I wanted was money, I could just cave in to Terry's demands and move back home, then I'd have access to more money than you could conceive of. I'm here, with you, because that is not the life I want to lead."

A spark of hope lit in Donovan's eyes, followed by a grim look. "And that's another thing." The anger vibrating through Donovan sent tremors of excitement through Mischa as well, and he leaned closer to the other man's heat.

"Who the fuck is this Terry that every time he calls you drop everything to answer the phone and run to do his bidding?"

Laughing, Mischa leaned forward and placed his lips against Donovan's. Breathing gently into the other man's open mouth, he whispered, "Terry, my sweet, jealous idiot, is my older brother. I just spent hours playing poker with my domineering older brothers, when I really would rather have been here with you, to prevent them from rushing over here to find me. Now make love to me before I die of spontaneous combustion."

Donovan sprang into action, scooping Mischa up into his strong arms and dashing toward the staircase.

"No! You can't carry me! I'm too heavy!"

"Shut up. I've been driving myself crazy imaging you with another lover all night. Now I'm going to enact some of the fantasies that I've been having since you moved in here. And every damn one of them takes place in my room, on my bed."

Heaven forbid he failed to fulfill those fantasies. Mischa shut up and concentrated on working his tongue and lips over all the exposed bronze flesh within reach.

CHAPTER EIGHT

REALITY

Donovan dropped Mischa on the light blue comforter on his king-size bed, and pointed a finger at him. "Don't move."

Mischa's lips parted and the tip of his tongue came out to gently worry the hoop in his plump lower lip. Donovan groaned. He wanted to explore the textural contrasts of soft lips and hard metal, dive deeper and seek the stimulation of the metal ball hidden inside the warm cavern. He tore off his clothes, flinging sleep pants, boxer briefs, and T-shirt to land haphazardly about the floor.

Mischa's laughter brought him to a standstill, and he quirked an eyebrow at the younger man. "You find my frustration amusing?"

Shaking his head, Mischa continued to laugh before sobering enough to choke out, "No. Now I know how your laundry problem builds! You're such a slob!"

Outraged at such a slur, Donovan launched himself onto the bed and on top of the slight figure. Reaching down to Mischa's waist he slid his hands in a smooth caress up his flat abdomen, loving the silky, smooth, hairless flesh he encountered. Pausing with his hands strategically poised, he leaned down close to Mischa's face and toyed with the silver lip ring with his tongue for a brief second. He enjoyed the flare of heat and widening of green eyes in response to his caress and gave in swiftly to the temptation to repeat it. Then he drew back slightly. "Take that back or else!"

Chuckling, Mischa stretched up and tried to press their lips together again. "Or what? You'll hold out on me?"

"Oh, no, no, no, no, no, no." Donovan laughed, "You're definitely getting what's coming to you!" So saying, he wriggled his fingers against the skin and muscle of Mischa's side ruthlessly.

Laughing hysterically, the two of them rolled and wrestled across the bed for a few moments before Mischa's hand landed on the hard length of cock throbbing between them. "I think I deserve a treat for working so hard all week."

Donovan stilled, twisting his body back to get a visual of the slender white hand caressing his throbbing cock. He gulped. End of playtime. He dove forward, pressing into Mischa's open, welcoming mouth with his tongue, demanding and getting a hot response. Their mouths melded, he pushed the T-shirt up as far as he could, and hungrily stroked all the warm flesh he could reach. Fuck. He'd suspected there might be more.

He pulled back from the kiss, ignoring Mischa's protesting whimpers.

"Where are they? How many more do you have?"

Donovan's teasing fingers toying with the nipple rings clued Mischa in. "Piercings? I have a few more that you haven't seen."

Donovan flung himself to the side. "That's it then." He pushed Mischa to the edge of the bed. "Get up. Strip. I want to see them all."

Smiling, Mischa rose in an elegant movement. He stretched his arms over his head, pulling the shirt off and tossing it with a smirk on Donovan's already discarded clothing. "You like metal?" he asked in a sultry voice that rippled over Donovan's skin like a caress.

"Oh, hell yeah, I like metal... on you. How many do you have?" *And can I play with all of them?*

"I have, let's see..." Mischa paused as though calculating in his head. "Eight."

Donovan studied the young man intently. "Strip," he ordered. He took in the piercing above the sparkling green eyes, the lip ring, the tongue piercing he could hear clinking against Mischa's teeth as he stood there unbuttoning and then unzipping his skinny jeans, then the two studs in his left ear, two nipple rings. Fuck—that made seven currently visible piercings. His cock throbbed again, demanding he do something about its overstimulated state. He reached down and stroked it lightly, tugging gently on his balls to relieve the urge to come right then. "Go on," he urged, as he noted Mischa had stilled, green eyes locked on Donovan's hand, licking his lips.

Mischa pushed his jeans down his legs, bending at the waist to pull them off. His position hid his cock from Donovan, who waited eagerly for the sight. *What kind of piercing did Mischa have on his genitals? A Jacob's Ladder? A Prince Albert?*

Mischa straightened and stepped toward the bed. Donovan squeezed his cock hard to still the rush of blood as his gaze locked immediately on the shiny silver horseshoe-shaped ring threaded through Mischa's cock.

"Fuck. Oh, fuck. Come here." He choked the words out. Reaching with both hands, he dragged Mischa to him. Pushing the man down on the comforter, he leaned forward and began with the top piercing, licking, sucking, and kissing it, then working his way down, giving each silver shape the same treatment. Soon Mischa was writhing and whimpering below him; twisting his hips to try to bring Donovan's attention to the place he wanted it most.

Donovan gripped his hip in one hand, holding him still as he teased first one nipple then the other.

"Please, please, oh, God, touch my cock. I need—"

"Shh..." Donovan whispered, moving back to steal a kiss before diving down to close his lips on the Prince Albert piercing at the tip of Mischa's cock. Mischa groaned in approval and tried to push forward, deeper into Donovan's mouth, but Donovan pushed him back down onto the bed, determined to give this piercing the same treatment as the others. As he licked and sucked salty drops of pre-cum from Mischa's leaking cock, he studiously ignored the demands of his own heavy and aching cock.

"Fuck! Fuck me now or I'm going to come without you!" Mischa's tortured demand from above him brought him out of his absorption with the cock in his mouth.

He crawled up the bed over the younger man and sealed their lips together. One hand fumbled under the pillow for the condom and lube he'd placed there a few days earlier. He swiftly coated his fingers with the lube and reached down between Mischa's legs to circle the tiny hole there. Applying steady pressure, he pushed one finger inside the heat and twisted it. Mischa cried out his approval into Donovan's mouth and lifted his hips, rubbing their cocks together.

With a groan, Donovan pulled back from the kiss and swiftly thrust a second finger in beside the first. He pumped his fingers, deep, hard thrusts, scissoring them open to prepare Mischa for his cock.

"Now, please, now!" Mischa begged.

"Now," Donovan agreed, pulling his fingers out of the tight haven. He unrolled the condom down his length and slicked it with more lube before pressing it to the eager opening. As he thrust slowly forward, he leaned down to kiss Mischa again. The tight heat enclosing him was maddening. He badly wanted to slam forward with all his might, but didn't want to risk hurting Mischa.

At last, he paused, fully seated in the clinging heat of Mischa's body. Lifting up, he stared down into passionate green eyes. "Are you ready?"

Mischa shifted below him. "Yeah, more than. Fuck me already."

"Ahh." Permission to move granted, Donovan couldn't hold

back any longer. His hips drew back, slammed forward, and Mischa moved to meet him.

Their combined groans and sighs of pleasure filled the large room. Soon, unable to prevent the orgasm that had his balls squeezed tight to his body, Donovan reached between them to grasp Mischa's cock. A few swift, firm strokes of his hand and Mischa yelled his release as thick spurts of creamy semen shot from his cock to land in gleaming streams on the pale flesh of his chest and stomach.

"Oh, fuck, baby, that is a beautiful sight." Donovan panted as he thrust harder, his cock enthralled by the pulsing of Mischa's inner muscles as he came. He groaned loudly as his own release flooded the condom and collapsed forward to rest on his elbows above Mischa.

"I think loving you is going to kill me." He rolled to the side and removed the condom.

"Don't you dare just drop that on the floor!" Mischa's demand made him chuckle. He'd never laughed so much in bed.

He tossed the messy thing into the trash can by the nightstand and handed Mischa his T-shirt to wipe off with. "What?" Why was Mischa looking at him like that, so hesitant and uncertain? "It's okay. My housekeeper will wash it." He joked, trying to put the smile back on Mischa's face.

"Do you? Really? Do you love me?"

Oh, fuck. He'd said that out loud, hadn't he? In for a penny, in for a pound. "Yeah. I love you. Don't ask me how. I know we've only known each other a few days, but—"

He didn't get the chance to finish his thought as Mischa launched himself in to his arms and began kissing and licking him at random, whispering into his ear, "I love you too. I wasn't going to say anything yet because I figured being so conservative and all, you'd think it was too soon."

Conservative? Too soon? "Baby, I'm only conservative at the office and in regards to the use of recreational drugs in my home. And it's not too soon; I've been looking for the love of my life for damn near twenty years."

"And that's me? The love of your life?" Mischa turned hopeful eyes in his direction and Donovan's heart melted all over again.

"Yeah, that's you. Not quite what I was expecting, but perfect nonetheless."

Sighing in contentment, Mischa curled in to Donovan's side and drifted off to sleep. Donovan stared at his lover's sleeping face. Karma was a wonderful thing. He wasn't sure what good deed he'd done in the past to deserve this blessing, but he would accept it with gratitude.

CHAPTER NINE

THE PAPARAZZI

The *clink* of china on a tray and the scent of coffee woke Donovan the next morning. He stretched his arms and sat up blinking slowly in the dim light. Mischa was crossing the room toward him with a tray of coffee and a covered plate. He smiled with pleasure and pushed his pillows up behind him.

"Breakfast in bed? You are going to spoil me." He couldn't believe how such a simple gesture warmed his heart. He patted the bed beside himself. "Are you joining me?"

Mischa nodded and sat in the indicated spot. He leaned forward and kissed Donovan briefly on the mouth. "I need to talk to you after work today about some things. I'd do it now, but you're going to be late for work if you don't eat and run."

Donovan glanced at the alarm clock and his eyes widened in shock. Sipping the coffee, he pushed the tray aside and climbed out of the bed. "Wow. You're right. I must have shut the alarm off instead of hitting snooze."

Mischa settled back against the pillows as Donovan went over to his closet and opened it, wondering if he had any clean suits left. The evidence of Mischa's visit to the dry cleaners met his eyes. He paused to appreciate the organized interior. Shirts, jackets, and pants hung neatly covered in plastic bags, arranged according to color and fabric. *Hmmm, for such a rebel, Mischa has a definite obsession with neatness and organization.*

He pulled out the items he needed and raced across to the bathroom, a quick once over with the electric razor, brushed teeth and he was back in the bedroom, pulling on a crisp, white shirt and stepping into dress pants. Mischa rose from the bed and came over to help button the shirt.

Less than half an hour after waking, he kissed Mischa at the front door, holding an insulated mug of coffee and a boxed lunch as well as his briefcase. The drive into his office passed quickly, his mind flooded with ideas that he couldn't wait to get down on paper—ideas for old clients, ideas for wooing new clients. His creativity was a river suddenly undammed.

He rushed past his secretary, who held something out to him and started to speak. He'd scarcely seated himself at his desk and pulled a sheet of clean paper forward to begin a sketch when Margo entered.

"Sir? You need to see this." She stepped forward, laid the object on his desk, and swiftly exited his office.

Humph, what was going on? He reached out and picked up the magazine she'd left on his desk. It was one of those grocery store gossip rags. What the hell could be so vitally important about this crap? His company didn't do print advertising with rags like this. Then he realized she wasn't showing him the magazine for the advertising, but for the articles. The cover picture showed Mischa getting out of Donovan's old Toyota in front of a dry cleaning establishment with an armload of laundry.

"Rebellious Blake Heir—Tame House Husband?" *What the fuck?* He turned quickly to the pages Margo had marked with tiny, sticky-note strips and began to read. Most of it was crap, but some of it he knew was true. The article mentioned Mischa's three brothers, and the name Terry stood out as instantly recognizable. That was the one who kept calling Mischa. Then there was the eviction—Mischa had told him about that. Sickened, he shoved the rag into his briefcase and left his office.

"I'm taking the day off, Margo. Reschedule my appointments, please." Did Mischa know about this article? Was he upset? His whole life was laid out there in snide innuendo and gossipy asides for the nosy masses. If this article were to be believed, then Mischa had inherited more money than Donovan could ever dream of making. A moment of disquiet stole over him. Could he provide for Mischa in the fashion he was accustomed to? Would Mischa leave him as soon as he realized that Donovan's wealth didn't compare to what he stood to inherit one day?

Concern for Mischa, as well as fear for their future, had him speeding down the interstate, and he arrived home less than two hours after leaving it.

He pulled into the garage and entered the house through the laundry room as had become his habit since Mischa began working for him. He liked walking immediately into the welcoming warmth of the kitchen where Mischa could inevitably be found at the breakfast bar, using his computer or preparing a meal.

Today Mischa jumped from the bar stool as Donovan entered. He started to cross the room to Donovan, but Donovan shook his head. He joined Mischa at the counter and took a deep breath.

"Shouldn't you be at work?" Mischa asked curiously.

"No. I should be here with you. Now." He took several deep breaths. Damn this was hard. "Those things you wanted to talk to me about after I got done working today, would they have anything to do with you being Mischa Blake?"

Mischa looked confused. "I told you I was Mischa Blake."

"But you did not tell me you were *the* Mischa Blake of Blake Family Productions. You did not tell me that you had a multi-million-dollar trust fund. What is this job for you, some kind of joke? What am I, a toy to amuse you for a while?"

Mischa lifted his head proudly in protest. He reached across the bar and pressed his hand to Donovan's own shaking fingers. "No! You are my love. I didn't expect to find you, but I did, and none of the rest of my life means anything without you."

"Then explain this to me, because I can't figure it out on my own," Donovan cringed at the nearly pleading tone of his own voice. Fuck. He sounded so needy.

"Remember when I came for the interview? I told you I didn't want to work, but my brothers dared me to get a job and support myself?"

He had vague memories of that, yeah. He nodded and clutched Mischa's hand in his own.

"They want me to clean up my image, work for the family business, and go to college."

"And you don't want to?"

"I like my image, and I don't want to be in the movie business. It's full of phony people, and you have to watch every hug in case the guy embracing you has a knife in his other hand. I wouldn't mind going to college, but they want me to study film or business, and I'm just not interested."

Strangely enough, Donovan could understand that. "I had the same problem with my parents. They couldn't understand why I wanted to go to college instead of living happily on the commune growing weed and organic vegetables."

Mischa smiled. "Not you, huh? The whole organic thing, I mean."

Chuckling, Donovan agreed, "No, it's not. So you don't want to do what your family wants, and getting a job gets you out of it? Then what?"

"Well, I have to actually support myself for a year with the job, so I'm hoping you aren't going to fire me for sleeping with the boss."

"I think I can overlook that. Would you go to college if you could study what you wanted to?" He sighed. Why offer

Mischa the opportunity to go out and meet other, younger, guys? *Because it's the right thing to do, asshole. He's a very bright kid and if he wants to go to school, I need to encourage him and get over my insecurities.*

"I'd like to study history, or literature maybe, but my brothers wouldn't approve. They think I need to apply myself to something functional so I can be useful in the family business. I can't go to college yet anyway. I gave up all access to my money until the year is up."

"What if I pay the tuition for you as part of your salary?" He had to make the offer. Mischa deserved the freedom to choose.

"Umm, I don't know. That doesn't sound like supporting myself."

"Well, think about it. If you want to go to school, you should." Funny, he'd have loved to have the interference and guidance of older siblings growing up, but if they had been as domineering as Mischa's older brothers appeared to be, he probably would have decked them.

Satisfied that the past few days as he'd lived them were real, and not some foolish rich-boy prank, Donovan braced himself for the hard part of the conversation. He flipped open the briefcase and extracted the magazine. "You know I love you, right?"

"I do. I love you too. What's that?" Mischa seemed confused again and reached for the magazine. As he took in the cover picture, his eyes widened and his face paled. "Oh, fuck. Oh my God. This is terrible!"

"Baby, don't be upset. My secretary gave me this when I got to the office this morning. It's not a nice article, but there's no naked picture or anything too terrible in it either."

"No, no, I'm used to this crap. Every few months one of those trashy reporters gets a burr up his ass to follow me around for a few days and try to catch me in some kind of illicit activity. You don't understand. This—" He thumped the picture on the cover, "shows the license plate of your car, and the phone number of the dry cleaner is on that sign."

"Yeah? So?" That was it? He wasn't upset about the innuendos about their relationship, but he was upset about Donovan's car in the picture? That made no fucking sense.

"So... we probably have about half an hour before my brothers descend on this place en masse to rip you a new one. Someone will have shown this to Brandon as soon as he hit the office this morning. Give him ten minutes to read it, an hour to gather the others, and he'll have had your address along with a detailed report from an investigator on his desk before ten o'clock coffee break."

Squealing tires and slamming car doors punctuated Mischa's matter-of-fact statement. *Fuck.* Either half an hour was an overly generous estimate, or the brothers were more pissed that Mischa realized.

"How many brothers?" This was beyond awkward.

"Three. All older, all bigger," Mischa responded. He wrapped his arms around Donovan's waist and leaned into him. "Don't worry. I've got your back."

Somehow, what had previously seemed a lovely dulcet doorbell tone just screamed testosterone when it rung repeatedly in conjunction with a heavy fist or two pounding furiously at the front door of Donovan's dream home.

CHAPTER TEN

Standing Together

At his front door, Donovan turned and bent to press another kiss on Mischa's lips. "You're sure we shouldn't just run and hide upstairs and wait for them to go away?"

Mischa chuckled. "That's not my way, or yours. Let them in and let's cut through the bullshit once and for all."

Donovan straightened his shoulders and girded his loins to stare directly into the eyes of the brothers of the man he'd made love to just hours ago. Fuck. Could anything be more difficult? What did he say? *"Hi, I'm Donovan, the owner of the hippie car your brother is driving in the photo you probably saw. Not to worry, I'm not a pothead, though I do fancy your brother's ass, as the article indicates."*

Before he'd clarified what exactly he was going to say, Mischa reached past him and tugged the door open. Donovan found himself face to face with three big, green-eyed, blond mountain gorillas masquerading as men. Blond? He peeked at Mischa out the corner of his eye. If that hair was dyed, he'd had his brows done too.

He held out his hand in the general vicinity of the brother in the middle of the group and forced himself to make eye contact. The heat rose across his cheekbones, but he held his ground. The gorilla battalion would cross the threshold of his home only after he ascertained their abilities to control themselves around their younger brother.

"Hi, I'm Donovan Holloway," he swallowed, "Mischa's employer and partner." Okay, maybe that assumed too much, but it sounded better than lover, and God knew it was the closest description he could come to what he wanted to be to Mischa.

Mischa's grip on his hand tightened and he tore his gaze from the piercing fury of green to the more welcoming sparkly depths he loved. Same eyes, different emotion entirely. His heart skipped a beat at the pleasure on Mischa's face, and he added, "If that's okay with you, baby."

"You know it is," Mischa responded, smiling broadly. "Okay, you guys can come in if you're going to be good, but if you're going to be your usual asshole selves, we'll have this conversation on the doorstep where any trashy reporters who followed you over here can get a better story."

"What the fuck is going on here, Mischa?" That came from the brother who'd just tried to outstare him. "This guy is old enough to be your father!"

"The doorstep it is, then." Mischa sighed. Donovan wrapped his arm around the young man's waist and pulled him in tight against his side. He scowled at the man who'd spoken.

"And you are?" He made his voice as chilly as he could, but the fury pumping through him at the guy's belligerent tone and patronizing glare at Mischa made remaining calm a difficult prospect. No longer reluctant, he met this asshole's eyes. Who the fuck did he think he was?

"I'm Brandon Blake, the oldest brother of the boy you've apparently been sodomizing. What the fuck is your problem? Can't you see he's just a mixed-up kid? Or is that what this is all about, huh? You figure out he's an easy meal ticket?" Brandon pushed forward, but one of the other gorillas grabbed his arm and pulled him back, stepping forward into his place.

"I'm Terry Blake, Mischa's older brother. We saw the article in the magazine, and I'm sure you can understand we're naturally concerned about Mischa." This one was reasonable at least.

Donovan met his gaze, pleased that his nerves had settled in the face of the older brothers' belligerence. "I'm glad to hear that because, to tell you the truth, I was beginning to think you all had rushed over here at the drop of a hat to browbeat your brother into doing something he doesn't want to do."

The third brother spoke up, "Now, there's no call to get nasty. Let's take this inside and discuss it like reasonable adults."

"As long as your pit bull is leashed, and you agree that Mischa qualifies as a reasonable adult, that suits me fine." He met each brother's gaze in turn before focusing directly on the belligerent one. He turned and led the way to the cozy sitting area Mischa had made by arranging his furniture in a neat horseshoe. He and Mischa dropped together onto the wide leather armchair, leaving the brother's to choose between a rocker, the sofa, and a beanbag.

Not surprisingly, they all crowded shoulder to shoulder onto the sofa. Donovan decided to steal their thunder and get the ball rolling. He really wanted to just boot the domineering assholes out of the house, but figured that if Mischa still insisted on playing poker with them every Wednesday night after all they'd put him through, they must mean a lot to him.

"So, I'm thinking you all came rushing over here to rescue Mischa from my evil clutches because you think I'm only interested in his money." He had their attention now.

"And you're saying that's not the way it is?" This from the third brother, what the hell was his name again? Daniel.

"Yeah, I am. I didn't know till that article came out this morning that Mischa had any money to speak of. Why would I? How many trust fund babies get jobs as housekeepers?"

"So, now you know he has money you plan to keep him around, hmm? Well, did Mischa tell you that he doesn't actually have access to that money without our approval until he's thirty-five?" That was Terry, Mischa's dickhead. Appropriate nickname now that he knew the guy a little better.

"No, as a matter of fact, he didn't tell me. Because it doesn't matter. I love your brother, with or without money, so you can take his trust fund and shove it up your tight ass." Cringing, Donovan instantly regretted the animosity of his response, but Mischa murmured in approval next to him.

The guy turned to Mischa and tried a different tack. "Come on, Mischa. I drove your Porsche over here today. You can have it back, and we'll forget about the dare, if you come home today."

Mischa stiffened and pulled away from Donovan's side. Donovan's heart lurched. Porsche? No way could he afford to buy Mischa a Porsche. Maybe he could replace the hippie car, but not with a Porsche.

"You are such an asshole, Terry. I love my Porsche, yes, but I love Donovan more. You can keep it. I've got everything I need right here." Mischa settled back and snuggled against Donovan again.

Amazed, Donovan pressed a kiss to his forehead before rising, "I think you all have outstayed your welcome. You can see that Mischa is where he wants to be, doing what he wants to do, and that we really aren't concerned about the trust fund, or the Porsche." He glared at Terry.

"But—" The third brother tried to speak, but Donovan had listened to enough bullshit.

"But nothing. You all need to figure out that Mischa is an adult capable of making his own choices and seeking his own path in life. He has strength of character and intelligence. Quit trying to force him into a mold you've made for him, and stop trying to manipulate him into doing what you want him to when he has the balls to tell you to go to hell." Breathing heavily, he came to a stop as he realized he'd been shouting at the thunderstruck brothers.

The eldest snarled at him. "We've heard a lot from you about letting Mischa make his own choices and letting him live his own life, but we haven't heard it from him. Do you really think an intelligent, strong character is best served by cooking your meals and scrubbing your toilets?"

Mischa leapt from the chair. "You have heard it from me! You just didn't fucking listen! I told you at the poker game yesterday, and I've told you here. I am where I want to be!"

"It's his choice. Freely made, and before we ever slept together at that. I didn't manipulate him into working for me, and I didn't manipulate him into sex. Your stupid dare put him in my path, and I'm not dumb enough to turn away from such a wonderful gift when karma brings it to my door."

The brothers ignored him and eyed one another. Kind of freaky, that. Looked like they were engaged in some kind of Borg collective mind meld or something. They rose and three hands were thrust in his direction.

He backed away and nearly stumbled over Mischa behind him.

"Aww," Mischa's voice oozed sarcasm. "Isn't that cute? They want to make friends."

What the fuck? A little dizzy, Donovan reached out and shook each hand briefly. "What the hell is up with you guys?"

Dan, spoke soothingly. "Just checking. We could tell at the game yesterday that something was up with Mischa. He even smelled different for Christ's sake. What were we supposed to do? Wait around for an invitation to the wedding?"

"Yeah," Terry interjected. "Clearly working for you was beneficial to Mischa, but he wasn't sharing the information, so we grabbed the opportunity to track you down."

"You mean you grabbed the opportunity to stick your noses in my business and check up on me!" Mischa dropped back down into the armchair and tugged Donovan down with him.

The brothers relaxed somewhat, though Donovan could swear he caught the eldest giving him the stink eye a few times. They scattered about the room, Terry opting for the rocker and Dan dropping onto the beanbag. Brandon plopped on the sofa and stretched his arm across the back.

"Okay, so we were wrong to manipulate you into finding a job. Since it worked out so well for you though, we figure you owe us now. Spill the story, bro. Damn, I love these things." Dan spoke from the beanbag.

"No. No manipulating inside the walls of my home!" Donovan voiced the command before allowing Mischa to answer, and then realized what he'd done. "If that's okay with you, baby?"

Mischa shrugged. "Your house, your rules."

Donovan started to nod, then shook his head. "No, *our* house, our rules. You get as much say here as I do."

That had apparently been the perfect thing to say because Mischa pulled his head down and licked his way into Donovan's mouth, pressing the shiny metal ball into the seam of his lips until they parted to allow his tongue inside. Donovan responded with a groan and pressed his tongue against Mischa's. He only realized they'd gotten carried away with the kiss when the brothers' catcalls and hissed comments broke through the haze of passion.

"Jesus, get a room."

"Oh, my God! Hello! Innocent bystanders here!"

"Wow! That's hot as shit!"

"You know Dan's taking notes for his next script?" Mischa whispered into his ear. Donovan groaned again.

"How long are they staying?" he whispered back before leaning back in the chair and tugging Mischa into his lap to cover his obvious erection.

EPILOGUE

Mischa surveyed the completed garden of his and Donovan's dream home. They'd spent weekends the last two months working on the yard, and finally it was ready. The entertainment area boasted an outdoor kitchen, barbeque and several conversation areas.

Friends and family had gathered in the backyard to christen the new space, and it amused Mischa to see his friends in their Goth garb mingling reluctantly with his family and Donovan's friends and coworkers. Bella hid in a lounge chair off in the shade, definitely intimidated by the testosterone in the yard. Now what had happened to—there they were. Dex and Trick, up to their old tricks, stood in the shade of a leafy palm tree, leaning together, absently petting and sharing casual kisses as they observed the gathering.

Other friends gathered in small groups, conversing and eating. Brandon stood with Donovan by the glass doors to the house, apparently trying once again to talk him into coming to work as the publicity director for Blake Studios. Donovan shook his head and responded calmly, but he'd apparently had enough of Brandon's rhetoric because he abruptly cut off the conversation by turning and stalking over to the grill to needlessly turn the steaks and burgers cooking there.

Grinning, Mischa sought his other brothers in the small crowd. Daniel stretched out on a lounger, chest bared to the sunlight and surrounded by cooing women from Donovan's workplace and a few coed's from Mischa's history classes. He'd wait till the crowd dispersed before he spoke to Dan. The idea he'd had for a historical miniseries based on the founding of New Orleans could wait a few more hours.

His gaze caught on Terry, who lay back on a padded chaise lounge staring off into the distance. His face looked dazed and flushed. *What the hell?* He strode across to Terry and dropped to his heels next to him. "Terry? Are you all right? Do you need a drink or something?"

"I'm fine. Fine. It's a little hot here, that's all." Terry spoke, but he didn't look at Mischa. Instead he whipped his head around to look at the outdoor kitchen. "Think there's any burgers ready yet?"

Mischa turned in the direction Terry had been looking when he approached him. That bit of misdirection on Terry's part was a dead giveaway. *Oh, now that was interesting. Very, very interesting.* From this perspective he had a clear view of two black clad figures entwined in an embrace that grew steamier by the second.

Pretending to buy Terry's dodge, he rose, "I'll check with Donovan for you." Humming, he strolled past Dan on his way to the outdoor kitchen and signaled his desire to speak to his brother with a rapid eye movement. A few whispered words in Dan's ear and his eagle-eyed brother took the bait and ran with it. Let the payback begin!

As the afternoon passed, Mischa observed Dan studying Terry, whose gaze seemed to be locked on the twins whenever he thought no one could see him.

At last, all the food had been served, and the time had come for him and Donovan to make their announcement.

Wrapping their arms around each other, they stepped in front of the grill and faced their guests.

Donovan spoke for both of them. "Friends, family members, we invited you here today to christen our new entertainment area, and we appreciate your celebrating with us. But while we've all been here having a good time, we just got a call. Mischa and I are going to be parents. Our request to adopt has been approved, and we're going to have to ask you to leave now, because we need to get on the road and pick up our baby in Oregon."

Whoops, cheers and Dan's familiar catcall resounded in the backyard as Donovan bent to kiss Mischa before ushering him off, leaving the capable Blakes to bring the party to a close.

TELLING THE TRUTH

CHRISTENING THE ENTERTAINMENT AREA

Terry Blake wandered aimlessly around his younger brother's newly completed backyard entertainment area. The kid had done a great job of creating a beautiful, functional space. It boasted an outdoor kitchen, barbecue, and several conversation areas. Spying an empty padded chaise lounge someone had moved away from the main conversation groupings, Terry moved off to claim it. He wasn't really in the mood to party, but under the circumstances he could hardly deny his brother his company. He settled into the lounge chair and surveyed the area. An interesting mix of people filled the large yard, gathered in small groups chatting, eating, laughing, and enjoying the sunshine of a perfect California summer day. Logically, he should be having a great time.

Terry sighed. There was no point denying it. He wasn't enjoying himself, and hadn't for a while. Marissa, his date for the occasion, had latched on to an actor and was fully occupied. Maybe he'd be willing to take her off Terry's hands. Luck would be a fine thing.

Brandon, Terry's eldest brother, stood with Donovan, Mischa's boyfriend, by the glass doors to the house, apparently trying once again to talk him into coming to work as the publicity director for Blake Studios. Donovan shook his head and responded calmly, but he'd apparently had enough of Brandon's rhetoric, because he abruptly cut off the conversation by turning and stalking over to the grill to needlessly turn the steaks and burgers cooking there. Terry shook his head in sympathy. Damn, Brandon just never knew when to quit, did he? He was going to piss off Donovan and Mischa again if he kept up the high-pressure tactics.

Daniel stretched out, chest bared to the sunlight on a lounger, surrounded by cooing women from Donovan's workplace and a few coed's from Mischa's history classes. *Impressive. Give Dan the chance and he'd fuck every one of those eager women.* A different woman every day was Dan's style. Somehow he never ran out of volunteers, either. Terry closed his eyes. Just the thought exhausted him. He'd never have the stamina.

When he opened his eyes again long moments later, he caught sight of two young men, nearly identical in appearance, standing in the shade of a leafy palm tree directly in his line of vision. Stunned, he stared in disbelief. They were absolutely beautiful. Were they actors from the studio? Pale skin, black hair, identical bright blue eyes, rosy-red-lipped mouths, the young men were slender and athletically built. They were so absorbed in each another they seemed alone in the crowded yard.

As he watched, the boys turned closer to each other, leaning forward to whisper together. Lowering his lids, Terry watched covertly. There was something illicit about the pair, something sexual. But surely they were related? Two young men who were so much alike had to be brothers.

One of the men tugged the other deeper into the shadows of a tree and the privacy fence. Their heads turned, and when one bright blue glance settled on him for a minute, Terry's heart rate increased, and his skin heated. They couldn't tell he watched could they? Apparently deciding that he was asleep and no threat, the two embraced, sharing gentle kisses and petting each other with slim, white hands.

Enthralled, Terry stifled a groan as his cock stirred against the zipper of his khaki shorts. Damn. That hadn't happened with so little effort in a long time. What the hell? He tried to glance away from the boys, told himself he should be disgusted, but he couldn't. Bottom line, he'd never been so turned on in his life. He'd spent his whole life doing and feeling exactly what everyone felt he ought, and what had it gotten him? A corner office in the family business and a lonely bed at night. Fuck it. He was done living for everyone else. If Mischa could find his own way, then Terry damn well could too. And he'd get started on doing that as soon as his erection subsided enough to get out of this chair without causing himself a lot of embarrassment. He crossed his hands over his lap and continued to watch the boys in the corner of the yard.

Mm, and why rush off? This lovely couple was really getting into their embrace now, and since no one else seemed to notice, Terry felt kind of included, almost as though he were participating in the act instead of witnessing it. He could practically feel the sweep of tongues in his mouth, the touch of two sets of hands tracing his shoulders, his abdomen. Damn, he really wished he had Dan's bold personality or Mischa's rebellious streak. He'd be over there in a heartbeat taking his share of kisses.

Down boy, he cautioned his newly overactive libido. *Baby steps; we'll get there eventually.* Jumping from mild-mannered, straight accountant to a gay threesome in seconds made for too drastic a change.

"Terry? Are you all right? Do you need a drink or something?"

Damn. Somehow Mischa had walked up and knelt next to him without him noticing.

"I'm fine. Fine. It's a little hot here, that's all." Terry spoke, but he didn't look at Mischa. He knew his voice sounded hoarse, but couldn't do anything about it. The best he could hope for was that Mischa wouldn't notice the rather large bulge under his hands. Thinking rapidly, he sought a distraction for his far too astute younger brother. He whipped his head around to look at the outdoor kitchen. "Think there's a burger ready yet?"

"I'll check with Donovan for you." Humming under his breath, Mischa rose and headed off toward the grill. As he strolled past Dan on his way to the outdoor kitchen, Dan rose and joined him. Terry watched as his two brothers spoke briefly. Dan turned a curious gaze in Terry's direction and he studiously ignored it.

Satisfied after a few moments that both of his brothers were thinking of other things, he turned his attention back to what he'd come to think of as his own little porn show. Startled, he found himself staring directly into two pairs of bright, blue eyes. The temptation to look away was an old habit that he'd have to work hard to break. He forced his eyes to maintain the connection, smiled hesitantly, and tipped his head in acknowledgment that he'd been busted true to rights, staring at something that should have been private.

Something in his expression must have met with approval, because both faces broke into wide smiles and the two young men nodded back.

CHAPTER ONE

POKER NIGHT WITH THE BLAKE BROTHERS

Terry Blake sat in his customary seat at the green baize game table, waiting for Mischa, his youngest brother, to arrive so they could start their weekly poker game. He tapped his wallet absently against the table and eyed the clock in frustration. Damn. Every minute dragged on.

Typically, Dan and Brandon argued nearby about the projected budget for a proposed miniseries portraying the founding of New Orleans. As expected, Mischa slammed into the room his habitual half hour late. The younger man glowed with happiness as he mumbled an excuse about his partner Donovan's late arrival home from work, leaving him without a babysitter for the couple's eight-year-old son Matthew.

Terry stifled the urge the ask Mischa about his friends Dex and Trick. After weeks of furtive glances and casual conversations about the weather and movies, Terry had psyched himself up to introduce a more intimate level of conversation than the weather, but the two had been no-shows at last Sunday's get together.

89

"Why didn't you bring Matt with you?" Dan asked, interrupting his train of thought. The Blake brothers were adoring uncles to the lively eight-year-old.

"Because he likes to spend time alone with his Dad," Mischa answered mildly, pulling hundred-dollar bills from his wallet to buy in. He turned to Dan as he spoke, and Terry noted a cryptic communication in the glance. Those two were up to something. "Deal."

Brandon, the eldest of Terry's brothers, sat to his left at the table, and true to form couldn't resist the opening to interfere in his brother's life again. He started in on the school Mischa and Donovan had chosen for Matthew, demanding to know why Matthew hadn't been enrolled at the West Haven Academy like his father and uncles.

Rolling his eyes at Brandon's continued efforts to micromanage his family, Terry interrupted. "Because we all hated that school."

"Precisely," Mischa agreed. "Besides, Matt has special needs and the school we chose will cater to those needs. Plus, it's close to the campus so I can visit or pick him up when I get out of class myself."

"Are we playing cards tonight or what?" Dan asked impatiently.

"Actually," Terry injected as smoothly as he could. "I have something I'd like to talk to you all about before we get started."

Three pairs of green eyes swung in his direction and Terry swallowed hard. Hell. He should have just blurted it out while their attention was elsewhere. Each responded according to his own personality and that was kind of reassuring.

"What is it? Is everything all right?" Mischa's sympathetic inquiry warmed his heart. Whatever the others might say—and he hoped he knew them well enough to predict they'd be okay with what he had to say—he knew he'd have Mischa's support.

"Are we losing money?" Brandon had a one-track mind. As long as the studio ran in the black and Terry played discreetly, Brandon wouldn't care who he slept with.

"Are you dying?" Trust Dan to go for the drama. "Cause if you're not, I'm dealing. And if you are, can I have the Porsche?"

"Actually, I'm gay." He made the announcement in his calmest board-meeting-financial-overview voice and settled back in his chair to view the results. His heart swelled at the responses. No rejection or base comments, just calm acceptance—in Blake brothers' fashion, of course.

Mischa nodded, patted his hand, and went back to counting out his chips and stacking the hundred-dollar bills in front of him. God, he loved that little shit.

Brandon grunted. "Don't scare me like that. If it's not important, send it in an email or something. You nearly gave me a heart attack."

"So, I can't have the Porsche? Can I borrow it on Saturday then?" Dan was already dealing.

"How about we make this a Truth or Dare hand to get everybody's attention?" Mischa suggested.

Terry stifled his groan at the suggestion. Since Mischa had lost the first Truth or Dare bet months ago, the brothers made it a habit to randomly suggest Truth or Dare stakes in their games. Terry had lost his share of games in the past few months and found himself involved in more than one stupid stunt as a consequence. Tonight it felt like a bad idea, but he could hardly refuse after Mischa had insisted on fulfilling the conditions of the first dare by continuing his role as Donovan's housekeeper until the year ended last month.

An hour and a half later, Terry was unsurprised to find Dan and Mischa pushing their cards to the middle of the table. Brandon stared at them all suspiciously. Whatever his two brothers were up to clearly Brandon had not been informed.

Sighing, he pushed his cards in with theirs. "Okay, Mischa, what's it going to be? Want me to help replant your flowerbeds? Wash your cars? Drive the hippie mobile to work for a week?"

Mischa shook his head slowly, green gaze dancing with delight. "No, tonight, Terry, I want the truth."

Truth? Mischa thought he had more truths to tell than he'd just divulged? He shrugged. "Fine. I just outed myself. What else compares to that?"

Dan's evil grin should have clued him in, but his brain didn't work in the out-of-the-box fashion Dan and Mischa were so good at. Give him a map and he could plot the way from point A to B with side trips to C and D and expense estimates for all rational variables. He couldn't pull shit out of thin air without a rational supporting argument. So naturally, he was floored when Dan and Mischa—the conniving little shit—demanded, "What's your darkest fantasy?"

His jaw dropped open and he stared at them, looking from one to the other in horror. No. He turned to Brandon, expecting God knew what kind of help from his eldest brother, but Brandon looked intrigued, and gestured him to answer. Fuck. Thirty-four years old. He was thirty-four fucking years old and he'd never discussed sex with anyone. Not his brothers, not his lovers, and not even his father after the horribly painful birds-and-bees talk he'd had with him on his thirteenth birthday.

And why hadn't he talked about sex with anyone in all this time? Because it fucking bored him, that's why. He'd always—up until recently, that is—had a low sex drive, and until six months ago, he could have quite truthfully answered that he didn't have any dark fantasies at all.

He felt his cheeks flush and his cock swell as he remembered what had started all his fantasies six months ago. Fuck. Now they were all staring at him even more eagerly than before. It must be perfectly fucking obvious from his expression that he had a hell of a truth to tell.

"I, ahhh, I wish you'd asked me that six months ago." Delay tactics. He couldn't hold them off forever, but maybe he could buy himself enough time to calm his heart rate and get rid of his sudden, painful erection. Those damn twins were going to kill him before he even got them into bed at this rate.

"Oh?" Brandon seemed willing to go along with Terry's line of bullshit.

Mischa and Dan exchanged knowing grins. Smug bastards.

"Yeah, because six months ago, I was dating Marissa, and I didn't have any fantasies to speak of." And what a fucking mistake that had been. Bitch. After the barbecue at Mischa's house, she hadn't handled the news that he didn't want to see her again very well at all. He fully expected to leave his office one day and find that she'd taken a Louisville slugger to Mischa's—now his—Porsche.

"So, that was six months ago. Shit happens. Things change. Then you were straight, now you're gay. You got fantasies, spill 'em." *Touching lack of concern for brotherly modesty there, Danny boy.*

"Right, well, yes. Now I'm gay." Already covered that ground.

"Right, so these fantasies, they would be about other men right?" *Thank you, Brandon.*

Mischa turned his intent gaze from Terry to stare in disbelief at his eldest brother. Terry wilted in relief before he remembered that Dan still had him in his sights.

"Fucking A, Brandon, of course he fantasizes about men if he's gay! Gay men don't fantasize about women! Do straight men fantasize about men?" Muttering under his breath he turned his sympathetic gaze back to Terry. "Don't mind him, Terry; he's always been a little slow. Now, what do you fantasize about these men?"

Cut straight to the bone in a single sentence, his little brother did. Was there some kind of knowledge of Terry's secret perverse desires behind that statement? Nah. It was an innocent question. Mischa had no way of knowing how it hacked away at his self-confidence and comfort with his new identity.

Inhaling deeply, he decided to just go for it. Be bold, be rebellious, he coached himself.

"I fantasize about men." D'oh. Mentally he smacked himself in the forehead.

"I thought we already covered that," Dan murmured *sotto voce*.

Girding his loins in expectation of the humiliation to be heaped upon his head when he finally found the right words to explain what exactly he fantasized about, he blurted, "I mean I fantasize about having two men, in my bed, at the same time."

Cheeks flaming, he subsided back in his chair and covered his eyes with one trembling hand. Visions of exactly which two men he wanted wrapped around him, under him, over him, in that bed lingered in his head a long six months after he'd first seen them. Those tormenting dreams and relentlessly recurring, waking fantasies had egged him on to come out to his family, to give up the phony life he'd been leading, and seek real happiness like Mischa had found by being himself. Now if he could just take that next step, get his courage together and ask Trick and Dex out for a drink, or coffee, or a movie, or something, anything more exciting than, "Do you think it's going to rain?"

It had taken him six months to reconcile himself to who he was. He never could make snap decisions. So even though he'd known six months ago he wanted those twins, he'd been slow to rearrange his life. He'd accepted who he was, come out to his family, studied, and prepared himself. Now, he was ready to stake a claim to the family he was certain he was meant to have.

"I don't get it."

Goddamn, Brandon. How did such an idiot ever get to be head of the studio? He slammed his head down onto the green baize of the table. Suddenly furious, he lurched upright and knocked his chair backwards.

"You fucking explain it to him," he snarled at Mischa and Dan who looked startled.

A half hour later he sat in an armchair in his large bedroom, pretending to read a book while he agonized over his stupidity. Why did he lose his temper? Brandon was as he was, dense about human relations, but brilliant in many respects.

He dropped the book into his lap to cover his ever-present semierection as a knock sounded at the door. "Come in," he called. No doubt one of his brothers had come to check on him after his unusual display of temper and bad manners.

Mischa came in and sat on Terry's bed. "I came to say good bye before I head home to Donovan and Matt. And to say I'm sorry for teasing you like that."

Terry forced a small smile. "It's all right. Shit, I've done the same. I'm just a little...umm...edgy lately."

Mischa smiled. "That's an understatement. Listen. I don't want to interfere in your life or anything, but in case you're interested, I can recommend a few places to help you, umm, take the edge off."

Terry stared at his baby brother. That couldn't have been what it sounded like. He realized he'd stared too long without responding when the kid flushed and spoke again.

"Fuck, Terry, there are clubs you can go to and get laid. Real casual hook-up kinds of places where everyone practices safe sex and you can work off some of that frustration that's making you such a joy to be around lately. Now, I'm getting the fuck out of here, now because I do not want to answer the question I can see forming in your brain right now. Goodnight, dickhead."

"'Night to you, you little shit." A picture of his baby brother club hopping in the hopes of getting some back-room action invaded his brain. *Get that image out of your head now.* It was replaced with a vision of two pale-skinned, dark-haired boys on their knees lavishing his cock with the attentions of twin rosy mouths. *That one too!*

CHAPTER TWO

The Club Scene

A month of soul searching and careful consideration had brought him to this place. Well, that and the threats from his entire staff to walk out if he didn't so something about his steadily worsening temper. He hadn't found any of the experience enjoyable though, and frankly that was beginning to cause him more than a little bit of concern.

His eyes burned and threatened to tear up every time they encountered the acrid smoke that the DJ seemed to feel enhanced the club experience. The flashing, colored lights made his head throb in agony. Was there latent epilepsy in the family? He'd better check with his mother on that before he made a habit of clubbing. The music—if it could be called that—battered his ears and contributed to the headache.

Worst of all, though, men crowded the place. Everywhere. All kinds of men: tall, short, thin, buff, sinfully handsome and sexily homely. They crowded the dance floor, the tiny tables around the walls of the room, and the bar itself. They gyrated on the dance floor in ones, twos, threes—a somewhat reassuring sight—and some tangles of limbs too numerous to sort out

TRUTH OR DARE

at all. Some wore tight leather and flowing pirate style shirts, some wore skinny jeans and too-small T-shirts, and others wore damn near nothing. Some even wore plain old Levi's and button-down shirts, just like Terry.

All these men, and he felt nothing. No spark of attraction for any individual or type. He stood here, leaning on the bar, watching things that should have sent his blood boiling and his cock cheering, in the hopes of gaining some experience and, to quote his younger brother, "take the edge off."

Instead, it cringed behind the buttons of his fly and gave no sign of being willing to play with any of the men aesthetics told him must be attractive to others.

He felt the slightest buzz of interest when his gaze caught two men entwined in a dark corner across the crowded dance floor, but the shifting throng of dancers obscured the view almost as soon as he caught it.

"Would you like another drink, or are you just hanging out here to provide entertainment for me?" The bartender—Calvin, according to his nametag—approached Terry for what must have been the third time in half an hour.

Smiling, Terry waved his still full glass. "No thanks. I'm good." He turned back to people watching. The bartender's hand dropped onto his own where it rested on the bar. Startled, Terry met the bartender's intent brown gaze inquiringly.

"I have a break in a few." The handsome young man quirked an eyebrow at Terry. "Want to take a walk out back with me?"

Ahhh, no, most assuredly he did not. "No, thanks anyway. I'm, um...probably leaving soon."

"Suit yourself." The bartender wiped the counter around his drink and strutted down the bar to chat with two guys at the other end.

Shit. This wasn't going well. *Did you really expect it to? Why? You didn't enjoy hanging out in clubs as a straight man, why did you think you would find the smoke, noise, and crowd more appealing now that you're gay?* Good point. He didn't like this scene, straight or gay. Nodding, decision made, he dropped a bill on the bar next to his untouched drink and headed for the door. No meat markets, gay or straight.

He had nearly achieved his objective when a hand from nowhere yanked him onto the dance floor and he found himself playing pole to a wildly gyrating dancer in a miniscule pair of black leather shorts. The dancer rubbed his obviously aroused cock all over whatever parts of Terry he managed to reach and draped his arms around Terry's neck.

Stunned, Terry waited for his body to respond. Nope. Nothing. Sighing, he raised his hands, looked at the other man's nearly naked body, and grimaced. He'd had this problem when his first prom date wore a backless, strapless dress too. No safe place to put his hands.

Finally, he settled for pushing the tips of fingers against the man's shoulders, trying to get some distance between them. "Thanks, but no thanks."

He backed away from the disappointed guy and then turned to make another break for the door. He assiduously ignored the straying hands that patted at his ass and groped his body, maintaining a steady pace toward the door.

At last he stood in the clean, sweet air outside the club, sucking in deep breaths. With fresh air came a return of sanity. What the hell did he think he was doing anyway? He wasn't some kid out looking to get laid. He was a grown man who'd had an epiphany. His personality hadn't changed. He'd just fallen in lust. Okay, maybe after six months he could consider the possibility that it might be more, but he certainly hadn't become promiscuous just because he'd admitted he was gay. He wanted two men, and only those particular two men would do. Searching for substitutes in bars was the stupidest idea he'd ever come up with. No, he could blame that idea on Mischa, the little shit.

Calm settled over him. Yeah, Mischa. He pulled his cell phone from his pocket and pressed the rapid dial button programmed with Mischa's cell. He'd met his twins any number of times at his brother's house in the past six months. If he stuck close to Mischa, he was certain to encounter his obsession again. Next time he met up with the twins, he'd be ready. No more wussing out.

Next time, he'd ask them out for a drink or something, anything that would mean time together without an audience.

"He was here."

Dex turned to stare into Trick's blue eyes. He smiled. His brother had such a beautiful face. "I saw him too," Dex replied, pulling his brother back down on the chair next to his at the tiny table along the furthest wall of the club. "He stood at the bar for a while."

Trick leaned forward across the tiny table to whisper in his ear in order to be heard over the loud music. "I told you he was gay."

"He was straight at that party six months ago. I saw him arrive with that slutty actress, Marissa 'Look I Have Boobs' Matinson." Dex shivered as Trick's warm breath caressed his ear. He swept a swift glance around the crowded club, but no one seemed to be paying any attention to them.

"We arrived at that party with Bella. Does that make us straight?" Trick flicked Dex's earlobe with his tongue, sending more shivers through his frame. "We should have gone over to him, said hello."

"Quit teasing," Dex demanded, twisting to press a kiss to the tormenting lips. "I want him, too. And I'll concede that his presence here does give a strong indication that he might be gay. But," he cautioned as he saw the fire light in Trick's eyes, "being gay doesn't mean he's going to be into both of us." Oh shit, he hated seeing that devastated look in those beloved blue eyes. Lifting a hand, he pushed straight, black locks behind Trick's ear and kissed him again, a little harder this time, trying to distract him from the possibility that their crush might not want them. Terry Blake always seemed vaguely startled to find himself with Dex and Trick. Every time they met he'd introduced himself as though he'd forgotten who they were, made some vague comment about the weather, stared around desperately, and made some shallow excuse to leave them. Sometimes, Dex thought he saw the slightest hint of heat, an ember of desire, but always it disappeared.

Sighing, Trick pushed him away, and then grasped his hand. "I know. But I didn't like seeing him here. I didn't like Calvin flirting with him; I didn't like that little creep dancing with him, and I didn't like seeing all those guys grabbing his ass. He's ours; I know it."

God bless Trick. He was always so certain things would turn out the way he wanted them to. No matter how many times life reared back and slapped them in the face, he always seemed to hold hope in his heart. Dex pulled Trick into a comforting embrace and whispered into his ear, "I didn't like seeing that either, doll. But I did like that he didn't seem to care about those other guys."

"What do you mean?" Trick gazed into Dex's eyes, seeking reassurance.

"I mean the hottest guys in this room gave him the eye, and he didn't even notice. I don't know why Mischa's brother came here tonight, but I do know he left alone and he didn't have to."

Fuck. Mischa's brother. There was a timely reminder. After years of rejection and snide remarks from family, friends, and complete strangers, Trick and Dex had finally found friends who accepted them for who they were. Mischa, Donovan, and Bella didn't look at them as though they were perverts because they loved each other. They didn't insist on looking the other way when he and Trick showed their affection for one another, and they didn't demand prurient details about how deep that affection went.

He looked over at Trick again. He wanted above all things to see his brother happy. Six months ago when they caught the gorgeous accountant watching them at a barbecue at Mischa's house, they'd both felt an instant surge of desire. Terry's expression showed fascination, not disapproval or disgust. The potential loss of Mischa's friendship made the price of taking Terry to their bed too high.

Damn, disappointment sank through him. Shrugging it off, he used Trick's grip on his hand to pull him to his feet. This called for distraction. "Dance with me," he pleaded. Trick loved dancing and threw himself into it. Wild music and drifting smoke, flashing lights and hot sweaty bodies provided an excellent distraction from the man they couldn't have, and Dex smiled as he watched Trick enjoying himself on the dance floor.

Leaving the club a half hour later, his unease returned when Trick leaned close to whisper in his ear again, "He's not going to come back here. I'm sure it's not his kind of place."

Desperately, Dex pulled Trick along to where they had parked their car along a side street nearby. At the car, he embraced his brother again, kissing him and running his hands through the silky black hair. He pressed closer, leaning hard into Trick's slender frame, dropping a hand to stroke the curve of his taut ass through tight denim.

He pulled his mouth from the wet heat, ignoring Trick's protest as he did so. "Please," he whispered. "Let this be enough, hmm? Let me be enough."

Trick stared back at him, desire darkened his blue eyes to almost black, but still, in the deepest recesses of those blue depths, Dex saw hints of loneliness, all the more devastating because he felt certain his own eyes reflected the same bleak look.

Determined to drive off thoughts of the man they couldn't have, he dragged his hand from Trick's ass to stroke his cock, hard beneath the zipper of his jeans. His own cock throbbed in response to the heat he found, and he moved to pull their hips together, rubbing, grinding, cock to cock, as he melded their lips again in a passionate kiss.

CHAPTER THREE

A Chance Encounter

Terry rolled his eyes as he listened to Brandon yammering on in his ear about some *important* budgetary crisis on a set. A movement in the rear view mirror caught his attention, and he turned to look at the street behind him. Shit. The couple making out against the Escalade behind him looked a lot like his twins. His previously stoic cock twitched and deigned to take note. That was one hot embrace.

Damn. They were *his* twins. "Brandon, I have to go. Catch me in the morning with this before you go to the office. Bye." Ignoring Brandon's voluble protests, he flipped the phone shut and shoved it in his pocket. Getting out of the Porsche, he pressed the lock button on the key fob and secured the car.

He crossed behind the car and approached the couple. They broke apart and turned to face him, one brother stepping protectively in front of the other. Terry stepped into the yellow glow of the streetlight so they would know they had nothing to fear from him. Instantly, the apprehensive expressions changed. With careful consideration, he guessed that the brother in front was Dex, who always seemed protective of his sibling. Trick pushed his brother lightly to the side and stepped forward. Terry blinked at the beauty of his broad smile. Dex seemed more subdued, not quite as welcoming. A few meetings and casual conversations at Mischa's house weren't much to go on, but nothing ventured, nothing gained.

"Hi, Dex, Trick. You might remember me from Mischa's house. I'm Terry, Mischa's older brother. My car won't start. Can I ask you for a lift?" He gestured toward the Porsche, maligning the magnificent machine without a twinge of conscience.

"I'm Trick, this is Dex, and we remember you. Where do you live?" Trick smiling was a gorgeous sight, but the hand gestures to indicate which brother was which were unnecessary.

"I know you're Trick. I live in Beverly Hills, but let me just call Mischa, and if you can drop me off at his place that'll be fine." Mischa could damn well drive him back to his car later.

"You know which of us is which?" Dex sounded dubious.

He nodded. "Of course. Not that you don't look alike, but it's more of a mannerism thing. Trick stays in the background more, you take the lead."

Trick shook his head. "If you say so. Anyway, we live in Beverly Hills too. We'll take you all the way."

Yeah, that sounded great. "Let me get my things from the car." He retrieved his briefcase and laptop bag from the passenger seat of the Porsche. As he strolled back toward the Escalade, he saw the brothers talking face to face. Were they arguing about him? As he watched, Dex took Trick's face in both hands and kissed him briefly on the lips.

"I love you." The intensity of the words, rather than their volume, made them audible to Terry as he moved down the pavement. He smiled. The boys exchanged hugs and Trick handed over the car keys to Dex as Terry approached.

Dex slid behind the wheel of the Escalade and Trick reached out to take the bags Terry held. He stowed them behind the rear seat then slid in. Instead of sliding across to the other side behind the driver, he stopped in the middle and fastened a lap belt. He patted the seat next to him, inviting Terry to sit close. Obligingly, Terry hopped in and slammed the door. He opted not to buckle the over the shoulder belt for ease of movement. Trick smiled approvingly at him. Terry met Dex's wary blue eyes in the rear view mirror. He wanted to be sure both of his boys were happy with the situation. Dex gave him a slow acknowledging grin, and then turned back to driving.

"You were at the club." Trick's soft, husky voice, full of hope and need gave him courage.

"I was. I wanted to check something out."

"Did you find out what you wanted to know?" Dex's inquiry from the driver's seat proved he followed the conversation.

"I did." With a deep breath, he took a chance on telling the truth. "I wanted to know if I was gay. Scratch that," he rushed out. "I wanted to know if I would be as attracted to anyone else as I am to the two of you." Again, he met Dex's assessing gaze in the rearview mirror.

Trick tugged on his hand, and Terry focused his attention on the more openly affectionate brother. Little fluttering touches from the smooth white hands caressed his fingers, petting and stroking his body wherever they could reach. Marvelous eddies of heat swirled through him, and he relaxed into the touches, finally raising his arm and sliding it along the back of the seat over Trick's shoulders.

Trick hummed in approval and raised his face to Terry's.

Maintaining the reflected eye contact with Dex, wanting him to know that as far as Terry was concerned he was part of this, Terry covered tricks mouth with his own. Slowly he traced the lips he'd dreamed about for over six months with his tongue, moaning in gratification when they instantly parted to allow him entrance. In the mirror, he saw Dex swallow hard and jerk his gaze back to the road ahead. Disappointed, Terry swept his tongue into the wet heat Trick had ceded to him.

He tasted the dark sweetness there, mingled with a slightly different flavor that might have been the residue of the kiss Trick had shared with Dex earlier. Mm. His cock thoroughly approved of that idea. It swelled and pressed eagerly against the zipper of his jeans.

Terry jerked in surprise when a hand dropped to his lap and pressed against his throbbing erection. *Shit.* That felt amazing. It had been so long since he'd felt any contact but his own hand there. That this touch came from one of the men he'd been fantasizing about had him on the verge of orgasm already.

Gently, he removed the hand and pulled back from the kiss. "Baby, not yet." He gestured toward Dex, who continued to steal peeks at them through the rear view mirror. "Let's wait till we can all play."

"Oh, my God, I can't believe you said that. Dex, did you hear that?" Trick's grin couldn't have been any wider. His eyes sparkled with true happiness, and Terry couldn't resist stealing another kiss.

"Yeah, I heard." Dex's hoarse voice drew his attention.

"Umm, is that okay? Am I assuming too much? I mean, I've...seen you...together." Damn. Was he making a fool of himself?

"No. It's fine. More than fine, actually," Trick insisted. "Please, we both want you, together. We do everything together."

Half an hour later, sexual temptation had yielded to sexual tension and rapidly transitioned to full blown frustration. He directed Dex to park in the circular drive directly in front of the big double doors to the mansion, jumped out of the car as quickly as his aching cock would allow, and pulled Trick out next to him. Dex dashed impatiently around the hood of the still pinging car and threw himself into Terry's arms. The frantic kiss he bestowed on Terry revealed the frustration he'd felt, relegated to the driver's seat while the other two played in the back.

TRUTH OR DARE

"I'm hiring a driver in the morning." Terry gasped, pulling away and tugging Trick into the kiss as well. Lips and tongues tangled, and Terry neither knew nor cared whose tongue caressed his own, he just knew he wanted to feel them both on other parts of his body, immediately if not sooner. "And buying a car with a privacy shield."

Wrapping a hand around each delicate wrist, Terry sped up the grand staircase, tugging a gently giggling Trick and smiling Dex behind him. He flung open the door to his room with a crash and shoved them toward the bed. Shutting the door behind himself, he locked it with a click and reached for a remote on the table by the door. He tossed the remote to Trick and ordered, "Choose some music." Turning to Dex, he ordered, "Strip."

Terry leaned against the door and watched as each brother scrambled to follow his orders. Trick had Tom Petty pouring from the surround sound speakers in no time, and then went to help his brother out of his clothes. Dex returned the favor, and in moments, the two gazed inquiringly at Terry. He surveyed them slowly, head to toe. Each head of sleek, black hair was styled in the same fashion, twin pairs of blue eyes glowed with desire, identical rosy mouths, swollen from the kisses they'd shared were parted in anticipation of more kisses to come. Smooth, white skin, taut, firmly muscled bodies, and hard throbbing cocks were a feast for his senses. The only visible difference between the two of them was a certain wariness in Dex's expression.

As always when they stood close, the twins' hands automatically sought each other out, stroking, petting, in constant contact. Terry sighed in pleasure. This he'd dreamed about. This was what he'd "come out" for. Watching his boys petting one another, he began unfastening his white shirt, shrugging it off and reaching for the button of his jeans. He pushed them impatiently down his legs, and eyes glued to the show, reclined on his bed, hands clasped behind his head.

107

Cheeks flushed and eyes sparkling, the twins rotated to face him. Their hands were more frantic now, their desire more pronounced. Terry, judging them to be as frustrated as he, opened his arms in welcome. In seconds, he had two armfuls of firm flesh pressed tight to his body, and two hands met around his cock. Fuck. That was absolutely perfect. One hot wet mouth latched onto a nipple and the other covered his own. His sorely tested will broke, and his hips jerked convulsively as the sweet touch moved from tip to balls and back again, jerking him tenderly. He groaned as the climax overwhelmed him and bursts of cum spurted over their hands and onto his chest. Moans of pleasure from the twins told him they approved his lack of control.

He lay panting for breath, hoping for a quick recovery, when he became conscious of hot tongues licking the cum from his body. When the twins had lapped all the liquid from his chest, they turned to one another. Trick brought Dex's hand, coated with Terry's juices, to his mouth and began to lick it clean, as Dex provided his brother with the same service. When each was satisfied, they met in a passionate kiss over Terry's abdomen. They broke apart to lean forward and include him in the kiss. Terry felt his cock stir in response. *Oh, yeah.* His recovery time as a gay man was a vast improvement over his recovery time as a straight man.

Growling, he rolled the nearest twin under him and began the leisurely task of kissing and licking every bit of the delicious flesh at his disposal. As he moved from slender, white neck to rosy, pink nipples, down a tight abdomen to a thick, throbbing cock, he felt the other twin's hands on his own body mirroring his path. As he took the leaking cock between his lips, a strong grip encircled his own and stroked it to full hardness again. Oh, yeah, this could definitely work.

Below him, Dex whimpered and thrust upwards, blue eyes begging for permission to come. Trick pulled away from Terry and dropped down next to his brother. He played with Dex's nipples and pressed hot moist kisses to his open lips. Dex groaned again, jerked convulsively, and Terry's sucking mouth was filled with hot, salty liquid. He struggled to both savor the flavor and swallow every drop, but found it impossible. He shrugged off the momentary tension he felt at not doing this perfectly. Screw it, it was his first blowjob, and he planned to enjoy it, not self-critique every moment.

When Dex had softened completely, he bestowed a final kiss on the delicate skin and crawled up the bed to kiss both boys again. He and Dex turned Trick onto his back and began the whole series of kisses and touches over again.

"Please, oh God, please, Terry, make love to me. I want to feel you deep inside." Trick's blue eyes blazed with scorching heat up at him, and Terry groaned. His cock approved that idea if the slick liquid drops of pre-cum leaking from its tip were any indication.

Rearing back, he spread Trick's thighs and moved between them. He stared down at the tiny puckered opening, feeling momentary concern. Though not huge, he was thicker than average Dex's touch while unrolling a condom down his length sent shudders of pure lust rushing through him, and he decided the twins knew what they were doing. If they thought it was possible, then he wouldn't argue. Terry ran a finger down the pulsing vein on the back of Trick's cock and dipped it into the pooling liquid at the tip. How would Trick taste in comparison to Dex? He brought the finger to his mouth and licked the drops of salty liquid. Mm. The flavor was different, but similar, earthier. Dex thrust lubed fingers in a steady rhythm in Trick's ass, and Trick moaned in pleasure. Terry waited as patiently as he could. At last, Dex pulled his fingers from the opening of Trick's body and guided Terry into place.

Gritting his teeth, he protested, "I don't want to hurt you."

In response, Trick squirmed closer, pushing against him. "You won't." He promised on a breathy whisper.

Gently, he pushed forward, feeling sweat bead on his brow and trickle down as his whole world narrowed to that one point where his body slowly merged with Trick's. At last, the thick crown popped through the ring of muscle and with a groan he slid home. Nothing had ever felt as good. The damp heat clung tightly, squeezing him so wonderfully he thought he might come right then.

He raised his eyes from the joining of their bodies to gaze deep into Trick's shining eyes. The younger man bit his lip, writhing impatiently beneath Terry's weight. Dex reached between them to grip his brother's hungry cock with a lubed hand. Groaning, Trick arched into the caressing hand, and Terry felt the movement as a caress along his entire length. Unable to wait he began thrusting into the heated grip of Trick's ass, reveling in the other man's gasps and cries of pleasure. Feeling his balls tighten ruthlessly, he knew he was on the verge of climaxing again and stilled briefly.

Dex jerked Trick with rapid, hard strokes. Terry tried to match the rhythm and power of his own body slamming into Trick's perfect heat. Trick reacted with an almost instantaneous shout as he came in long bursts of creamy liquid.

The rhythmic pulsing of his passage around Terry sent him over the edge as well. With a strangled cry, he followed his lover in to hot ecstasy.

Lying in a cocoon of warm limbs and sticky bodies, heart still pounding, and gasping for breath, Terry decided sex had never been so good.

CHAPTER FOUR

Trick woke in momentary confusion. The firmly muscled chest under his cheek boasted a fine sprinkling of hair, and Dex's chest was as hairless as his own. A touch of panic set in and his eyes popped open instantly. *Where is Dex?* Inches away, Dex's sleeping face, flushed and innocent, more relaxed in sleep, rested on the same broad, golden-tan chest.

Smiling, Trick remembered the details of the previous night. He gently pulled back from where he and Dex lay cuddled against Terry's warm body. His lovers protested as his movements disturbed them, but he wanted a moment to admire the way they looked all curled up together. Terry's body was big, well muscled, and an all-over golden tan that suggested he sunbathed naked. He had sprinklings of fine blond hair on chest, groin, arms, and legs that glinted a bit in the early morning light. By contrast, he and Dex were pale, with creamy white skin, nearly hairless, small, and finely muscled.

A sudden thought sent him scrambling for his pants pocket and his cell phone. He switched it to camera mode and snapped a quick shot of the two men he loved more than anything.

Smiling, he searched Terry's room and came up with his cell phone as well. A few minutes tinkering and he had programmed the phone with his and Dex's numbers and snapped a number of photos with it as well.

Setting the phone on Terry's nightstand, he shook Dex's shoulder. Time for them to get out of Terry's house and off to their own before anyone noticed their Escalade blocking the main drive. He smiled indulgently as his brother grumbled about waking up and getting dressed. In this respect, he and Dex were not alike. Trick enjoyed mornings as much as nights, especially mornings after great sex, like last night. He woke energized and feeling fantastic. Dex faced every morning as though it were a mortal enemy, no matter how amazing the night before had been.

He bundled his sleepy brother into his clothing and hustled him out the bedroom door into the spacious hallway. Having shut the door carefully behind him, he turned to gather his brother to his side and guide him down the stairs.

"What the fuck?" Brandon's belligerent, deep voice demanded. "Oh, hell no! You two did not just come out of Terry's room!"

Trick felt his happiness fade and pulled his twin closer. Dex jerked fully awake in a second, which was a damn good thing because the shouting and waves of anger emanating from Terry's brother made his own stomach lurch violently. They had to get out of there quickly or he was going to be violently ill.

"What do you care? We're leaving now anyway." That was Dex, tough guy in the face of adversity. Why could Trick only be strong when things were going well? He hated feeling this way, but confrontation was not his thing.

"I care because I love my brother. Unlike him, I know exactly who you really are, Destiny John Hyatt!" Brandon's face reflected the fury in his eyes. His hands clenched into fists, his face flushed with anger.

Dex appeared taken aback to hear his birth name spoken aloud for the first time in probably a decade. It kind of surprised Trick, too, but worse, it made his nausea more acute. He really was going to lose it right here on this gorgeous Persian rug if they didn't get out of there soon. He covered his mouth with one hand and clutched Dex tighter with the other. His twin got the message because he pulled his hand away and wrapped a supporting arm around Trick's waist. The strength in that embrace shored him up a little, and he prayed they could make a fast escape, but apparently the tirade wasn't over yet.

"I know the whole story of your sordid pasts, and you are not what my brother needs. He's just admitted he's gay for Christ's sake, and that alone is going to cause a furor of publicity that he'll hate. Do you really think he needs to come out in the middle of an incest scandal as well? Just get out of my house and don't come back!" Brandon scowled in disgust.

That did it. Trick couldn't hold back any longer. His stomach gave a particularly forceful lunge and he doubled over retching and spewing vomit across the carpet, spraying Brandon's trousers and shoes with the foul stuff as well. Shivering with horror and on the verge of tears, he turned to his twin and begged, "Please, let's go. I can't..."

Dex wrapped both arms around him, but Trick couldn't take any comfort from the embrace. Dex had been right. There really wasn't a permanent place for them in Terry's life. Tears trickled down his cheeks, and he buried his face in his brother's shoulder, trying desperately to hold back the sobs in Brandon's presence.

"I could cheerfully kill you for that," Dex sneered. "Trust me, we are well aware that judgmental, half-informed people would make Terry's life hell if we pursued a relationship with him."

Trick leaned heavily on Dex as they made their way down the grand staircase they'd flown up so exuberantly the evening before. Sick and tired, he just wanted to curl up and sleep and forget about the disastrous ending to the most beautiful sex of his life.

In the Escalade, he reclined his seat and covered his sore, red eyes with polarized sunglasses. Trick held tight to Dex's hand and struggled to stop the tears, to stop the downslide into what promised to be the worst depression cycle he'd ever experienced. Trick was exhausted from the emotional strain of bouncing from high to low and the turmoil of the morning. He slid into sleep, wishing he wouldn't have to wake up to a world of loneliness again, a world where it was him and Dex on one side and the rest of the world on the other.

Dex drove carefully through the morning traffic. He should have just taken Trick, Loki James Hyatt, to give him his birth name, over to the Hyatt estate and let him sleep there. Neither of them enjoyed being in their parents' home, though, so he had telephoned Bella and asked if they could crash at her place for a while.

Bastard. He fucking hated that bastard. How dare Brandon Blake threaten them? Ten years ago he and Trick had been lonely, scared thirteen-year-olds abandoned by their parents and sent off to boarding school away from the home they'd grown up in. Was it so strange that they would cling to each other for comfort?

Of course, having a bigoted homophobic bully for a roommate hadn't helped Trick any. He'd crept into Dex's bed for comfort, and the next thing they knew, despite their protests of innocence, they'd been expelled for reasons they couldn't quite comprehend. A flurry of publicity had hounded them for years, reporters sneaking pictures and printing innuendo. Rags published sleazy stories from former schoolmates or roommates testifying to the supposed incest, and offering doctored photos as proof. It had been a long time before they'd escaped the stigma, and they'd only managed it by adopting new names, new images, submersing themselves in a culture of defiance. That was how they'd met Mischa and Bella, and finally discovered friendship.

He knew Trick had hoped that Terry's open acceptance of the two of them meant that they could be together, just as he knew that Brandon's anger had destroyed that hope.

He fought back his own tears today just as he had all those years ago. With their parents gone, maybe even dead after all this time, Trick was his responsibility. He needed to be strong to take care of his brother, to keep him from slipping over the edge into the depression that clearly threatened.

Parking outside Bella's apartment block, he opened the glove box and rooted around a bit. Finally he found the small pharmacists bottle of anti-depressants and shoved it into his pocket. He gathered his cell phone and laptop bag and jumped down from the Escalade. Hurrying to the passenger side, he opened it and gently shook Trick to wake him. Heart aching in sympathy, he unfastened the seatbelt and tugged his brother forward. Shifting his burdens so he could wrap his arm around his brother's waist, he led him gently up the path to the steps leading to Bella's door.

Bella must have been watching for them because the door swung open, and she rushed out to help him get Trick inside.

"What happened?" she whispered softly, guiding Trick to the bed in the corner of the studio apartment. Together they pulled back the covers and rolled Trick to the center of the bed. "Is he sick?"

Bella must have caught the whiff of vomit that still clung to Trick's breath. He shook his head. "No. He has a weak stomach. Stress-induced nausea. He just needs some comforting." Bella nodded and crawled across Trick to the side of the bed shoved against the wall. She snuggled next to his brother without further probing and pulled the blanket up to cover them both.

Dex watched her calm acceptance of the situation and felt the tears he'd held back trickle slowly down his cheeks. He turned slightly away, hoping she hadn't noticed. His voice, when he spoke, was hoarse. "I'll be right back. I have to make a call."

He hurried over to the balcony that overlooked the inner courtyard of the complex. Gulping in fresh air, he struggled to get his emotions under control. He had to make the call to Mischa before Terry got to him first, and the hour-long drive had given Terry plenty of time to wake up.

CHAPTER FIVE

Terry came awake slowly with a welcome sense of peace. His body ached in places, but damn, he felt good all over and completely relaxed. Memories of caressing hands, hot lips, and hard cocks flickered through his mind as he recalled the hours of lovemaking that had contributed to his current state. His eyes snapped open and he scanned the huge bed for his lovers. No pale-fleshed, dark-haired twins lounged at his sides. When he had at last drifted into sleep, too sated with sex to stir, they had been cuddled up next to him. Twin heads of dark hair rested on his broad chest, petting each other and himself in open affection and as they whispered softly together. That soft, sexy murmur of nearly identical voices had lulled him to sleep securely in a bed that had been far too lonely.

They were gone. Sighing, he sat up, shifted his pillows, and then settled back to sit against the headboard. *What did you think? That they'd move in? That you'd wake up and they'd be here waiting for a repeat performance before breakfast?* Of course they left early in the morning. Their car blocking the drive would have been sufficient reason. Imagine the field day the reporters/

stalkers would have if they'd been discovered!

His gaze fell on the cell phone on the nightstand by the bed, and he smiled. He'd left it in the pocket of his jeans last night, too anxious to get naked and on the bed to properly put it away. One of the twins must have taken it out for some reason. He picked it up and his smile broadened as he took in the new screensaver picture. It showed one of the twins, Dex, he thought, sleeping with his head resting on Terry's chest. Terry slept obliviously, one hand curled in Dex's hair. Both wore contented expressions. On a hunch, he checked his contacts and saw that two new cell phone numbers had been programmed into his phone.

Without hesitation, he dialed the first number, impatient to speak to his lovers. He waited while the phone rang four times and then drew in a breath as it went to voice mail. Deciding to leave a message on the spur of the moment, he spoke. "Hey, Trick, it's Terry. Thanks for the picture. I loved waking up to it. I have to go in to work at the studio today, but hope to leave the office by seven. I'd like to meet up with you two tonight. Call me anytime, okay?"

Feeling happier and more at ease with himself than he ever had before, Terry slipped from the bed and headed to shower. He was running awfully late, but he had some other things he needed to do this morning. One of which—he looked around his comfortably elegant bedroom in the family home—was to get the ball rolling on finding a home of his own. And two—he smirked wickedly, remembering the long car ride yesterday evening—hire a driver and buy a car with a really big, comfortable backseat and privacy glass.

Placing help wanted ads and calling his car dealership to place an order for what he wanted went pretty quickly. Finding a real estate agent to show him houses was a little more difficult. He hadn't been able to reach Trick or Dex on the phone, and since he really wanted them to view the houses with him, it put him at a standstill. His old insecurities came back too. Maybe he assumed too much after a night of great sex. The twins might not even want to see him again, let alone consider helping him choose a home with the view to living there with him at a later date. Maybe he assumed too much in thinking that the sex was as great for them as it was for him.

Shaking off the self-doubt—he couldn't have been mistaken in that intense emotional connection he'd felt—he went in to the office and tried to get as much of his work done as possible so he could leave.

When no return phone call came before lunch, he tried calling both numbers on his cell again, and again it went to voice mail. At seven o'clock, as he packed up to leave the office and head home, he tried both numbers again. Shrugging off the nagging concern he felt, he reminded himself that they might well have had plans already, or be working. He really didn't know much about Dex and Trick. He couldn't help thinking, though, that at some point during the day, one of them could have picked up a phone and called to tell him that they couldn't meet.

He lounged on the sofa in the TV room, flipping through channels, unable to settle on any one show to watch. Nothing caught his interest; nothing distracted him from thoughts of the twins, wondering where they were, who they were with, and why they hadn't called. Memories of the excesses of the night before kept him more than half hard. When ten o'clock came around with no call, he headed up to his room, stripped out of his clothing and jumped into the shower.

Quick wash-off accomplished, he crawled into bed and studied the picture on his cell phone. Why leave him the picture and their numbers if they didn't want to see him again? Reassured, he studied the photo. One hand drifted down his body to lightly clasp his cock, stroking firmly as he replayed the memories of the best night of his life. Gasping, he felt his balls tighten close to his body. A tingling heat pooled at the base of his spine, and Terry stroked himself to orgasm. He wiped the sticky mess from his hand and chest with his T-shirt and rolled to his side to pick up the phone again.

He wouldn't call again. Couldn't. If he had been mistaken, if the emotional connection he had felt hadn't been there for them, he had to maintain some dignity. No doubt he'd be encountering the twins again—at Mischa and Donovan's frequent gatherings, if nowhere else. If he made a fool of himself now, he'd never be able to look them in the eye.

As he drifted into a restless sleep, he wondered if preserving dignity should still be a goal. After all, dignity had been a byword for straight, unhappy, everything by the book Terry Blake. Damn this cold, uncomfortable, lonely bed.

Another day passed without contact, and he restrained himself, leaving only one voice mail—this one on Trick's phone—asking the twins to meet or call him. Still no response came. By the third day, he decided dignity be damned, he wanted answers. He needed to know if he was blowing a one-night stand out of proportion. They at least owed him a face-to-face kiss off, didn't they?

Feeling desperate, he caved in to the impulse that had been driving him mad the last two days and called Mischa. When this call, too, went directly to voice mail, he decided to give his brother the benefit of the doubt and assumed he was in class. Certain that Mischa would pick up his son Matt from school and head home by three thirty; he decided to stop by Mischa's house on his way home. He didn't know exactly what he expected Mischa to be able to tell him, but he figured he could cross-examine his baby brother at leisure in the privacy of his own home. Mischa would have a hard time lying straight to his face, though why he thought Mischa might try to hide something from he him, he didn't really know either.

So at seven fifteen he found himself standing outside Mischa and Donovan's house, admiring the newly planted flowerbeds while he waited for a response to his knock. As the door swung open, he heard the shrieking laughter of his nephew Matt in the background and Donovan's deep voice in counterpoint.

He met Mischa's gaze quizzically. Instantly, his eyes narrowed and his smile turned to a scowl. It was blatantly obvious from Mischa's expression that he knew something, and that whatever that something was, Terry wasn't going to like it. "Spill it, Mischa. What do you know that I don't?"

"Oh. Come into the house. I don't know why all my brothers think I want my neighbors to know the most intimate details of my life." Mischa turned and gestured him into the hallway, then waved him to the living room. "I'll just go tell Donovan that you're here. He's playing with Matt. Are you staying for dinner?"

"I don't know. It depends on what you have to say." He strolled restlessly over to the sofa, remembering a time not so long ago when he and his brothers had crowded into this room, determined to protect their little brother from Donovan's greedy clutches. Well, more like eager to judge the character of the man who had had such a huge impact on their youngest brother's way of life in such a short period of time.

"Well," Mischa returned and curled up in a corner of the couch. "What can I do for you, Terry?"

"You can cut the crap and tell me what you know about the twins."

Mischa's eyes rounded in pretended innocence. "I know quite a bit about them actually. We've been good friends for over a year now, so you'll need to be more specific."

The little shit was hiding something from him. Using misdirection to piss off his brothers was a key character trait of the old Mischa. The new one usually relied on brutal honesty and cut through the bullshit. Sounded like a good policy for the new Terry to adopt as well. "Cut the bullshit, Mischa. If you guys are such good friends, I'm sure they told you we hooked up the other night."

All pretenses at innocence dropped from Mischa's expression. He turned a serious gaze on Terry, speaking softly. "Yeah, I know. Dex told me."

"And?"

"And he doesn't want me to tell you how to get in touch with them." Mischa looked almost regretful.

Fuck. That was brutal. They didn't want him to get in touch. "Why? I mean," Heat rose in his cheeks. "It was amazing. Nothing has ever felt so right before. Why would they leave me their numbers if they didn't want to do it again?"

Disgust replaced the sympathy in Mischa's gaze. "If all it's about is a great lay, then I'm not surprised. There's more to life than sex, you know. And when I said you needed to work off some of that frustration, I did not mean that you should take advantage of my best friends!"

Sinking onto the opposite corner of the couch, Terry rubbed his hand over tired eyes. "It wasn't. I didn't. I mean the sex was great, but it was more than that! I fell in love with your friends at that damn barbecue you had six months ago! I didn't drop my old life style and come out publicly to my family for a one-night stand. I could have done that without the publicity."

Mischa crawled along the couch and put a hand over Terry's shaking fingers. "So, it wasn't a one-time thing for you?" Now the sympathy was back in his voice.

"No! You know me, Mischa. I may be gay, but I'm just not interested in casual sex with strangers. I don't do spur of the moment, and I don't do rash and impetuous. For the past six months, I've thought about nothing else but Dex and Trick and how we could be together!"

Mischa nodded. "I know you. Relationships are important to you, but Dex and Trick have only met you a handful of times, mostly here in my home. They don't know these things about you. Did you talk to them about what you wanted, what you expected?"

Damn. No, he hadn't; he'd typically assumed in his arrogant way that they wanted the same things he did, that he knew what was right for all of them.

"Fuck, Mischa. I never got the chance. Never made the chance, I guess. I had plenty of time that night to talk, but loving seemed more important. When I woke up, they were gone. Left me phone numbers, but never answer when I call. How can I tell them what they mean to me if they refuse to talk to me?"

"You're a dickhead, Terry, but I love you. And I think that my friends feel something for you too." Mischa stopped talking and paused, considering.

Terry felt a spurt of hope in his chest, a lightening. "Really? So, you'll tell me where to find them?"

"Ahh, no. I can't do that."

"Why the hell not? You just said you thought they felt something for me too." *Fratricide is against the law. Besides, Donovan is bigger than I am, and I don't want to traumatize Matt, do I?*

"Because three days ago, Dex called up here and made me promise not to tell you where to find them. Oh, cool down, he didn't give me any fucking details about when or where or why or how you guys hooked up, or why he didn't want to be found. I just assumed things didn't work out and said okay. To be perfectly honest, I thought you were being your usual dickhead self and said something to piss him off."

Chest expanding in an extravagant sigh, Terry pressed back against the arm of the sofa. "I don't think so. My memories are of a lot of action and not much talking, but the talking I remember was very...sexy. Maybe I should have been more open about how I felt, but I didn't realize I wouldn't get another chance to talk to them. Please, Mischa, I'm begging here. Help me out?"

"Go talk to Donovan and Matt. I can't make any promises, but I'll call around and see what I can do, okay?"

CHAPTER SIX

Dex stared at his chirping cell phone with loathing. Finally he snatched it up and checked the display. Thank God it wasn't Terry. Every time the man called he had to fight the urge to answer, to beg him to give them a chance. Trick was still curled up in a tight fetal position on the bed in the corner, and Dex knew he couldn't risk it. One night of fantastic sex and parting from their lover had sent Trick into a depression. How would it be if they spent more time together?

The phone shrilled again, and he flipped it open. "Hello, Mischa." He knew he'd been neglecting his friends, but Trick's needs took precedence.

"Hey, Dex." Mischa sounded hesitant, and Dex felt immediate concern.

"Is something wrong? Are you all right? Matt and Donovan?" Oh, fuck, what if something had happened to Terry?

"We're fine. Terry's fine, too. In case you're wondering." Mischa sounded a bit annoyed. Shit, he knew messing around with Terry would screw up his relationship with Mischa.

"I'm glad to hear that." His heart pounded frantically. He stared across the room at his sleeping brother. Trick had slept about twenty hours a day for the last three days. The antidepressants should kick in soon, but even so, he worried about his brother.

"Are you? Because I have to tell you, there's a lot that fine doesn't cover."

Damn it. He didn't want to hear this.

"Dex? Did you hear me? I've talked about things with my brother tonight that I would rather never have known about. And if you know Terry at all, you know what it cost him to come over here and talk to me about this shit."

Yeah, he did. Because unlikely as it might seem, he did know Terry. Terry was private, calm, and self-sufficient. He loved his brothers, the family firm, and— Dex suspected—, him and Trick. That's what made this all so hard. He wanted that love, and Trick desperately needed it, but Terry didn't need the shit that would hit the fan if any of the reporters that constantly hung around the Blake brothers figured out exactly who they were.

"I'm sorry, Mischa. It should never have happened. What do you want me to say?"

"Well, fuck, Dex. I'd like you to say that you give a shit. My brother, the tough, silent guy who blushed like a virgin when anyone even mentioned sex, just unloaded on me about his gay threesome, and now, if I'm not mistaken, he's in the other room crying on my lover's shoulder. Doesn't that mean anything to you?"

Dex was getting pissed. Fuck. He did not want to hear this. "I'm sorry, Mischa, but Trick has to be my first concern."

Mischa drew in an audible breath. "Good. That's great. I'm glad to hear you say that. How is your brother? Because I love my brother too, and this is fucking killing him."

Dex groaned. Did Mischa think this was easy for him? "Mischa, please. Trick is, well, you know. He's in a downward spiral right now, but he should be cycling up by the morning. What do you want me to do?"

"I want you and Trick to meet Terry, talk to him. He just wants the chance to see where this thing between you is going. Frankly, I think if you gave him a chance you'd find it's going somewhere you want to be. Other than that, I think you owe the man a face-to-face to tell him thanks but no thanks, if that's the way it has to be."

Shit. Shit. Shit. It was pretty shitty to just keep ignoring the man's phone calls and hoping he'd give up and go away. To be perfectly honest though, Trick had been in no condition to meet anyone the past few days, and Dex could hardly leave him on his own to go see Terry and tell him things between them were a no go.

"Okay. Not yet though. Trick needs another few days to recover from this." And he needed a few days to gird his loins and shore up his defenses.

"So, I can tell him you'll call him?"

Dex sighed. There really was no way around it. "Yeah, we'll call him when Trick is better."

"You know, he's going to be pissed that you didn't tell him Trick wasn't well. That you kept him from seeing him."

Fuck. Yeah, he kind of knew that, too. "Fuck. I know Mischa, I'm fucking sorry. But tell Terry, would you, that we'll call him in a day or two. And Mischa, tell him that whatever else might come of this, neither of us regrets it."

"Right. So, Dex, we're good, right? You aren't going to pull a disappearing act on me next are you? 'Cause you guys are my best friends, and I really don't want to think about the hole it would leave in my life."

Heart overflowing, Dex smiled. "We're good, Mischa. See you soon." Flipping the phone shut, he bowed his head, overcome with gratitude that whatever else their one night with Terry had fucked up, they still had a strong bond of friendship with Mischa.

"Tell me that wasn't what it fucking sounded like." Trick's caustic voice caused his head to jerk upright again. He jumped up and headed toward the bed, pleased that his brother was awake and seemed alert.

"Trick, how are you feeling, doll?" He reached out to press his fingers against Trick's pale forehead, but Trick brushed his hand away furiously.

"What was that all about? What did Mischa say?"

How much to tell his brother? Shit. How much had Trick heard? "That was Mischa. He called to see if we wanted to meet with Terry."

"I gave him our phone numbers, Dex. If he wanted to meet with us, he could have called us directly. Why do you think I've been so depressed? I thought it was more than a one-night thing for him."

Truth time. Dex gathered his brother into a close embrace, feeling him tremble with tension. "He did call. Several times. I didn't answer. I thought it would be better if we didn't talk to him or see him again."

Trick put both hands on his brother's face and turned it to stare deep into his eyes. "I don't fucking believe it. Terry called? And you, in your infinite wisdom, decided it would be better for me not to see or talk to him?"

Shocked, Dex pulled back. "But, you were—"

"I am quite capable, even on the verge of depression, of deciding whether or not I want to see someone. I definitely wanted to see Terry again. I can't believe you didn't tell me he called. What are you, taking lessons from Brandon Blake now?"

Ouch. That fucking hurt. "Trick, I love you! You know I would never do anything to hurt you. I just wanted to protect you from what would happen later!"

"Oh? What's going to happen later, Dex? We find out the man we love, loves us? We have a real relationship? Is that what you were really protecting me from? You don't want to be part of a threesome for real, do you? You want to keep it just the two of us, because that way it's safe and secure and neither

of us risks getting hurt. I understand that, Dex, really I do."
Trick's voice ran the gamut from loud and furious to soft and
soothing.

"I don't want you to hurt any more, Trick. It tears me up to
see you sad and hurting. You are more important to me than
anything." Surely Trick could understand that his intentions
had been good?

"I understand that, Dex, I do. I don't want to see you hurt
either, but this is one risk I'm going to take. I want more for us
than we've been settling for. I think we have a chance to have
it all with Terry."

Trick's blue eyes pleaded with him to say yes, to take that
risk as well.

"But, what if he finds out about us? About the past, our
parents, all the shit that keeps following us around?" Dex
couldn't handle it if they had a real relationship and it fell apart
because of the nasty publicity and rumors.

"Dex, honestly! When we meet him, we tell him all about
our pasts, and let him decide if he thinks he can weather the
publicity, if it should arise. We don't get to make that choice for
him any more than his brother Brandon does. And, much as I
love you, brother, I'm in love with him, and I hope he decides
we're worth the risk."

"Me too." Damn. He really hoped he hadn't fucked things
up too badly by ignoring Terry's calls. "I think, though, that we
should take things slowly. No jumping into bed first chance we
get, okay?"

Trick looked at him curiously. "Really? Why? The sex was
fantastic. I'm kind of looking forward to repeating it, to tell
you the truth."

"Something Mischa said. He said if we knew Terry at all,
we'd have known he wouldn't just jump into bed with people
he didn't care about. I think we should date first, get to know
one another other a little better."

"So, you're going to give this a chance? Really?" At his nod, Trick launched himself off the bed and into Dex's arms, where he covered his face with tiny affectionate kisses and stroked his fingers through his silky, black hair. "Oh, fuck, Dex. I love you. I really, fucking love you! We'll take this as slow as you want, but I know it's going to work out beautifully."

Dex held his brother tight, enjoying the exuberant kisses and caresses. This was Trick as he loved him best, as he always should be. "Hey." He avoided a kiss on the lips. "We should find our phones and listen to Terry's messages."

"You didn't even listen to them? Where is my phone?" Trick glanced around the tiny studio apartment. "And where's Bella?"

"Bella is at work. The phones are on the table." He pulled Trick over to drop down onto the sofa. Each of them picked up his own phone and listened to the messages Terry had left. By the last message, both were teary-eyed.

Dex looked over at Trick, without trying to stop the tears that trickled down his cheeks. "I'm sorry. I'm really sorry."

CHAPTER SEVEN

Terry glared at his silent phone on the desk next to him. Every time it rang, his heart jumped and his cock swelled, even though he knew damn well the twins wouldn't call for a few days. Mischa had specifically said that Dex would call when Trick felt better. Therein lay part of the reason for his anxiety. He stupidly kept worrying about what illness had befallen his lover. Reassurances that if Trick was recovering already the illness couldn't have been too serious weren't effective. Dex should have told him Trick was ill. He should have been able to hold his lover and offer comfort.

He struggled to work through his pinging emotions. He felt like a bouncy ball shot from a cannon into an empty room. That, right there, was why his best writing was signing the checks that paid the bills. He had no talent for self-expression. Words were not his friends. And without the right words, how could he convince the twins that he wanted what only they could offer?

In sudden hope, his gaze snapped to his opening office door. His expression froze into a pleasant snarl as he recognized his brother Dan, the guy who got the family's gift for words. This damn emotional roller coaster was making him nuts.

"Come on, your secretary told me to take you out for a three martini lunch. Apparently you're slashing budgets and refusing to spring for good coffee in the cafeteria. Let's go."

He flushed. Had he really been that bad? Terry stood and grabbed his jacket. He contemplated picking up his phone as well, but decided to leave it behind.

"Aren't you bringing your lifeline?" Dan asked.

"Nope, every time the damn thing rings my heartbeat accelerates and my hands get sweaty. I'll never relax if I take it with me." Reluctantly, he turned his back on the phone and followed his brother out the door.

Terry couldn't say so much that he'd woken up as that he'd become aware slowly that he was awake. The pounding in his head made the prospect of opening his eyes unappealing, and so he kept them tightly shut to keep out the tormenting sunlight from the window. He'd apparently stumbled in so drunk last night he'd forgotten to close the drapes the maid always left open after cleaning his room. What the fuck had he been thinking?

Oh, yeah. He'd been thinking he didn't want to think. He and Dan had hit that three Martini lunch, then headed to the golf course to shoot a few holes —accompanied by more martinis— then stumbled into the clubhouse.

An aborted movement nearby sent a tremor of fear trickling through his brain to his heart. Fuck. Someone else lay in the bed with him. What the fuck had he done? Just how much had he drank? Wait, he could swear that he'd come back to the house with Dan. Had he gone out again afterward?

Frantically trying to remember what had happened, he reached across the bed with one hand. His hand closed around a hairy arm. Gross.

"Get out. Get out of my bed. Get out of my house." His voice was gravelly as he forced the words out despite the painful ricochet they made in his head. His heart pulsed painfully. How could he have done such a thing? Drunken one-night stands were not his thing. Shame and sorrow seeped through him. How could he face the twins now? What could he say? He'd have to tell them about his drunken binge and throw himself on their mercy. He really couldn't imagine what had possessed him to pick up some guy and bring him back to the bed he'd last shared with Dex and Trick. Oh, God. He needed to puke. He swallowed desperately, because getting up wasn't an option.

A corresponding groan from the other occupant of the bed drew his attention. His bedmate hadn't left as ordered. Fuck. Channeling Brandon in a bad mood, he resorted to insults to get the guy to leave. "Fuck, buddy, get the hell out! What are you waiting for? A tip?"

The deep, hoarse voice that answered caused his eyes to shoot open painfully wide. "Fuck you, Terry. Shut the fuck up. You're killing me, here."

Snapping his eyelids closed relieved the darting agony of the piercing sunlight. Tension eased from his body and the nausea receded. Fucking Dan. His brother lay sprawled across the bed near him, fully clothed and clearly hurting as badly as Terry. He breathed slowly and deeply for several long moments before whispering as softly as possible.

"You scared the shit out of me, Dan. What the fuck are you doing in here?"

Dan's whimpered response grated on his exposed nerves. "Dude, please, shut the fuck up. Your voice is like a cheese grater on my brain."

Asshole. Basking in agonized gratitude that he hadn't turned out to be a cheating prick after all, he allowed his brother a few moments to recover.

"Seriously, Dan. Get the fuck out. I need to get up and shower and head in to the office. Do you have any miracle hangover cures?"

"What, you think I do this all the time or something?" Dan still whispered.

Terry snorted, then groaned and grasped the top of his head to keep it from falling off. "I know you do. Please pull the drapes on your way out." He pulled a pillow over his face and listened to his brother's reluctant movements as he edged to the side of the bed. Dan's muttered curses were muffled by the pillow, but still sent tremors of pain arching through Terry's skull. Never again. He could handle the uncertainty of his position with Dex and Trick better than the aftermath of alcohol.

"Meet me downstairs in the kitchen in thirty minutes for your miracle cure." Terry hoped the door slamming hurt Dan as much as it did him. He pulled the pillow off his face and slowly pried one eye open. Sighing with blessed relief, he managed to open the other in the gloomy darkness. Dan had just risen to the rank of number one brother for the day. Holding his head with one hand, he trudged off to the attached bathroom. A shower and shave later, he felt slightly more human and headed down to the kitchen to meet up with Dan. He needed to ride into the studio with Dan because he'd left his Porsche there yesterday. Leaving the cell phone behind as well had been a mistake. Who knew how many important calls he'd missed? *Don't lie to yourself. You know damn well you could have fifteen messages, and if one of them isn't from Trick or Dex, you're going to be down all over again.*

Checking his messages would have to wait a little longer, he realized, as Dan pulled his car into the personalized parking space next to Terry's Porsche. Rather, what was left of Terry's Porsche. The front windshield had been shattered. The headlights smashed in, the tires slashed. The previously sleek, sexy body of the car had been battered and dented. Worst of all, someone had spray-painted *I know about you!* in ugly red letters across the hood. What the fuck was that all about?

He stood next to Dan, surveying the damage while he waited for a tow truck. Dan eyed him sympathetically. "What the hell happened here? Who'd you piss off?"

Terry shook his head wearily. "Hell, if I know. Don't tell Mischa yet, okay? He'll have a fit if he finds out this happened here of all places after I warned him repeatedly about parking on the street near that loft he used to rent."

Dan chuckled. "Yeah. But how did anyone get in here? There's a damn security guard at the gate twenty-four hours a day."

Terry shrugged. "I don't really care. Maybe some nut climbed the fence. I needed a bigger car anyway."

He turned to the nearby security guard. "Send the police up to my office when they get here, would you? I have to get to work or none of us will get paid this month."

Strolling into his office, his gut clenched and his pulse raced as he noted the blinking light on his phone that indicated he had messages. All thoughts of the damage to the Porsche and what the hell the cryptic message spray-painted on the vehicle might mean disappeared. He caught his erratic breathing and urged himself to be calm. The odds of a call from Dex and Trick today were better than yesterday, but still, there was no guarantee. He forced himself to approach his desk calmly, unpack his briefcase and laptop as he normally would, and then reach for his cell phone.

Hand trembling, he scrolled through the phone numbers for the missed calls. His brows drew together in a frown. A call from Marissa Matinson had come through in the early hours of the morning. What the hell could she want? He hadn't seen her since Mischa's barbecue six months ago, had broken off his relationship with her that night as a matter of fact. There were several business calls including the car dealer he'd spoken to the other day and a few real estate agents. And yes! Trick had called, twice. Dex had called after Trick's second call, and finally Mischa had called late last night.

Elated, he dialed the message retrieval function and skipped through the first calls to get to the ones that interested him. Trick's first message made his heart sing. He sounded so happy, and eager to see Terry again. "Terry, it's Trick. I'm calling to see if you want to get together with Dex and me tonight. There's a coffee shop we can meet at and talk. Call me when you get this message."

Fuck. Goddamn Dan and his three-martini lunch! If he'd stayed at work, not only would he feel better right now, he'd have gotten to see the twins last night instead of the inside of a vodka bottle! *Can't really blame Dan, though. He did tell you to bring your cell.* Another stupid decision made on the spur of the moment. When would he learn that he did better when he took the time to think things through?

Trick's second message dimmed his smile a little. "Terry? It's Trick again. I guess you're not available tonight, but could you call me when you get a minute? I'd really like to talk to you." Trick didn't sound quite so happy in that one.

Fuck, as soon as he listened to Dex's message he'd call them back and clear his schedule for the day. Unlike Trick, Dex's voice was tense and hurt. "Terry, I'm sorry we didn't call you earlier, but please, it wasn't Trick's doing. It was mine. I didn't even tell him you called. If you don't want to see me, I understand. Please at least see Trick."

Christ. That was jumping the gun a little. Dex seemed to jump to conclusions and make snap decisions. And that seemed to work as well as Terry's impetuous decision had. That was to say, not at all. Holding the phone to the side, he buzzed his secretary and told her to clear his schedule for the day. He had to stay until the police came to take the report on the vandalism to Mischa's Porsche.

Mischa's message left a lot to be desired. "Quit acting like a fucking asshole, Terry. I went out on a limb for you, now do something about it!"

He closed the phone and drew in a deep breath. *Make haste slowly. Your worst decisions have been those you failed to think through properly.* Did he want to pursue a relationship with the twins, despite the emotional trauma it was likely to cause? Look at all the ups and downs he'd endured in the past week. Look at how the twins had suffered when they hadn't heard back from him yesterday. He closed his eyes, thinking of the joy he'd felt when they'd smiled at him across Mischa's lawn all those months ago. He'd never felt such pleasure in anyone's company as he had with them the other night.

Oh, yeah. After only one night, he'd missed them like hell. Did he really have any choice to make? *Just take it slowly this time and don't rush the physical side of things. Let them know you and that sex isn't your only interest.*

Decision made, he called Trick.

"Hello, Terry!" Trick sounded like he was pleased to hear from him. That was good.

The sound of Trick's mellow voice rippled through Terry, and he found himself relaxing back against his chair. He pushed it away from the desk and smiled into the phone. "Hi, baby. How are you? What happened?"

Trick laughed huskily. "Nothing important. I missed you, though."

Terry's dick liked that idea—a lot apparently, as it swiftly hardened in a head-lightening rush of blood that had him hard and pulsing against his zipper. His own voice had hoarsened when he replied, "I missed you both. I wanted to be with you every damn minute of the last few days."

Trick's approving moan came through the air, loud and clear. "Are you terribly busy, darling?"

Terry groaned. He pressed his hand against his cock. Trick tempted him to break the promise he'd just made to himself to take things slowly. "Unfortunately, I have to hang out here for a while. I have to file a report with the police who should be coming any minute now."

"Oh," Trick's disappointment was hard to bear. Then his breath hitched, and he moaned again. "Terry, I ...want you so much."

His hand moved mindlessly to lower the zipper on his trousers and he freed his aching cock, breathing a sigh of relief as the pressure eased slightly. "I want you. Is Dex there with you?"

"Oh, yes, he's right here. Let me put you on speaker phone." A few fumbling noises later and Dex's panting breath was as audible as Trick's.

"What are you two up to?" As if he didn't know. His voice was a husky purr as he slowly touched himself.

"Well," Dex answered. "We've been waiting to hear from you, and thinking about you...and we got a little...eager."

He smiled. "I'm...eager, too, baby." Almost beyond eager, damn it. He stroked himself, feeling the tiny drops of liquid beading at the slit.

His lovers' voices murmuring in the background sent frissons of awareness flickering along his taut nerves.

"Are you hard, Terry?" Trick's breathless voice felt like a caress along his cock; he closed his eyes, reveling in the sweet, sensual sound.

"Oh, yeah. So hard, baby. Talk to me," he whispered. "I want to come to your voice. Tell me what you're doing."

"Oh, fuck," Dex responded. "We're lying on the bed at Bella's place. We just woke up, and we'd both been dreaming— about you."

Umm. He liked the sound of that, too. Blood pulsing thickly, roaring in his ears, he stroked himself harder. "Yeah," he groaned, urging them to continue.

Trick's voice took over; his sexy whisper harder to distinguish over Dex's panting breaths in the background. "Want you...ooh...didn't know when you'd call. So, we've been...remembering...that night... stroking each other off. The phone rang at the perfect time."

Fuck, oh yeah. "Perfect," he groaned, feeling his balls tighten painfully as tingling heat pooled at the base of his spine. "I'm close, so close, baby. Are you ready?"

"Oh, yeah, we've been holding on, waiting for you to catch up."

"Now then. Come with me!" he groaned, hearing matching cries of pleasure and feeling his own release spill hotly over his hand. Struggling to catch his breath, he wiped his hand and the front of his trousers on a handful of tissues from his desk before tucking himself away and zipping up. "Shit," he choked out. "The cops are coming any minute and I just messed up my trousers. What am I going to do with you two?"

"Hmm," Trick's contented purr soothed his turmoil instantly. "More of the same, I hope."

"When are you done there?" Dex's strained voice told him the older brother still felt some trepidation about his welcome.

"As soon as the police get here and I can file a report. Want to go to my house and I'll meet you there as soon as I get done?"

Absolute silence. Then, Trick's voice, sounding a little panicky. "Police? Never mind. You can tell us about the police later. No. We don't want to go to your house. How about meeting us at Mischa's, and we can go to the coffee shop or something from there?"

Something was seriously wrong there. His intercom beeped and his secretary announced the responding police officer had arrived to take his report. *Later. I'll get to the bottom of that later.* "Okay, the police are here now. So I'll meet you there as soon as I can. It'll take at least an hour, though." He raised a brow at the policeman and gestured the man to take a seat. The man nodded, indicating the accuracy of his estimate of time. "Right, I'll see you in an hour." He flipped the phone shut and scooted his chair under the desk, wondering if the room stank of sex, or if his guilty conscience merely magnified the scent that clung to his hand and trousers. So much for abstaining from a physical relationship until they knew one other better. He hadn't made it through a damn phone call without whipping it out. How would he handle a face-to-face encounter?

CHAPTER EIGHT

Trick lounged on the daybed in Mischa's study. It had started out as Mischa's bedroom when he'd been just Donovan's housekeeper, but that arrangement hadn't lasted long. The room still housed Mischa's books and the antiques he'd inherited from his grandmother, as well as some of the treasures he'd picked up on his own.

Dex was tense; he paced around the room, occasionally flopping on the daybed near Trick and stealing a kiss or two, but he couldn't hide the nerves that had him popping up and making the rounds of the room again and again.

He sighed. His brother tried too hard to make everything perfect, to keep the outside world from intruding on their lives just in case one of them got hurt. He wished he could make it easier for Dex, but all he could do was hold his brother when things were bad, and let him know he'd never be alone. Hopefully, now Terry would be there to help convince Dex that he was worthy of being loved.

The ringing doorbell brought Dex to his side again, a worried expression on his familiar face. "Come on, Dex," he whispered into Dex's ear, feeling his brother tremble slightly in his arms. "That's got to be Terry. Let's say goodbye to Mischa and go." Standing, he carefully adjusted the suddenly prominent erection that developed at just the thought of seeing Terry again. Smiling, he tugged his brother up as well and noticed he had a similar issue.

He whispered encouraging words in Dex's ear all the way through the kitchen and into the living room, where he found Mischa, Donovan, and their son, Matt, entertaining Terry.

Terry spun in their direction as soon as he became aware of their presence and the pleasant smile on his face immediately broadened into a huge welcoming grin. His green eyes lit up with an inner light that sent tingles of pleasure racing through Trick's body. Oh, how gorgeous the man was! Trick felt Dex relax next to him at the warm welcome. Terry clearly held nothing against Dex for not answering his calls.

Terry came across and embraced both Trick and Dex, and Trick felt his cock throb hungrily in response to the brief contact. He noted a brief strain in Terry's eyes as he pulled away from the embrace more quickly than Trick would have liked. The twinge of concern vanished as Terry bent to press a hot kiss to Dex's mouth before turning and doing the same to Trick. Immediately, Trick opened his mouth and tried to deepen the kiss, desperate for the taste of his lover, but again Terry pulled away.

"Hey, baby." Terry's husky voice told him he was as affected by the kiss as Trick had been, but still, he'd pulled away. Trick pushed the doubts out of his mind.

"Hey, yourself, lover. Ready for some coffee?" The coffee shop was a tiny little hole in the wall a few streets over and run by a misanthropic guy who baked the best pastries Trick had ever eaten. The place would be empty at this hour and the owner would leave them to their conversation without the constant in-your-face helpfulness so many establishments seemed to favor.

"Did you drive the Porsche over?" Dex asked. "We can take our car or you can follow us."

Terry blanched and cast a quick, apprehensive glance at Mischa. "No, I didn't. Dan dropped me off. I'll ride with you."

"Oh, that's great." Trick smiled. Remembering their first drive, from the club to Terry's house, he'd planned ahead. Instead of the Escalade with its bucket seats, he'd driven his 1949 classic Plymouth Deluxe, primarily because of its very roomy bench style front seat.

"Come back and join us for dinner later," Mischa instructed.

Trick met Dex's eyes, uncertain what to answer.

"Maybe," Dex finally said, gazing cautiously at Terry. "I'll call you later to let you know." No sense promising to be here if Terry didn't want anything to do with them after he knew the truth.

Mischa glared at Terry. Terry glared back, before huffing, "Fine. We'll be back for dinner later. Then you can give me a ride to the poker game."

Damn. Encouraged by the fact that Terry included them in the dinner invitation and disappointed that he still intended to leave them for the poker game, Trick wrapped an arm around Dex's waist and grabbed Terry's hand. "That gives us a time limit, so let's head out. Thanks, Mischa, Donovan. See you around, Matt."

He studied Terry. He was so giving, so loving, the man deserved to have children. For so long Dex had been his only family and, as grateful as he was for the love of his brother, he did want more. Being with Terry had opened his eyes to what could be. Maybe later, in a few years, they could consider the issue of children. Terry would make an amazing father, and Dex would try to guard the kid from all harm. He'd like to start with a baby though, not a full-grown kid like Matt, even if he was cute. Maybe they could hire a surrogate, use Terry's sperm, and have a bunch of little blond-haired green-eyed babies. He smiled. Yeah, a few kids would make their family perfect.

Outside, Terry surveyed Trick's car with a rueful expression. "You aren't going to make this easy on me, are you?" he asked, chuckling.

Trick felt liquid heat spread throughout his body and pool in his throbbing groin at the sound of his lover's sweet laughter. "Nope, I don't know what you really mean by that, but I can tell you, I like it hard." He palmed his cock through his tight jeans as he spoke and watched the answering flare of heat in Terry's gaze. He glanced toward Dex and saw a reciprocal heat in his blue eyes.

Terry groaned at his bad pun, and opened the passenger side. "It's hard, all right. I'll sit in the middle if that's okay with you." He addressed the last remark to Dex, who seemed a bit hesitant about getting into the vehicle.

Trick gave Dex a quick hug before jogging around to the driver's side. "Go on, he's not mad. He loves you, too." Dex nodded and slid onto the seat next to Terry, closing the door with a solid thud.

By the time Trick made it to his seat, Terry had pinned Dex against the passenger side door and devoured his mouth in a hungry kiss. Trick stared, enthralled. Damn. That was fucking hot. His face flushed and his cock hammered against his zipper uncomfortably. Shit. He scooted across the bench seat and climbed onto Terry's lap to join in the kiss.

Gasping for breath, they all broke apart in response to a thump on the roof of the car. Settling back, eyes glazed with lust, they peered out to see Mischa standing next to the car, arms crossed and scowling.

Trick sighed, fastened his safety belt, and waved to Mischa as he pulled out of the driveway and headed to the coffee shop. "Your family is...nice." He concluded lamely. He loved Mischa like a brother, really, but ...would it kill the kid to give them a little privacy?

He drove with one hand on the wheel and one eye on the road. Terry held his right hand and Dex's left, cradled together in his lap, seemingly content to wait until they reached the coffee shop before beginning the serious discussion.

As expected, the coffee shop was empty. The owner scowled at them and grudgingly rose to get their orders as they seated themselves at a small table in the farthest corner. The man ran a dark, narrow eyed gaze over them. "Three coffees, black. I got a half-dozen fresh-baked squares of orange glazed shortbread. That good enough for you?"

Trick choked on his laugh at Terry's expression. His lover clearly wasn't used to this quality of service. "Yeah, that would be great, thanks."

The shop owner nodded shortly and stalked away. He returned with a laden tray and deposited it sharply on the table. "Stuff's over there," he stated harshly before dropping a tab on the table and ducking off behind his protective counter.

Dex smiled at Terry's appalled expression. "He's always like that. But the coffee is great, and the baked goods are better. Want me to get cream and sugar in that for you?"

Terry shook his head, obviously still dazed by his encounter with the brisk shop owner. "No. I take it black; as I see you do, as well. But how did he know?"

"He doesn't. He serves every cup exactly like that."

"Oh, well, no wonder the place is empty." Terry looked down into his cup, then raised his gaze to meet Trick's then Dex's. "I...um...need to tell you about a decision I've made. I think we should cool the physical side of things for a while."

Trick felt a tremor of fear at Terry's first words, swiftly followed by relief and anger. What the fuck was up with the people in his life making decisions for him? "Don't you think that's something we should talk about and decide together?" He asked more sharply than he intended.

Dex placed a comforting hand over Trick's, where it rested on the table, then bent to press a kiss against his brother's cheek. "Doll, before we get upset about Terry making choices for us,

LEE BRAZIL

we need to tell him about ourselves. It may not even be an issue." Dex's voice shook a little as he tried to be the strong one yet again, and bring up the subject that had to be brought out into the open. Trick knew it had to be done; he just really didn't think it was going to be an issue for Terry. Being so exposed to his lover caused him some concern, yeah, but not as much as the sudden wholesale ban on physical relations between them.

Confusion spread across Terry's face. "Does this have something to do with your disappearance the other day, or your refusal to meet me at my house?"

Cringing at the reminder, Trick nodded. Dex looked really worried, tapping his finger on his lower lip. He tightened his grip on his brother's hand and decided to take the initiative for once and spare his brother the agony.

"Yeah, both, actually. First of all, I should say, I'm actually Loki James Hyatt, and this is my brother, Destiny John Hyatt."

Terry didn't seem impressed. "Yes?" He tapped his fingers impatiently against the table top, briefly drawing a belligerent stare from the coffee shop owner. "Sorry," he called to the barista. "We're good."

Fuck. He'd kind of hoped that Terry would recognize their names and realize the rest of the story himself. "Our parents are John and Moonbeam Hyatt. The Hollywood actor and his wife accused of being involved in the bombing of a federal building in Orange County when we were ten. They left us in the care of nannies and took off. We haven't seen them since. They might well be dead by now, for all we know."

Concern etched across Terry's face, and he leaned over to press his hand against his and Dex's. "I'm sorry, baby. That sucks. What happened?"

Feeling tears gathering in his eyes, Trick looked desperately at Dex. Dex squeezed his fingers and then drew in a deep breath, taking up the story. "We were sent to boarding school. The estate paid for it out of our trust funds. At the school, Trick

144

had a real bastard of a roommate. They split us up, wouldn't let us room together. It was horrible. We'd never been separated before. One night Trick came to my room. He was upset, crying. We fell asleep on my bed together."

Trick picked up the story when Dex paused for breath. "Only I wasn't the only one with an asshole for a roommate. Dex's roommate took pictures of us on the bed and posted them online. When he was busted by one of the other students, he claimed we were behaving inappropriately. We were expelled from the school for 'lewd and obscene behavior.' The rags picked up the story, and it followed us around for years. Reporters snapped pictures, photo-shopped them to show 'incest,' and the publicity was pretty bad. Even now, every few years we get a resurgence of the Hollywood Activists' Sons' Twincest Scandal."

Terry sighed sympathetically. "It wasn't true then, I take it?"

Dex snorted. "Hell, Terry, it's not really true now."

Trick rolled his eyes at his twin's outburst. "It doesn't matter. We were young, our parents had disappeared, no one took care of us, and we were wards of an estate. Of course we clung to each other as tightly as we could. It was the only stability in our lives. And it's stayed that way ever since. People have come and gone. We settle in and the publicity rises up again. People look at us as though we are disgusting. You didn't. You looked at us as though you wanted to be with us."

"I did. I do. There's nothing I want more than to be with you. And I don't give a damn who your parents are or what you do together—in fact, I think you're hot as hell together and even hotter with me."

That was exactly the right response as far as Trick was concerned. He jumped off his chair and into Terry's lap, covering his face with tiny kisses. Staring down into his lover's hot green eyes, he licked his lips. "Really? The thought of the reporters finding out and splashing us all three across the front pages of the gossip magazines doesn't bother you?"

"I wouldn't love it." Terry didn't hesitate. "But I love you, both of you," he added with a purposeful glance at Dex—who flushed. "And I'd deal with it if it came up."

"If you love us," Dex ventured. "Then why are you cooling off the physical relationship?"

Terry sighed again. "Because you two don't know me well enough. You didn't trust me. That hurt. You should have known that I would never indulge in a one-night stand. It's just not me. So, I think we should date for a while, let our relationship progress from there as we get to know one another better."

Dark anger surged in Trick. Brandon Blake was such a prick. "Terry, we never thought you wanted a one-night stand."

"Then what the hell was last week all about?"

It only took a minute for Trick to go ahead and throw Brandon Blake under the bus. The fucker deserved it and Dex definitely did not. "Your brother can probably answer that question for you better than we can."

"My brother? Mischa? What the hell does he have to do with this?"

Dex cut in bitingly, "Wrong brother."

CHAPTER NINE

The shrill noise of his cell phone cut through Terry's furious silence. Without checking the identity of the caller he flipped it open. "Blake."

He caught Mischa eyeing him warily out of the corner of his eye instead of watching the road. They were on the way to the weekly poker game, where Terry intended to beat some answers out of Brandon. His twins had refused to tell him more, insisting that Brandon could answer his questions. He fully expected not to like what he heard.

Just as he didn't like what he heard on the phone right now. Hell, it was Marissa. He should have checked the caller ID before answering. He cut off her flow of inane conversation. "No. Marissa. I do not want to meet you for coffee to talk about anything tomorrow morning. I have absolutely no influence over casting. All I do is sign the checks."

In the seat next to him, Mischa winced as Marissa's shrill voice came through the wire, "I want that part, Terry Blake, and if you don't see that I get it; then I'm going to have to make sure that the whole world knows about your dirty little secret!"

Terry stiffened in his seat, meeting Mischa's incredulous eyes. "What did you just say?"

"I said I want the female lead in the New Orleans saga, and you'd better see that I get it or I'm going to the press with what I saw outside that club last week. You and your tawdry little gay threesome ought to make nice headline news."

Enraged, Terry forced his voice to icy calm. "That's what I thought you said. Are you working on something for us now, Marissa?" Had the bitch been on set the day his Porsche was trashed?

Her voice lowered, apparently feeling like she'd gotten her way. "No. I just finished up this morning on that baseball thing. So, you'll do it then?"

Shaking with anger, Terry tried to hide his feelings. He was no fucking actor, though, and his voice shook slightly, "I'll arrange a meeting for you in Brandon's office tomorrow afternoon." He flipped the phone shut and cursed loudly.

"That bitch!" Mischa sounded indignant. "Did she just threaten you?"

"Yeah. Worse, she threatened Dex and Trick. That woman just bit off more than she fucking realizes. I fucking did *not* need this now." He contemplated his brother as he pulled the minivan into the family garage. "I don't suppose that you know what Brandon has to do with any of this, do you?"

"Nope. Trick and Dex didn't confide in me, and if they did, I couldn't tell you. This isn't going to be an ongoing problem is it? You expecting me to spy on my friends for you?"

Shit. Was that what he was doing? "I—no. No, of course not. I respect your right to keep their confidence. I'm just a little anxious; knowing Brandon, it could be anything. I keep hoping whatever it is, they overreacted, but that just doesn't seem like Trick. Dex, yeah, but Trick always looks on the bright side."

"I know," Mischa conceded. "Knowing how controlling Brandon is, I'm a bit concerned myself."

"And now this. What the fuck is Marissa thinking? You know, she fucked up your Porsche, right?" he confessed to Mischa.

"You mean your Porsche. It's not mine any more, remember?" Mischa shrugged. "It's insured, right?"

"Yeah. The police will want to know about this. Damn it. How does she think she can get away with this shit?"

"Brandon will eat her alive for daring to think she can dictate to him."

Mischa had that right. For a moment there, he almost felt sorry for Marissa, then he recalled her threats to expose his twins to public scrutiny and all sympathy faded.

He seated himself in his usual chair between Mischa and Brandon and pulled out his wallet, automatically handing it to Mischa after he'd removed a stack of hundred dollar bills for himself.

Mischa's snort called his attention to what he'd done and he flushed slightly. "That's all right, Terry. Save your money. You've got a big family to support now. Donovan and I do just fine."

Blinking, Terry caught on to what his brother meant. "You mean you don't know? They don't need my money any more than you do. Trust fund babies, just like you."

"Seriously? I had no clue. They just seemed so genuine and down to earth. Never made an issue about money, not when I had it, and certainly not when I didn't have any to spare."

That made him feel inordinately proud for some reason, as though he'd had a part in the development of the twin's character. "I know. It's just one of the things I love about them."

Silence dropped instantly over the room. Terry felt himself once again the center of attention, as he had been weeks ago when he made his grand announcement. What the hell had he said this time? Oh, yeah. That was quite an announcement to just blurt out in casual conversation, wasn't it?

"Oh, fuck." Brandon seemed especially stunned.

And that reminded him. He locked eyes with Brandon, who had suddenly assumed a startling resemblance to a deer caught in the headlights. "And that reminds me, Brandon. Do you have something you'd perchance like to share with me regarding my choice of partners?"

If it weren't so infuriating, it would have been amusing. Brandon actually looked panicky. "I...umm..."

Now all the green eyes that had been staring at Terry in shocked surprise, turned to Brandon with interest. Dan in particular seemed fascinated.

"Yes?" he encouraged. "You...what?"

Brandon tore his gaze away and let it skitter about the room. Terry had a sinking feeling this was going to be worse than he thought. "Yes?" His voice now was as cold as the tone he'd used on Marissa.

"What exactly did you do?" Mischa demanded.

"I may have met Destiny and Loki outside your room one morning."

Dan raised an incredulous eyebrow. "You mean you don't know for sure who you met?" He turned to Terry inquiringly. "Just how many threesomes have you engaged in, brother dearest? I thought you were only interested in two men in particular, not any two men in general."

"I am only interested in two men in particular, and you know damn well *Dex and Trick* are the only two men I've invited into our home."

Brandon turned a bit pale. "Shit. Okay, I met them outside your room when I went to discuss the budget crisis on the set of the baseball thing—which you never got back to me on, by the way."

Nope. Not going for the dodge. "Screw the baseball thing. What the hell happened outside my room?"

"I ahh...told them I knew who they were"

Terry blanched. That would have been enough to send Dex into a tailspin right there. But would it have been enough to send

Trick into a depression? Or, he thought, even enough to have both brothers refusing to come to his house to meet him? Hardly.

Dan stared from Terry to Brandon in fascination. "Who they really are? And who are they really?"

Mischa reached across and smacked Dan on the head. "Shh..." But Terry noticed that Mischa listened just as avidly as Dan. Shit, what the hell? The twins were going to be part of his family, so his brothers would all have to know the story eventually anyway. But those details could be shared later. There was something that Brandon still wasn't telling him, and he had a sneaking suspicion what it might be.

"So, you warned them off me, didn't you?" And naturally, sensitive to rejection, they'd taken it to heart. Damn it. Brandon really had a lot to answer for.

Brandon shook his head. Voice soft, he confessed, "I told them you didn't need the publicity of a twincest scandal on top of coming out as gay. Then I told them to get out of my house."

Terry stared at his brother. He heard the words, but comprehension came slowly. He knew Mischa and Dan understood a lot sooner than he did, because Mischa gasped and grabbed his arm, and Dan sucked in an audible breath, before breathing out, "Oh, shit."

"You told them I didn't need a twincest scandal. Because you knew who they were. Didn't you consider how they would feel about that? They were kids ten years ago for fuck's sake!"

"It might not have been true ten years ago, but it's true now." Brandon had the nerve to attempt to defend himself.

Terry lunged out of his chair, crunched his hand into a fist, and slammed it directly into Brandon's jaw. Brandon's head flew back as the blow connected with a solid *thunk*. "And it's not just your house, asshole!"

Terry turned to Mischa as Dan jumped up to inspect the moaning Brandon's jaw. "Let's get the fuck out of here. Can I stay with you while I find a house of my own?"

Brandon moved as though to stop them from leaving, but Mischa took Terry's hand and led him away, shaking his head and frowning at Brandon over his shoulder.

Un-fucking-believable. Brandon was lucky Terry didn't kill him. He wanted to go back in there and beat the shit out of his older brother. For years he'd worked his ass off to live up to Brandon's expectations. Get the MBA, take over the family finances, wear the right clothes, and date the right women. One thing. He finally did one thing for himself, to make himself happy, and Brandon, the control freak, had nearly ruined it without a second thought.

"He meant well," Mischa offered.

"I don't fucking want to hear it. If I hadn't just spent the afternoon ironing out this relationship with Dex and Trick, I'd have killed him right there. I guess now I know how you felt all those years."

"Nah, you don't, not really," Mischa teased. "You just got it from Brandon. I got it from all three of you."

CHAPTER TEN

Dex sat up in bed, watching his brother and their lover sleep. They moved together in some strange symbiotic manner across the mattress, each turn or movement reciprocated so they remained entwined, snuggled as closely as two men could get.

Acting on a wicked inspiration, he reached out to grasp a corner of the silky sheet where it lay near his foot. Trick and Terry together made a beautiful sight, but he needed more. He tugged the sheet gently, drawing it slowly down and away from their bodies. His breath caught and he stared at what was slowly being revealed. Terry's thickly muscled limbs, lightly furred with fine blond hair, interlocked in sexy display with Trick's more slender, sleek muscles. Golden skin rested next to creamy white in a sultry invitation to touch, to taste. Mouth watering, pulse speeding up, cock stirring with interest, Dex tugged again. The black, silk sheet slithered slowly away, baring Terry's muscled chest with its large copper nipples, Trick's head resting just over his heart, one slim white hand clutching at his waist.

Dex tugged again, harder, and the sheet pooled to the side, revealing the long, hard curve of Terry's erect cock arching up from the nest of fine golden curls, and nestled next to Trick's bent thigh. Years of waking beside his brother lent the certain knowledge that Trick's smaller cock was in the same state of arousal as his own. He studied his lover and his brother. What the hell had he done to be so lucky? Despite his stupid mistakes, Terry still wanted them, wanted him. Love was a beautiful thing.

Crawling up the bed, cock aching, heart pounding, he shifted limbs until he rested on his knees between Terry's legs. He turned his brother until he knelt, looking down on two gorgeous cocks, each fully aroused and waiting, begging for his touch. Terry might be thicker and darker, but Trick was no less beautiful. The two were a direct contrast, milky-white to flushed-gold, long and thick, both enticed him to touch, to lick, and to suck his lovers awake.

Rising from the bed, he walked around to the nightstand to retrieve the bottle of lube and strip of condoms. Definitely would need those later. The pleasant ache in his ass served as a reminder of the pleasures of the night before. The thought sent a powerful tremor of need, of desire through Dex, but he pushed it aside. His wants could wait for later. His needs were second to seeing to the needs of his lovers.

Using both hands, he reached down and traced each cock with a fingertip, from base to crown. Smiling in approval, he noted that each tip was moist with pre-cum. He bent and pressed open-mouthed kisses to first one then the other. Trick whimpered in immediate response. Terry's large, hard hand threaded through Dex's hair, trying to hold him in place over his cock.

Voice husky from sleep and lust, Terry begged, "Please, baby. Suck me."

Dex pulled away, continuing to stroke the firm, hot flesh, "I have a plan," he announced.

Leaning up and bracing himself on his elbows, Trick locked

a heated, blue gaze on the hand stroking his cock, shifting to take in the identical grip as it stroked up and down Terry's cock as well. "As long as your plan includes all of us coming in the near future, count me in." He reached over with one arm and pulled Terry into a hot, wet, open-mouthed kiss. Dex shifted restlessly, barely maintaining the rhythm of his strokes as he became lost in the passion of that kiss. He licked his own lips, tasting the residue of flavors left over from the previous night's kisses. Breathing deeply, he let go and reached down to squeeze his own balls to stave off his orgasm. Dex edged backward on the bed and held up the condom and lube.

Blue and green eyes followed his movements with hot interest as he sheathed his cock in the condom and offered the lube to Trick. Trick accepted it with a raised eyebrow. Dex grabbed the pillows scattered around the bed and stacked a few of them against the headboard. "Lie down here." He suggested to Trick, who obeyed, stroking his own cock all the while.

Dex turned to Terry. "Crawl up over him on your hands and knees. I want to fuck you." He cringed at the baldness of that statement. "I mean...if you want to, that is." *Please, please want to.*

The bigger man drew in a sharp breath. He'd fucked both Trick and Dex more than once, but neither had topped him yet. Maybe it was something he wasn't really interested in. Dex could live with it if that was the case, but he hoped it wasn't. He wanted to feel the tight heat of Terry's ass enclosed around his cock, wanted even more to show the man the dark pleasure that he had given Dex the night before.

Slightly apprehensive, Terry nodded then crawled up the bed until he was positioned across Trick's lap, face to face with the younger man. Pleasure shown in Trick's eyes and he instantly took advantage of their positions, drawing Terry in for more intimate kisses and massaging his hard muscles with both hands. Dex surveyed the sight laid out before him in delight. The long clean lines of Terry's back swept down into tight firm buttocks, lightly dusted with the same fine golden hairs that curled around his groin.

He reached for the buttocks, massaging the muscles, then smoothly separating the cheeks. The tiny puckered entrance to his lover's body beckoned, and he pressed closer, tracing the tender flesh with a gentle finger. Terry quivered slightly, and Dex repeated the movement with more pressure. Leaning back, he reached forward. "Lube?"

Trick squeezed a bit of the liquid from the bottle onto his fingers, and Dex paused to note that Trick and Terry were still exchanging wet, sloppy kisses. Terry had a strong hand wrapped around Trick's throbbing cock, and jerked it slowly, rubbing his thumb over the moist tip with every upward pull.

Smiling, Dex brought his lubed fingers up to trace the opening again. He applied a bit of pressure and Terry tensed, then slowly relaxed. Encouraged, Dex pressed forward, wiggling his finger a bit until the ring of muscle stretched and his finger slid smoothly into the clinging heat. Fuck. That would feel incredible on his cock. Terry stiffened again, and Dex paused, waiting for him to relax before proceeding. Slowly, he began to thrust his finger in and pull it out. Terry moaned into Trick's mouth. "Feels good, lover?" Dex reached around Terry's body to stroke his cock, and sighed with gratitude when he found his brother's hand already there. His concentration back on the task at hand, he pulled his fingers back and this time pressed two forward. Fortunately, he and Trick were not so generously endowed as Terry. Twisting and scissoring his fingers, he pumped into Terry's ass. With each thrust, he gently stretched the opening to allow his aching cock entry.

At last, Terry's groans and Tricks whimpers urging him on, he pressed his condom-covered tip to the quivering opening and pressed slowly forward. He gripped Terry's golden hips tightly. Everything inside him convulsed, wanting more, urging him to move deeper, to take more. Shuddering, he held back, feeling the muscles stretch and give as he slowly slid forward. Raw lust spiked and he was nearly overwhelmed by the potent urge to drive forward and fill Terry in a single thrust. He struggled to control himself, control his breathing, to stave off the threat of imminent climax. First time. He reminded himself. Terry's first time. If he wanted the chance to do this again, he had to make it good. For himself, for Trick, and for Terry, he had to make this an experience to remember. Maybe he'd bitten off more than he was capable of chewing by moving their relationship along to this level so quickly.

Terry wiggled frantically beneath him, and Trick's sultry whisper pierced the veil of lust and self-doubt clouding Dex's mind. "We're ready, move."

Ready. Thank god. He pushed forward, slowly feeling the squeezing heat of Terry's inner passage massaging his full length. Pressed deep inside, he added his hand to Trick's as it jerked Terry's cock steadily.

Trick pulled his hand away and called, "Wait." Terry turned his head to capture Dex's lips in a kiss, nibbling his full bottom lip before thrusting his tongue inside. Dex moaned, loving the powerful sweep of that talented tongue as it stroked against his own. Fuck, he had to move.

He felt movement between his legs, heard Terry's raspy moan. Looking down, he saw that Trick had wiggled down the bed and rearranged himself so that he could lick and suck Terry's leaking cock. Umm. The sight alone sent powerful surges of lust through him and his skin prickled with awareness. Balls drawing tight to his body, he gritted out, "I can't wait any more. That's so fucking hot." He moved, pulling back slightly before thrusting forward again.

Terry's moans of ecstasy and Trick's full-mouthed whimpers spurred him on as he thrust harder, faster. He pulled back and slammed forward with all the force he could muster. Forcing his eyes open, he sought Trick, wanting them all to come together.

Relieved he found Trick jacking himself strongly, thrusting smoothly into his own fist as he licked and sucked Terry's cock. "Oh, fuck. I'm coming. Coming now," Terry moaned, as Dex ground against his ass frantically. Thank God. Oh, thank God, released from restraint, he spilled himself almost immediately, collapsing forward on his lover's strong back to watch as Terry's beautiful cock erupted in long creamy streams. Gripping the condom at the base, he pulled gently out and removed it, tying it off before tossing it in the general direction of the trash can.

He and Terry, as though of one mind, crawled over Trick's supine body and began licking the slick cum from his flesh, laving him with rough tongues.

When the last salty, sweet drop had been licked away, they all curled together with contented sighs. Lying in a sated tangle, Dex petted his lover and his brother absent-mindedly. Could anything be more perfect?

"I want a baby." Trick's dreamy admission stunned Dex. They'd barely managed a sexual partner who didn't consider them a one-night novelty, now his brother was thinking about an emotional investment that would last a lifetime.

Dex met Terry's eyes over Trick's head in disbelief. He could see Terry comprehending and then considering the idea. Thinking about it, Dex decided he kind of liked the idea too. "A baby? Are you sure?"

"We probably wouldn't have much luck adopting." Terry added, gently running his fingers soothingly through Trick's hair. "Unless we wanted an older child like Mischa and Donovan."

"No, I want a baby with black hair and green eyes, or blue eyes and blond hair, a baby that is us," Trick mumbled, blushing slightly.

Terry sighed. "Baby, I don't want you to be disappointed, but where are we supposed to find an agency that will let a gay threesome adopt a baby?"

Trick's eyes opened, and the stunning, blue depths sucked

Dex into believing in the possibility. "Don't be silly. Bella would have the baby for us. She could be the surrogate because her hair is black like ours, and her eyes are blue as well. Plus we know she's healthy, intelligent, and wonderful."

Dex somehow found himself agreeing to discuss the possibility with Bella and saw Terry just as bewildered by his own sudden desire to have a child. Clearly, making Trick happy was as important to Terry as it was to Dex.

CHAPTER ELEVEN

In the tense, thick atmosphere of Brandon's office, Terry glowered at Brandon who ducked his head and gazed unseeing out the tinted window across from his desk. Mischa sat near Terry, on guard and ready to intervene if necessary. Dan lounged conveniently next to Brandon's desk, apparently with the idea he could prevent any significant damage in the event Terry was unable or unwilling to exert the self-control that being in his brother's presence right now demanded. If it weren't for the need to show a united front to the bitch who would be arriving any moment, Terry wouldn't even have deigned to enter his overbearing, control-freak brother's office. Oh, he knew he'd forgive Brandon eventually; he just wasn't willing to do it until he'd made his point.

"Are you sure this is how you want to handle this?" Dan's inquiry forced Terry's attention back to him and away from Brandon.

"Yeah. I'm sure."

"We'll do it your way. It's your call," Brandon inserted eagerly. "I..."

The door burst open and the whirlwind that was Marissa swept into the room. Her blue eyes flashed in triumph, silicon bosom extravagantly exposed in a vest style jacket worn with skintight jeans. She posed with one hand on a thin hip, a sneer on her lip. "I'll take my copy of the New Orleans script, Dan. Terry, I'll sign the contracts in your office after this. What the hell is the kid doing here?"

Mischa glared at the brunette.

Terry wondered what had ever possessed him to date someone like Marissa in the first place? "Are you sure that you want to go down this route with Blake Productions? Blackmail is pretty nasty."

"So's a gay threesome. I can just picture the headlines and the sympathy my story will get me. My boyfriend dumped me for a one-night stand with gay twins. Charming, isn't it?" She stalked toward Brandon's desk in what Terry assumed she imagined was a seductive manner.

The previously silent Brandon sat upright in his chair and swept her from head to toe with a withering glare. "Sit down." His voice was hard enough to chip granite and for the first time, Marissa faltered.

She edged sideways and lowered herself into a waiting chair. "What is it? We all know you aren't going to risk the bad publicity. Blake Studios is family friendly and image conscious. This story would be terrible for you all."

Brandon's brows rose. "I don't follow you. Surely you realize that it would be even worse for you?"

Never the brightest candle in the ballroom, Marissa cast a confused glance around the room, lighting on each brother in turn. Each met her gaze full on, Mischa with loathing, Dan with sardonic amusement, Terry with disgusted anger, and Brandon with icy resolve.

"What are you talking about? I'm the injured party here!"

Again, Brandon filled the breach. "You're an idiot, Ms. Matinson. If you hadn't just finished your last contract with us, we'd have fired you on the spot yesterday."

"You can't do that! I want that part, and I dated him for four months. He cheated on me, turned fag. You owe me that part!" Marissa was making no sense in her rage.

"I did no such thing. We never even slept together. Maybe that's part of the problem here, a bit of jealousy. But you should have known better." Terry felt no sympathy for the bitch who had threatened his twins. He knew what was coming, and it would be the end of Marissa's career in California.

"This is a family business, as you so kindly pointed out, Ms. Matinson, and we take care of our family. The 'fag' you refer to is our brother, and the 'gay twins' are his partners. That makes them family, too. Threatening any of them is a threat to all of us," Dan's mocking voice chimed in.

"In short, your services will not be required for the production of *my* miniseries, New Orleans," Mischa announced baldly.

"But...you can't...I'll go to the press!"

Brandon slapped a manila file folder down on the desk in front of her. "Perhaps you'd like to take a copy of this with you."

Marissa eyed it as though it was a snake. "What's that?"

Terry laughed, a soft warm chuckle. "That's the police report of the investigation into the vandalism to Mischa's Porsche, Marissa. It makes for interesting reading. I haven't decided yet whether or not to press charges against the person responsible."

Marissa paled under her makeup and two rosy circles of blush stood out on her cheeks. "I don't know anything about that," she blustered. "Why would you think I took a baseball bat to your Porsche?"

Brandon scooted his chair back. "If we didn't already know, based on the police reports, that you had done it, you just confirmed it nicely. The evidence is all in the file, along with the documentation outlining your attempts to blackmail the studio. You're welcome to tell your story to the press if you like. Blake Studios and the Hyatt twins have survived bad publicity before. We will again."

162

Enraged, Marissa shot upright and leaned forward over the desk, thrusting her nearly bare bosom under Brandon's nose. The disgust on his face as he jerked back set Terry off and he laughed again. Mischa met his eye and joined him.

Marissa's previously pale face flushed an unbecoming red, and Dan watched in apparent fascination as the flush mottled the skin of her neck and chest. "Fine! Then I'll be seeing you from the talk shows!"

Sobering up, Terry laid a hand on her arm as she stalked past him. "Marissa."

She flung his hand off abruptly and glared at him. "What the fuck do you want?"

Terry smiled pleasantly. "I just wanted you to know that we have copies of that file printed out and ready to send to the heads of every studio. How many of them do you think will be willing to hire someone who vandalizes private property on site after a relationship ends?"

Marissa halted, shocked. "You wouldn't!"

"I would," Brandon answered. "Terry is too much a gentleman to be as ruthless as is perhaps necessary in this industry. But I'm not. I don't give a fuck about you. You're a bitch. If you expect to work in this town again, you will see that no such stories are ever published in any venue. If any article is brought to my attention, then I'm calling in my colleagues and sharing this file."

"Bastards!"

The four brothers watched as Marissa stalked toward the door. She was savvy enough to realize the game was up. She'd never work for Blake Studios again, but she still had a chance at other studios if she kept her mouth shut.

Sighing, Terry hugged Mischa and Dan, and then approached Brandon. Instead of the hug he'd given his other brothers, he held out his hand, offering to shake.

Brandon, tears in his eyes, grabbed the hand and used it to

pull him into a tight hug. "Damn it, Terry! I said I was sorry. If I had any idea you were in love with those boys, I would have kept out of it!"

Terry hesitated, and then returned the hug. "I know. You really think of them as family now, don't you?"

Brandon squeezed him one last time and then shoved him away as though he had developed a sudden case of the plague. "Of course, they're your family, just like Donovan and Matt are Mischa's family, and that makes them our family as well." He waved to include a nodding Dan in that statement. "Now, are you done being stubborn and moving back home?"

"Ahh, no." Terry grinned. "I actually bought a house this morning." He turned to Mischa. "We're going to be neighbors. I got the house across the street from you."

EPILOGUE

Trick lounged on the deck of his, Terry's, and Dex's new home. Terry had insisted on purchasing the house himself, though it was in all three of their names, claiming that he had been raised to "support" his family. Trick and Dex had given in, agreeing to keep their trust funds for their own personal use. Trick smiled, which really just meant that he and Dex had spent a lot of their own money on remodeling, decorating, and landscaping their new home.

The yard was a lush, green oasis with tinkling waterfalls, colorful flowers, and lots of hidden nooks for lovers to tryst. Footsteps on the gravel path from the front of the house attracted his attention, and he felt himself tense as he looked up into Brandon Blake's eyes. Shit. After all these months, Brandon still made him nervous and tense. His stomach churning, he opened his mouth and whispered, "Hi. Would you like to have a seat?"

Dex slept soundly on the lounger to his left, thank God, so if Brandon chose to sit, it would have to be in one of the chairs on the opposite side of the low table.

"Thank you." Brandon's usually vigorous voice sounded subdued and taut. He seated himself in the nearest of the chairs, then leaned forward, tenting his hands in his lap and staring down at them.

"Terry won't be back for at least an hour." What had brought Brandon to their door? Usually the twins avoided contact with this brother, though they knew that Terry had resumed the weekly poker games and reestablished the close family ties. Family gatherings were slightly awkward, but they were getting to be a big enough crowd that it was easier to avoid one Blake when necessary.

"I know. I came to see you, both of you," Brandon included Dex in his glance, who had stirred at the sound of voices.

Dex kept his expression carefully neutral. "Why is that? Trying to scare us off again?"

Brandon winced. "I deserve that. I apologize. I never should have interfered in Terry's life. You have every right to be upset with me still, but I'm asking you, please, can get past this and try to be friendly for Terry's sake?"

"It bothers him." It was a statement, not a question.

"I think he sees you avoid me, and even though he says he's forgiven me, he knows you're still hurting because of my actions. It's creating a rift in our family."

Dex sat upright and studied Brandon. "Does he know you're here? Is this another one of your little control-the-world things? You think something's wrong in your brother's life so you're going to go charging in and fix it for him?"

Brandon nodded. "That's a fair hit. Yes, he knows I'm here. He drove me over. I told him what I wanted to do, and he approves of it. It occurred to me that I apologized to my brother for interfering in his life, but I never apologized to you for hurting you. I'm sorry for the pain that my words caused. I want us to be family, just as Donovan is my family. Please forgive me?"

166

Trick felt the tears coming again. Damn it. Bella had just confirmed her pregnancy with them yesterday, and already he was feeling surrogate sympathy pains. He felt nauseous, tired, and emotional all the time. He studied his lover's brother. Brandon seemed sincere, and for the sake of the baby they would have in eight months, a unified family would be best. He held out a hand to Brandon and noticed that Dex had done likewise. "I accept. But you have to stop interfering in your brothers' lives. Apologies don't mean a lot if you keep committing the same offenses afterward."

"I know." Brandon clasped his hand. "I'm getting therapy and making some changes."

The soft *clink* of the sliding glass door drew his gaze to Terry, who stepped out with a tray of cold lemonade and the iced cookies he and Dex had fumbled through making earlier. The tightness in his heart Brandon inspired eased as he took in his beloved's smiling face. Dex melted into a state of relaxation next to him in Terry's soothing presence, and Trick felt the last vestiges of tension melt away. They were loved, and they loved, and that was enough.

GIVING UP

PROLOGUE

Brandon white-knuckled the elegant leather armrest, fighting the urge to protest as his brother whipped the sleek black Porsche to the curb in front of his house. He wanted to reprimand Terry for parking such an expensive vehicle on the street, but his brother had made it perfectly clear that unsolicited advice would be unwelcome. *Let it go. You made it here alive. Be grateful for that.* Parking on the street might be a fond "fuck you" to their youngest brother Mischa, but they were both grown men and Brandon had to let go of the father role he'd assumed when they were young.

Terry clicked off the engine and swung to face Brandon in the passenger seat. "You don't have to do this you know."

"I know. I need to though. The tension is aggravating my ulcer." Terry's partners, Dex and Trick, had cemented their place in the family months ago, and not just because the twins moved in with Terry. All three men were anxious about becoming new fathers. "I'd really like your partners to regard me as family, especially with the new baby on the way. Congratulations on that by the way." Trick in particular still seemed nervous around

Brandon, and Dex frequently became defensive when he realized his brother avoided Brandon. Brandon wanted the twins to be comfortable around him for their sakes, and his own, but mainly because when the new nephew or niece arrived he had every intention of being a favorite uncle, not a wicked step-uncle who was included in family gatherings as an afterthought. Also, he really liked his expensive Italian shoe collection and lived in dread of Trick vomiting all over them again.

"Well, if you must, you must," Terry agreed. "However, I should warn you," He flicked a glance toward Brandon's shoes, "Trick is convinced already that he's suffering sympathy pregnancy symptoms, including morning sickness. I'd keep a safe distance if I were you while you talk to him. Go on through the garden gate, I'll be inside."

Brandon walked slowly down the gravel path to the garden gate, listening to the crunch of his loafers on the gravel as he went. He could do this. Dr. Arden Grey—God, he repressed an aroused shudder at the very thought of her—had emphasized the importance of realizing he had a problem and then apologizing to the people who'd been hurt by his actions. Though she claimed to be more accustomed to teaching people how to take control of their lives, her assertion made sense, as had her urging him to take a step-by-step approach to his problem. It was unfortunate that his body reacted to the mere thought of her with the same enthusiasm it did to her presence.

He stopped outside the gate and drew in a deep breath. The stirring arousal that thoughts of his therapist caused weren't welcome. Something about Arden Grey called to someone inside him that had been kept hidden for a long time. Someone he wasn't sure he could be any more. The petite, red-haired doctor was sleek and professional and bore no resemblance to the buxom aspiring actresses he normally dated. He had more than a sneaking impression that she had no interest in men. Too bad, but reassuring in a way because it made her safe.

TRUTH OR DARE

Arousal subsiding, he lifted the latch and walked into the lush backyard paradise that Trick and Dex had created in their new home across the street from Mischa and Donovan's place.

Trick and Dex lounged on the deck, which faced out over the yard, a lush green oasis with tinkling waterfalls, colorful flowers, and lots of hidden nooks for lovers to tryst. Brandon's footsteps on the gravel path from the front of the house attracted Trick's attention, and Brandon felt his stomach burn as he saw the slight young man tense up when he realized who approached.

Shit. After all these months, with Brandon going out of his way to be soft-spoken and polite to the man, Brandon still made Trick nervous and tense. His stomach churned as he tried to move carefully and appear nonthreatening.

Trick paled, opened his mouth, and whispered, "Hi. Would you like to have a seat?"

Seeing that Dex slept soundly on the lounger to Trick's left, Brandon chose to sit in one of the chairs on the opposite side of the low table, unable to repress the snide gratitude that if the other man threw up it wouldn't be on his shoes this time.

"Thank you." He seated himself in the nearest chair then leaned forward, tenting his hands in his lap and staring down at them.

"Terry won't be back for at least an hour." Trick ventured.

Usually the twins avoided contact with Brandon, though Terry had resumed the weekly poker games. Family gatherings were slightly awkward. Brandon wanted the awkwardness over; his health demanded it, and he needed his brothers now more than he ever had in the past.

"I know. I came to see you, both of you." Brandon included Dex, who had stirred at the sound of voices.

Dex kept his expression neutral. "Why is that? Trying to scare us off again?"

Brandon winced. *Fuck.* Nothing in his life had been easy since he'd turned sixteen and his mother had been inspired to include him in her circle of friends. Why should this be any different? "I deserve that. I apologize. I never should have interfered in Terry's life. You have every right to be upset with me, but I'm asking you, please, can get past this and try to be friendly for Terry's sake?"

"It bothers him." Trick's statement was not a question.

"I think he sees you avoid me, and even though he says he's forgiven me, he knows you're still hurting because of my actions. It's creating a rift in our family."

Dex sat upright and studied Brandon. "Does he know you're here? Is this another one of your little control-the-world things? You think something's wrong in your brother's life so you're going to go charging in and fix it for him?"

Brandon nodded even though Dex's words felt like a twisting of the knife that tore at his guts constantly. "That's a fair hit. Yes, he knows I'm here. He drove me over. I told him what I wanted to do, and he approves of it. It occurred to me that I apologized to my brother for interfering in his life, but I never apologized to you for hurting you. I'm sorry for the pain that my words caused. I want us to be family, just as Donovan is my family. Please forgive me?"

Trick's eyes watered, and Brandon cringed. *Oh, fuck.* Terry would absolutely fucking kill him if he made Trick cry. *Damn it.*

He and Dex held out hands to Brandon to shake at the same time, and the churning in his gut eased a trifle.

"I accept. But you have to stop interfering in your brothers' lives. Apologies don't mean a lot if you keep committing the same offenses afterward." Trick offered the advice solemnly.

"I know." Brandon clasped his hand. "I'm getting therapy and making some changes." He shuddered again. Just the word *therapy,* brought images of Arden to his mind, his skin prickling in awareness.

CHAPTER ONE

That now familiar awareness caused Brandon's palms to sweat and his skin to tingle as he stepped through Dr. Grey's office door. The attraction he felt for the petite redhead embarrassed him to no end, not least because she gave no sign of finding him attractive in return. Dr. Grey addressed him professionally, her voice cool and her blue eyes indifferent. While he believed she sincerely wanted to help him, she'd made no secret of the fact that she normally worked on helping people take control, not get over their obsession with control.

This was his third meeting with the doctor, and he had high hopes. Her approach of treating his need for control as breaking an addiction appealed to him, mainly because she had emphasized the fact that such an approach put him in control of the solution. Maybe that seemed counterproductive, but he liked it anyway.

Running a hand through his sandy blond hair, he checked his loafers for scuffs, and straightened the drape of his pant leg before approaching the receptionist. The young man surveyed him coolly before waving him to a seat.

"Dr. Grey will be ready for you in a moment, Mr. Blake."

Stifling an impatient desire to urge the young man to remind the doctor that his time was valuable, Brandon seated himself in an uncomfortably stiff chair and picked up his iPhone. He scrolled through his emails, noting with an inward curse several that would require personal attention. The longer he waited, the worse the burn in his stomach became. He had reached the point of walking out and rescheduling his appointment for a later date, after he'd dealt with the crises of the day, when the door opened and the faintest whiff of a sultry perfume announced Dr. Grey's presence.

He stood automatically, reaching out to shake her hand in greeting and murmuring a polite good morning. A slight heat rose in his cheeks, and he hoped to hell the blush wasn't visible. And why the fuck a simple handshake with the doctor should cause him to blush, he didn't know. Something about her made him feel self-conscious and uncertain in ways he hadn't felt since he was a wild sixteen-year-old serving as his beautiful mother's escort to wild Hollywood parties.

He stiffened his spine and forced himself to meet those sharp blue eyes, unwittingly squeezing her hand just a little too tightly. He watched as the blue eyes flared wide then narrowed, and Dr. Grey gently removed her hand from his. The heat in his cheeks grew, and he felt his stomach churn alarmingly. He and Trick were about to have more in common than he'd ever thought possible if he couldn't calm down soon.

Dr. Grey led him into her office, and he took his usual seat on the plush leather chair in front of the desk. Somewhat surprised, he noticed that instead of taking the chair adjacent to him as she normally did, Dr. Grey seated herself behind the neat steel and glass desk. Crossing her hands on the desktop, she met his questioning gaze calmly, and Brandon let out the breath he hadn't realized he held. His roiling emotions calmed as he took in her stillness, and even his churning stomach was soothed. This was different, but not wrong.

Or so he thought until she spoke.

"I'm afraid, Brandon, that I can't keep you on as patient any longer."

Panic flared. "What? Why not?" His stomach heaved, and he forced himself to breathe deeply through his nose, swallowing rapidly to prevent the consequences of the sudden lurch. He was sure nothing of his feelings showed on his face. He had twenty-three years of practice since his mother's death at making sure of that. He couldn't have heard correctly.

"Because I can't help you in a professional capacity. I've given you the tools to manage your problem; you're an intelligent man, and you can resolve your issues from here on your own." Her voice remained the same as it always had, soothing and cool, her gaze untroubled and calm.

Damn. How had he come to depend on that calmness in so few meetings? How would he deal without the soothing effect her voice had on his nerves and stomach? Quickly pulling in resources to hide the shocking sense of abandonment he suddenly felt, Brandon grasped the tiny thread of anger and blew it up.

He surged upright and waved his phone in her face. "Fuck. I could have been at the office heading off a dozen major crises! See this? It's called a cell phone. I have it with me all the time. Next time you need to change our plans, use it!"

He stormed out of the office slamming doors behind him as he went. On the bottom floor of the building, he raced frantically toward the men's room where his upset stomach finally emptied, before heading into his office feeling shaken, cut adrift, and terrified that he wouldn't find his way to shore.

Facing his brothers again over the green baize of the poker table that night, the burning ache in his stomach had receded to a manageable level, and he had himself under control, even if he had the terrible feeling that the rest of his life was spiraling out of control at a rapid rate.

Terry and Mischa had their heads together sharing recipes or some such. Dan shuffled the cards absently, staring off into space with a cat-that-ate-the-canary grin that hinted at some wicked plot Brandon had to avoid for his own health. Heart aching, Brandon studied the three men covertly. His brothers. He'd been taking care of them for twenty-three years—ever since the day he'd promised their dying mother as the two of them lay trapped in the wreckage of the car she'd drunkenly wrapped around a telephone pole. Now, they didn't need him, but he needed them more than ever.

Remembering a similar night some months earlier when Terry had made his own startling announcement, he cleared his throat and forced the words past the constriction in his throat. "Need to talk to you all about something before the game starts."

As expected, he had their immediate attention; three green gazes, inherited from their father, fixed on his face. "I'm reducing my responsibilities as CEO of the studio." He paused briefly but not long enough for any of them to utter the confused comments he sensed in the offing. "I'm having some health issues that I need to take care of and reducing stress levels is an inherent part of the cure, according to my doctor. Dan, Terry, I need you to take over as much of the day-to-day stuff as possible. Please." He added the last in the hopes of turning his command into a request.

Stunned looks met his, and he held himself carefully still, projecting reassurance as best he knew how.

"That's what this therapy is all about isn't it? Reducing the stress to improve your health?" Terry's thoughtful response stripped away a layer of his confidence. Damn the man. He'd always been too perceptive by far, even as a young teen.

"Yeah, except that I'm not in therapy anymore as of this morning." And damn it if that didn't hurt still. "Arden Grey said that I had the tools to manage my problem and I was on my own." He swallowed hard again. "I'm going to need your help with that too. I know I've spent too much time micromanaging your lives, and I'm sorry for that. I'll try to do better. Please tell me when I'm being too controlling. I don't want to ruin anyone else's life like I almost did Terry's."

Terry adjusted the stack of bills in front of him before meeting Brandon's gaze. "You didn't almost ruin my life."

"I did. I nearly cost you the relationship you have with your partners. I thought I could protect you from the gossip."

"Brandon, you did protect me from the gossip, remember? And I have a wonderful relationship with my partners, a job I love, and the life I want, because of you. Because since I was fourteen years old, you've been there for me helping me find myself, helping me become comfortable in my own skin. You saw my talent for numbers and money and handed it all over: the family finances, the studio finances, all of it, to a kid just out of college with an untried MBA. That kind of belief is inspiring. And fuck, yeah, when you need me, I'm stepping up to the plate. I'll do whatever needs doing at the studio while you recover your health."

Brandon caught Terry's glare at Mischa and Daniel and saw their jaws clamp shut immediately before the two of them chimed in with their own words of encouragement.

The buzzing of his cell phone drowned out their garbled words, and from long-ingrained habit, he answered immediately.

The calm, soothing voice washed over his nerves, settling something deep inside that had been frantic since the morning. "Brandon, this is Arden Grey." The irrational hope that she had reconsidered surged through him, as did the prickle of awareness he couldn't stifle. He only hoped the heat in his cheeks wasn't visible to his brothers. He shifted in his chair, trying to hide as much as possible from too many pairs of perceptive eyes. *Damn the timing of this call!*

"I took your advice, Brandon. I'd like to change our arrangements, so I called you on your cell phone." The faintest hint of amusement colored Arden's voice, and Brandon stiffened; his stomach reacted to her voice with a delicate flutter—nothing like the agonizing turmoil he'd been experiencing, more of a pleasant anticipation.

"What can I do for you, Dr. Grey?" He forced his voice to a normal professional tone when it wanted to be husky, forced it to level confidence when it wanted to tremble in uncertainty. Why was she calling?

"Will you have dinner with me tomorrow evening, Brandon?"

Shocked, his mouth dropped open, and his brain scrambled to find an acceptable answer. Before his suddenly eager libido and a tentative inner voice could cast their votes for yes, his pride forced its way to the fore. "I don't think so, Doctor. As I am no longer your patient, I see no reason for us to meet again."

"I see. Thank you for your honesty, Brandon." His words seemed to have had no effect on her at all. Arden's voice remained calm and soothing, faintly amused, and dependable. *Idiot. You want to see her again.* When the phone went silent, he stared at in horror. What the hell had he just done? Chopped off his nose to spite his face again? The sudden lurch of his stomach had him hastily practicing the deep breathing exercises his primary care physician had recommended and reaching in his pocket for an antacid tablet.

He slowly became aware that Dan had dealt the cards, and all his brothers regarded him in varying degrees of fascination.

Dan quirked an eyebrow. "Truth or Dare?"

"Oh, fuck you, Dan. The gimmick has lost its novelty. Just tell me what you want me to do because we all know you'll maneuver me into the loser's seat anyway." Playing coy hadn't saved Mischa or Terry from Dan's machinations, and Brandon wasn't in the mood for bullshit. He may well have just screwed himself out of the chance to explore the strange attraction he felt for his therapist, and his mood deteriorated rapidly as a result.

Mischa and Terry overrode all Dan's attempts to protest his innocence, and the evil bastard finally admitted his plot. "I want you to call her back and ask her out. But I'm perfectly willing to beat you at a few hands of cards first if it'll make you feel better about doing it."

Fucking evil bastard.

CHAPTER TWO

Lying back against the pristine white of her 800-thread count cotton sheets, Arden contemplated the length and thickness of the flesh colored vibrator she held. *Not nearly as enticing as the real thing*. Brandon Blake was the man of many an actress's fantasy. The real thing would be even better. She hadn't actually expected that Brandon would fall in line with her plans for them. He'd had twenty-three years to create his structure of command and the persona he hid behind in his interactions with others. Just because she had a clear view of the man he should have been didn't mean that she'd be able to bring him to the surface with a single phone call. *Oh, this will be a challenge. Brandon will be a challenge.*

The seductive image of Brandon, naked and bound, sent a shiver of desire coursing through Arden's thin frame. His golden-skinned body would stretch the full length of the bed. Those deep green eyes, usually so remote and unreadable, would beg for her touch. Raising the vibrator to her lips, she flicked her tongue across the tip. The thrill of the tiny prickles on her soft skin sent new shivers down her body. Casting a glance at the antique, oval, mirror angled in the corner of the room, she watched herself draw the vibrator from lips to chin, down her neck to the beating pulse at its base. Amused by the blatant contrast between the Arden on the bed and the Arden she showed the world, she rose up to her knees and surveyed her body. The most generous of critics would be hard pressed to call her anything but short and skinny. She barely topped five feet, and her curves would be better defined as gentle slopes. Still, everything was firm and gravity had treated her forty-five-year-old frame kindly. Her skin retained the resilience of youth and her thrice-weekly workouts kept her muscles sleek.

Intrigued by the reflection, she traced the vibrator over her collarbone and down to the pink tip of one breast. Instantly her flesh trembled and the peak tightened. *Mmm, too bad Brandon hadn't been more amenable.* Her own company wasn't so bad either.

The gentle vibrations of the purring toy left prickles of awareness in its wake as she traced it over the most sensitive areas of her body, pausing here and there to repeat a movement that was particularly intriguing or exciting. All the while, her eyes locked on the woman in the mirror, eagerly tracing the flush of pink that spread across the creamy white flesh, and noting the telling signs of arousal and desire. There was a time when she wouldn't have done such a thing. In her early years she had believed that her husband owned her sexuality, though she had never thought of it in exactly those terms.

Twenty-three years after his death, she had long since reached the point where his inhibitions and moral strictures in the bedroom ceased to be an influence. If she wanted to engage in any sexual activity, alone or with a partner, she had developed the self-confidence and strength to explore and indulge herself. She relished the fact that she'd gone from being the victim, the controlled, and had taken control, usurping the mantle the men of her life had worn so callously.

She had learned on her own what pleased her, and in the

doing had discovered that part of that was having that ability to control her partner's orgasm as well as her own.

Shaking introspection aside, she gently pushed the vibrator through the neatly trimmed red curls that scarcely hid the slick pink lips of her pussy. More shivers racked her body as its ridges brushed over her stiffened clit. She gasped aloud, pausing to stroke the full length of the seven-inch cock against her moistness in several slow caresses. She threw back her head, flinging tiny drops of sweat to the side from her brow where sleek red curls had dampened as the heat of her body rose. Her blue eyes drifted shut, and the muscles of her thighs flexed as she rose higher off her heels.

A slight adjustment in the angle of the vibrator, and it slid without effort through pleasure-slick folds of sensitive tissue and muscle. Sighing, she flicked her tongue across her open lips, and watched again as the woman in the mirror— the woman she had struggled for years to become—began a pattern of shallow thrusts and twists. It was familiar, soothing, and exciting simultaneously, like making love to an old lover you encounter unexpectedly years after the affair was over.

When the tension of her body built to an unbearable degree, she bit her lip and arched her back into the easy hand movements, before sliding her other hand over to her clit. A few quick strokes started the explosions, and her body pulsed, clenching rhythmically around the hard length of silicone.

Sudden inspiration led to a quick sharp slap of her hand against her clit, and her mouth opened on a cry of ecstasy as she fell backward on to the bed panting.

"Oh, Brandon," she whispered through shaky breaths. "This could be very good for both of us, so don't take too long making up your mind."

Laughing at her own impatience, she rose from the bed and quickly restored her room to rights, pushing the mirror back into place and cleaning and storing her toys.

She headed into the cozy kitchen. Brandon would call, she was certain of it, and when he did she had no choice but to refuse whatever he offered. She almost regretted the hurt he was sure to feel.

The phone rang just as she poured steaming water over the tea bag in the delicate china cup. Briefly Arden considered the advisability of not answering the phone. Determined that it would be acceptable to let Brandon know that she hadn't sought an alternative to his company for the evening, she answered.

"Hello, Brandon." She deliberately pitched her voice to be carefully smooth, calm, and slightly amused. She wanted to project reassurance, to let him know she was a known quantity that he could count on to make steadfast, trustworthy decisions.

"Arden?"

She smiled. The man on the phone was the ruthless executive, not the seductive, vulnerable man she'd met in her office who worried about losing his family and the future of their business. This was the man who quelled arguing writers with a single glare, kept recalcitrant producers on a budget, and smooth-talked leading men and women alike into behaving on the set and off. She'd bet real money that the brothers were in the room and possibly behind the phone call.

"Yes, Brandon, what can I do for you?" Not that she had any intention of doing anything he might suggest at this point.

"I wondered if you would like to attend the New Orleans premiere party with me tomorrow evening." Smooth, confident, and oh, so unappealing! Hollywood parties might become a staple of her future, given that she intended having a relationship with a studio bigwig, but it was definitely not the place for a first date with Brandon. The venue he'd selected made her answer even easier to give.

"No, I have other plans. Thank you." Before he could respond, she hung up the phone. Of course, since she had just asked him to dinner a few hours earlier he might doubt the veracity of her claim. The truth couldn't be denied though. Just because she wasn't going to be out wining and dining some man didn't mean she had no plans. She had plenty of them and most all of them centered on the man she'd just hung up on.

CHAPTER THREE

Brandon placed his phone on the table next to his cards. "There. I asked. She said no. Can we play cards now?"

Dan looked stunned. "Why'd she say no? She just asked you out. That doesn't make any sense." He restlessly shuffled the cards with his long elegant fingers. "Sorry, Brandon. I just thought a little play time with a nice girl would help you relax."

"I don't know why she said no. Deal, or let's call it a night." He had a niggling suspicion that he knew perfectly well why Arden had said no. Her answer would always be no if he asked. A tiny trickle of warmth glowed inside, and he smiled at his brother. He didn't like aggressive Hollywood starlets, society tramps, or pushy working women and always made a point of turning them down, sometimes with less consideration than he should, perhaps. Dr. Arden Gray's appeal though was undeniable. He might have to reconsider his policy of never saying yes to an importunate woman.

Mischa dropped his cards face up on the green baize table, and Brandon tapped his fingers restlessly on the table as his brothers stared at him again. He quirked an eyebrow in irritation and watched in amusement as his baby brother unconsciously echoed the expression.

"Who was that, Brandon?" Mischa demanded.

"Just the therapist." He met Mischa's gaze blandly. *Just. Like five foot nothing of slender, sexy redhead could be called just anything.*

"The therapist you just assured Trick and Dex you would be seeing for help with your control issues?" Terry scowled.

"Now we know why you said no to her. Aren't there ethical conventions in psychiatry that prevent doctors from dating their patient?" Dan seemed perplexed. Or maybe he was just pretending to be perplexed. *Wouldn't put it past him.*

The deeply hidden part of Brandon that seldom saw the light of day found something of great interest in Dan's words. It drew them in, ran them around, and considered them from all angles. Decided to ignore them.

"Yes, Terry. That therapist, although, she fired me as a patient today, as I said." Damn. That trickle of warmth grew a little more, and he made an instant decision that when—not if, when—Arden called him back he would accept whatever invitation she offered. A therapist couldn't date a patient. Had she fired him so she could date him? His cock twitched in approval of that idea, but he hastily shifted and dismissed the thought. Arden had no sexual interest in him Pretending that sex had a role in her desire to see him was self-delusion. Frankly, as someone who practiced deception on a daily basis, he recognized it when he saw it. In some cases it was unavoidable, and in others, he absolutely couldn't function without it, but in Arden's case, letting his cock control his actions would be disastrous.

"Okay, we're clearly done here." He shoved his heavy oak chair back from the table and stood. "When you all are more interested in my life than cards, it's time for me to give up." The irony of his comment wasn't lost on him, or any of his brothers. Mischa and Terry, however, agreed with alacrity, rising and leaving the game room bickering amicably as they headed out

TRUTH OR DARE

to Terry's Porsche to carpool home. Since Terry had bought the house across the street from Donovan's, the brothers had grown even closer. While Brandon enjoyed seeing their relationship deepen, he regretted greatly that it seemed to come at the cost of distance between his brothers and himself.

Dan protested a bit but Brandon ignored him as he headed out the door and up to his own suite of rooms. Arden's words from earlier played on a new loop in his head, only this time instead of filling him with dread, they filled him with hope. *"I can't help you in a professional capacity."* Maybe she intended to help him in a different capacity. His heart lighter, his mind less troubled, he strolled into his room and into the attached bath. Shower, medication, and he could sleep well and wait for Arden to call again.

Crawling into bed a while later, he couldn't quite push away the twinge of guilt over the fact that Arden Grey's calm eyes and gently smiling mouth had accompanied him into that shower. His heated imagination had been unimpressed by his admonishment that the doctor wasn't interested in the length and thickness of his cock as he stroked it with a soap-slick hand. Her tiny frame would never crowd his in the expanse of his shower, and her pink lips would never close around his cock the way he imagined. Her eyes would never glow with lust as she watched him play with himself for her benefit, and certainly she would never offer up her body as a canvas for his seed as he'd just pictured.

Keep your lust in check. He combed out his blond hair, making a mental side note to have a barber from wardrobe sent over to give him a trim tomorrow. *A friend you can talk to is more important than getting laid.* He most needed Arden's willingness to help him with mastering his control issues and hold on to his family. Shit. Even that came out making him feel like a freak. He really needed her help with this. Besides, just being around Arden relaxed him, which in turn improved his constant nausea.

Settling back against his pillows and pulling a blanket up to his chin, he rested his head on the crisp white sheets and closed his eyes. Instantly a riot of images and thoughts flooded his brain, and he jerked them open again. Staring at the ceiling, he breathed in slowly and deeply, held his breath for a count of five, and then exhaled just as slowly. Repeating this process several times slowed the sudden leap in his pulse that had accompanied his anxiety, and he hesitantly closed his eyes again. *Examine each issue consciously and put it away for the night.* Arden's advice guided him.

Randomly, he concentrated on Matt—Donovan and Mischa's son was a joy to be around. He had some issues stemming from a bad start in life, but Donovan and Mischa were meeting the boy's needs, and the whole family loved him dearly. *Put Matt to bed for the night. In fact, put all your worries about the family to bed. Everyone was doing very well.*

Bella, his subconscious insisted. *Do you know how many things can go wrong in the first few months of pregnancy?* No, he didn't. *Put that on the agenda for tomorrow. Research pregnancy.* Being prepared would make dealing with any crisis in Terry's child's birth easier. There, that's Bella put to bed.

Breathing easier, he quickly cycled through the concerns about work and the house and soon drifted into a restless sleep.

She met him there, as she so often did, smiling up at him, telling him how handsome he was. She was beautiful and vibrant, easily the life of the party, the center of everyone's attention. Her friends surrounded them, laughing, shrieking, drinking, and to his horror, smoking, shooting, and popping pills. He tried to protest, but she shoved one drink after another into his hands, patted him on the head, and said he was a good boy. At last he hid behind a column, peering around occasionally to watch as she moved about the room, chatting, drinking, and finally screaming.

Heart pounding with sickening terror, he ran as fast as he could to see what had happened, why she screamed. When he at last found her, she was no longer beautiful and vibrant, no longer the life of the party. He collapsed, panting for breath, to the ground. She lay on the grass by the side of the road like trash thrown from a car window. Screams ripped through him, but now they were his, not hers. Her body lay lifeless and still, grotesquely coated with vulgar thick streams of pulsing lifeblood. As he sobbed in protest, the sounds caught strangely in his throat, her eyes flicked open, and he stared into lifeless, green depths. Bloodless lips parted as he struggled to force noise from his tight throat, but her words came to him clearly. "Should have driven."

When he snapped awake, he found his mouth dry, throat aching from attempting to force out sound. He hoped none of the screams of his nightmare had made it into the waking world, hoped no one had been disturbed by his dream but him. Sweat from his hair and his body drenched the damp sheets. Muscles aching, head throbbing, he sat upright. Wiping tears and sweat from his face, Brandon headed into the shower. Sleep wouldn't come back tonight. The only thing to do was to get ready to face the day. The same thing he'd done every time the nightmare visited him for the last twenty-three years.

He knew his reason for doing so was foolish, but he grabbed his cell phone and put it in his trouser pocket before heading to work. If Arden chanced to call him today, he wanted no delays. He didn't actually expect that she would call; he just wanted to be prepared if she did. *Such a good little Boy Scout I am.*

That same vague desire to please had him choosing a tie carefully, inspecting his Italian loafers for minute scuff marks, and combing his hair into precise position. The green tie brought out the color in his eyes, and the glossy finish of the shoes met with his approval. A smile twisted his lips as he considered changing his shirt. *She isn't going to be able to see you through a phone call! Fucking idiot. You're primping like Terry this morning!*

Pushing aside the desire to strip and start over, he shoved the sense of insecurity to the back of his mind and headed to the office.

Two hours later, in a grueling session of numbers and what-if scenarios, he struggled to make intelligent comments, ask insightful questions, and keep his face from betraying the impatience he felt. He kept unconsciously reaching for his cell phone, and Terry went on and on. Finally, unable to care about the cost of coffee in the cafeteria, he growled a low warning then grimaced as he caught his brother's disbelieving look.

"Did you just growl at me? During a finance meeting?" Terry's amusement irritated Brandon, but he couldn't really say anything without looking like an even bigger idiot.

Making an unprecedented spur of the moment decision, Brandon announced, "I think that it's silly for you to keep reporting to me about this stuff. You've been handling all our financial stuff for over ten years. I trust you."

Brandon's cell phone ringing interrupted Terry's very amusing flapping jaw routine. He turned his back on Terry while shoving the documents on his desk aside.

"Hello? Arden. It's great to hear from you." His heart raced, and he closed his eyes, letting her soothing voice wash over him, leaving trails of calmness in its wake. The pleasant acceleration of his pulse and the cessation of his nausea and tension were more than welcome. He listened with only half an ear to Terry packing up his briefcase and quietly leaving his office.

CHAPTER FOUR

Waiting before calling Brandon had been the right decision Arden decided as she hung up her cell phone and turned to the stack of memos her secretary placed on her desk. A pink phone slip marked urgent from her brother Bastian topped the stack.

"Oh, Rick! What does Bastian want this time?" Bastian lived every moment courting disaster with a *joie de vivre* that exhausted Arden. Rick, however, seemed to find Arden's brother amusing, a fact that Bastian took shameless advantage of.

"He'll tell you all about it, but honey, you have to get a move on. You have a full schedule this afternoon, including a six o'clock group counseling session at New Hope. I blocked you forty-five minutes for yoga in the salon on the ground floor. Then you have clients until five." Rick edged toward the door as he spoke, but froze when Arden pinned him with a stern gaze.

"Yoga?" Skepticism colored her soft voice.

"Yes, yoga is so much more relaxing and…elegant than kickboxing. You'll enjoy it."

"I don't kickbox to relax, Rick. I do it to keep in shape." She rolled her eyes. Elegant exercise. What a concept. Still, though Rick had her best interests at heart, he knew well enough that arranging a class for her stepped outside the bounds of his authority. When Stephen died, she'd been left floundering, unable to fend for herself. She'd learned the hard way to assume control of her environment. It had taken years before she had become comfortable enough with her issues to turn control of some aspects of her life over to others. Allowing Rick control of her schedule was a concession to being unable to do everything herself. She'd never regretted it before, but yoga?

"Please," Rick scoffed, sweeping her tiny 110-pound frame with a snide grimace. "You don't gain weight. If I didn't love you, I'd hate you. All you need is to keep toned, and yoga here in the building will more than do that for you. Plus, it's a nice little class, an activity you can do outside of your apartment, nice as it may be."

She cast him another steely glance. "Don't get pushy. What time am I meeting you and Bastian for dinner tonight?"

Rick flushed and looked away. "Well, I wasn't planning on attending myself, but I made reservations for seven thirty."

"Nice try. If I'm enduring Bastian's exuberance after a full day of work, then you are too. Pick me up at New Hope at seven. And make a reservation for lunch tomorrow at Ecole for two."

Apparently deciding to throw discretion to the wind, Rick leaned forward, studying Arden intently. "Who are you having lunch with tomorrow? I don't have anyone on the schedule."

Smirking, Arden threaded a hand through the pure white streak in her bright red hair. "Brandon Blake."

Rick stared at her, eyes wide in disbelief. "I thought you said you couldn't help him?"

"I said I couldn't help him professionally. This is not a professional meeting."

Chuckling, Rick turned back to his desk to make a notation in the appointment book and make the reservation. "Shall I cancel a few appointments and give you a nice long lunch break?"

"No, you should not you cheeky little..." *Bastard*, she finished silently. Feeling a little impatient with what she knew would be a slow courtship, Arden grabbed her bag and headed down to the fitness salon on the ground floor to test drive the yoga class.

Later, at the nondescript New Hope building with its discreet plaque on the door, she admitted that the yoga class had been more effective at relaxing her than the kickboxing tapes she normally did in the privacy of her own home. The class had been small, the instructor dulcet and charming, and the other students welcoming professionals who worked in the same building. After class, she'd made arrangements to meet several of them for lunch the next week. The afternoon had flown by.

Now she had arrived at what was one of her favorite parts of the week. Inside this dull little building in a small room, with cracked peeling paint and no windows, seven women waited for her.

Once a week these women came from shelters and safe houses around the city for guidance on how to take back their lives from the men who had destroyed them. Each woman who found a job, a home, and the courage to live on her own was an affirmation of the victory Arden had achieved so long ago. These women came to her, battered emotionally and physically, unable or unwilling to trust another man, and with careful coaching, she gave them the tools they needed to go out into the world and be successful, independent women. Each woman who turned her back on her abuser and took charge of her life counted as a victory for Arden.

She wiped her hands down the legs of the jeans she'd changed into for the counseling session and stepped into the room. Seven pairs of eyes locked on her, some startled, some scared, some wary or defiant. She brushed her hands again. *Brush off the guilt. Help these ladies help themselves.*

"Hi." She projected calming reassurance into her voice and saw some of the women visibly relax. This was a new group, and she needed to convince them that she knew from personal experience what they were going through.

The women mumbled vague responses, some looking away and to the side. Others deliberately met her eyes.

"Twenty-three years ago I killed my husband." Chairs clanged and shocked gasps filled the room. Although a bit misleading, her confession never failed to get their attention.

"Why? What did he do to you?" That, too, was inevitable. Every woman at these sessions assumed that if a woman had committed violence, a man had been the cause of it. In reality, she had simply failed to call in 911 as quickly as she should have when Stephen had fallen down the basement stairs of their home. He'd fallen trying to push her, and she'd been in shock, or so the paramedics had said.

Satisfied that her icebreaker had brought a degree of trust, Arden led the ladies in her group to talk about themselves and what brought them to the New Hope center.

An hour later, Arden lounged against the rough, gray, stone fence that bordered the tiny strip of grass in front of New Hope. She flipped with amusement through a series of text messages from Bastian ranging from a threat to kidnap Rick for a night of hot sex—leaving her stranded for the night—to a plea for her to rescue him from Rick's straitlaced, unadventurous ideas on how to pass time.

Her chuckle died abruptly as a firm hand gripped her shoulder. A lightning-quick glance and the tension in the air told her that this wasn't Rick or Bastian. She'd have seen their headlights if it had been, anyway. Smoothly, she turned toward the person who held her shoulder in a tight, painful grip, and shifted sideways, shaking off the grip as she did so, rising from her slouch to her full five feet. She found herself looking up into a furiously angry face, and striving to maintain a calm expression while not inhaling the foul alcohol fumes that the stranger breathed out.

"Where's Mary?" the burly man demanded, reaching for her again.

"I don't know anyone named Mary." Though she spoke softly and assertively, she couldn't help the tiny feeling of relief inside as headlights swept the parking lot and Rick pulled forward to park her car in front of them. Both the driver and the passenger side doors opened. Rick and Bastian stepped out, two very different men, each commanding attention in his own way. Bastian tall, broad of shoulder, and physically intimidating, Rick slender, shorter, but just as well built.

The stranger backed away at their approach before turning and walking off into the darkness. Bastian's narrowed gaze followed him as he disappeared into the shadows. "Who was that?"

She shrugged nonchalantly, holding her hand out to Rick for the return of her car keys. "He was picking someone up. She obviously already left. Where are our reservations?"

Rick flushed slightly as he climbed into the back seat of the little car. "Umm, my apartment?"

Her eyes met his in the mirror and widened slightly as she noted Bastian folding his much larger physique into the seat next to Rick instead of taking the front seat, which offered more legroom. With a tiny smile she acknowledged Rick's progress in forging a relationship with her wild younger brother, and simultaneously let him know that she didn't mind being used as a means of getting closer to Bastian. His sigh of relief in response let her know that she'd made the right decision. Bastian and Rick would be a great combination. Her brother's adventurous spirit would be good for Rick, who could be too serious at times, and Rick could temper Bastian's wilder starts. She wouldn't interfere, and as long as Rick knew that she knew what he was doing, she'd be happy to lend herself to his plans.

CHAPTER FIVE

Brandon took in the Grecian style of the restaurant frontage. White marble columns and fern-filled urns graced the portico. He followed the marble walkway to the maître d's desk and informed the host that he was meeting Arden Gray. The tuxedo-clad man nodded respectfully and led him to an alcove where Roman couches lined three walls interspersed with more leafy green ferns in tall urns. He noted the man's gaze taking in his attire, lingering on his polished black loafers. A nod granted approval of his Italian silk tie.

Slightly irritated at being made to wait for Arden again, he settled onto one of the velvet-cushioned lounges and pulled his phone out. Moments later the sound of the host's approaching footsteps drew his gaze from the tiny screen of the phone to see another man being led to the alcove as well. He dropped the phone to his lap and stared. This new arrival contrasted drastically with the environs and with Brandon's own appearance. His head had been shaved and tattoos decorated his broad, bare chest, shoulders, arms, and torso. As his sole concession to clothing, the man wore a pair of skintight leather pants and disreputable looking combat boots that made Brandon shudder.

The maître d treated him with the same distant respect he had shown Brandon, and the newcomer seated himself on the lounge opposite. He met Brandon's gaze with a smirk, "You're a pretty boy, aren't you?"

Brandon allowed his brow to rise, and then deliberately returned to his phone. The maître d's slight cough caught his attention "Dr. Grey will be in to get you in just a moment. Your table is nearly ready."

Brandon nodded abruptly. What kind of place was this? Tuxedos, business suits, and near nakedness were apparently all deemed appropriate attire, despite the classical elegance of the setting.

He was spared further confusion as Arden strolled into the room on the *maître d's* arm. He rose when she stepped into the alcove, and reached out to take her hand as she offered it to him. Her petite figure was clad in a dark blue suit with a neat short skirt, which ended above the knee. Her shiny blue high heels with their thin piping of red trim added a few inches to her delicate height. Taking in the effect of the shoes, he swallowed hard and drew her hand through the crook of his arm. He cursed the flush he could feel crossing his cheekbones as he traced a visual path back up her body from heels to head and found himself looking into laughing blue eyes.

"I love the shoes," he blurted cursing inwardly as he did so.

"So I see," Arden murmured in response, making an obvious reciprocal visual map of his own body.

Embarrassed, Brandon tried to apologize, but Arden brushed it off with a laugh. "Brandon, I'm not the kind of woman to be offended by a man approving of my taste in footwear. Truth be told, I like your shoes too." Arden was as ever, calm, amused, and encouraging.

What did that mean? She had to have noted his physical reaction to her footwear, to her, damn it. He'd probably have the same reaction if she wore goddamned combat boots like the guy on the lounge, but these were fuck-me shoes if he'd ever seen any. With Arden's tiny hand on his arm feeling more right than anything he'd felt in a long time, Brandon followed the maître d' as he led them down the white marble floor into a large chamber divided into small intimate alcoves for diners.

He led them to a secluded table then withdrew respectfully, passing a single menu to Arden and telling her that their waiter would be with them shortly.

Mystified, but content with the company, Brandon let his gaze wander around the room which had been carefully arranged to allow all diners the maximum amount of privacy. He couldn't see much of anything. He turned back to Arden for the answers to his questions, and found her studying him intently.

"I've never been here before." Casual conversation while he willed his body into submission. He clenched his hands together in his lap, unwilling to let her see them shaking. *Control your body; control your urges. Learning not to control other people doesn't mean you don't have to control yourself.* Hard as he tried, though, he couldn't ignore the prickling arousal that the intimate setting and the beauty of his companion inspired.

Arden smiled in response, and he stifled a groan.

"I'm not surprised. This is a rather exclusive club. Membership is limited." Brandon forced himself to focus on Arden's words.

The waiter stopped at their table, putting a momentary halt to the conversation. Brandon watched bemused as the elegant young man deferred to Arden without even acknowledging his presence. Arden kept her gaze locked with Brandon's as she ordered wine, appetizers, salads, and entrees. He kept silent, watching curiously. In ordinary circumstances, he'd have resented the waiter's rudeness and Arden's usurpation of control, but he had a feeling she had a purpose in her actions and in choosing this very odd club for their meeting.

The niggling little voice inside that protested her domineering actions was beat into submission by his need for her companionship and guidance. Let her order lunch for him. She knew this place, knew what was good here. He could allow this; it was safe enough. Talking himself into allowing Arden to choose his meal certainly took care of the ever-present semi-arousal he felt in her presence, though. He turned back to her as the waiter left.

"Is this all right, Brandon?" Her soothing voice stroked across his nerve-endings, and the churning in his stomach slowed. He couldn't help but nod. Her presence reassured him in ways he hadn't felt since he was a very young man, and if it made her happy to order food he probably wouldn't be able to eat, then what difference did that make?

"It's fine. I can't really eat a whole lot, you know? This ulcer thing." He didn't want to offend her by picking at the meal she'd ordered for him.

Sympathy shone in her bright, blue eyes, and she reached across the table to him. Automatically he lifted his hand from his lap, and she clasped it on the tabletop, stroking gently with her thumb along the edge of his wrist.

"That's one of the things I think I can help you with Brandon, reducing your stress levels."

Relief flooded him. "Oh, that's great. When you said you couldn't be my therapist anymore, I didn't know what to think. So you can still help me?"

"I think so, yes, but in a different capacity, Brandon. You weren't always like this from what you told me before."

Brandon nodded. "When I was younger. Before the accident I told you about. But after that, Dad was devastated, worked a lot, and I had to take care of the boys. Then, when he married again, there was Mischa. Sasha was an actress; she and my dad worked together all the time, so I took care of Mischa too."

"So you see, Brandon, this is learned behavior for you. It is not who you really are. I saw who you really are in our therapy sessions, and I can help you find that man again. Finding him will ease your relationship with your family and give you an outlet for the stress and frustration that being the head of the studio causes you."

Well, that sounded good. Theoretically, at least. "I'm hoping you can help me, Dr. Grey. My family is very important to me, and I need to be on good terms with them, especially with the new baby coming. I really appreciate this."

Arden tilted her head to the side and studied him again. "Brandon, you know I'm not interested in doing this as your therapist, right? I'm going to just come out and say this. Honesty is the best policy, and I believe in going after what I want. I want a relationship with you."

As quickly as the words were spoken, the usual calming influence of her voice was lost in a rush of blood and the throb of his groin. "Fuck." The word spilled out of his mouth before he could stop it.

Her laughter greeted his profanity. "Exactly. Only, more than that. I think we could really have something between us, something special. I felt it the first time you walked through my office door."

Try as he might, Brandon couldn't quite get his head around the idea of the delicate woman across from him returning his interest. "But, you're a lesbian, aren't you?" he protested dubiously.

"Ahh, no. No, I'm not. And I'm not even going to ask what gave you that idea. I'm a widow, have been for twenty-three years now. My husband died when I was twenty-two. I'm quite a bit older than you are, you should know that."

Forty-five? Brandon slowly studied the bright red hair with its single white curl, the delicate features of her face. The skin was unlined except for a few crinkles about the corners of her twinkling blue eyes and at the corners of the ruby red of her mouth that seemed too wide for her tiny face. God, had that mouth haunted his dreams! Although partially hidden by the table, he knew her body was slender and gently curved.

"I don't care about age. Donovan is almost twenty years older than Mischa and they are perfect together." His struggle to control his physical response to her bold declaration made a nonchalant response to the revelation of her age easy enough. In fact, he sounded a hell of a lot calmer than he felt.

"Please, Brandon. I'd like to share a little of my past with you, not that I'm looking for sympathy, but so you'll understand why I need things to be a certain way."

Brandon nodded absently while still wrestling with his own demons. Did he want a relationship with Arden Gray? His body certainly did. His mind said that it might not be such a great idea; she was too domineering and controlling. A relationship between them would be full of conflict as each tried to get his or her own way. The conflict would aggravate his health issues at the very least.

The silence from across the table got his attention. He shifted focus from his inner conflict to Arden's patient expression.

"Thank you." She granted him an icy smile in response. "I need to tell you these things, Brandon, because they may well be deciding factors in your decision to have a relationship with me. They are in part why I chose this venue for our lunch today."

"I see." He didn't, not really, but he trusted her, for whatever reason. If she thought he needed to know something he probably did.

"I was a victim of domestic abuse, Brandon. My husband was violent, verbally abusive, and controlling. I had no access to transportation, friends, or money. If he hadn't fallen down that flight of stairs, I truly believe he would have eventually killed me." Arden's voice hadn't changed. It was the same calm, reassuring tone that had coaxed him into sharing the story of his mother's drunken-driving death and his fears for his brothers' futures. The same tone that usually soothed his soul sent rage tearing through him in an overwhelming tide.

"What the fuck?"

"Shh." She clasped his agitated hand again, soothing him with stroking soft fingers and that calm voice. "He's dead and gone for a long time now, Brandon. I didn't tell you about Stephen in order to gain sympathy or to enlist you to fight my battles. That's my job. I fight my own battles now. It's a privilege I worked hard for. You have your issues with control, Brandon, and I have mine."

Swift and sudden, comprehension dawned. Brandon got it. She'd been at some bastard's mercy for years and now Arden needed to control her own life—every relationship and every decision—even what was served for lunch.

"I don't really know what to say here, Arden. I mean, I'm flattered, and I return your…interest…absolutely. I just don't know that I can deal with that. Surely you can see that we'd fight all the time. Between my control issues and your control issues, we'd never have a moment's peace." Sexual satiety aside, he did need peace.

"I know. So, if this attraction between us is to lead to anything, then you have to accomplish your goal, Brandon. And I have a vested interest in helping you to do that. You can agree to giving this affair between us a chance—letting me make the decisions for us, for you, then the rest will come. Just think about giving it a trial, all right?"

CHAPTER SIX

Visions of a muscular, partially clad man being led on a leash looped through the leather collar around his neck passed the dining table where he ate lunch with Arden Gray flashed in and out of Brandon's mind all afternoon as he signed contracts, shuffled papers, and delegated responsibilities to underlings he barely trusted not to fuck up.

"That's not what she meant," he chided himself as he banished the image for the umpteenth time. *No woman would be fool enough to believe she could lead you around on a leash like that. Not a real one anyway, I think she meant more of a metaphorical leash.* Sighing, Brandon was as tempted to call Arden and say, "forget it" as much as he was to call and say, "Here I am. Where do you want me?" He forced himself to leave the work on his desk and exit the building at a reasonable hour. How that would reduce stress when he'd just be worrying about it while he was at home, he didn't know.

Leaving the office was a necessity, but going home to the nearly empty estate was impossible. Sitting in his car in the parking lot, he considered his options. He could go to dinner in a restaurant, alone, where possibly journalists and wannabe starlets would recognize him. He could go get a drink at a bar, with even greater likelihood of being recognized, or he could go home to the house where the empty rooms just reminded him of the days when his brothers used to run wild through the place laughing and creating havoc. Then, he hadn't minded leaving work.

He could head over to Donovan's house, where he could play with Matt and annoy his brother, or Terry's house, where he could spend a few hours protecting his shoes from imminent destruction if Trick hadn't gotten over his morning sickness.

Decision made, he drove swiftly through the early evening traffic to the quiet neighborhood where his younger brothers lived. One of them had to be home and willing to endure a visitor. Grimacing, he wondered when his status had changed from hero to someone to be endured. At one point his brothers had looked up to him, loved him, and sought his company and his advice. Now, he felt like a simple visit at Terry's house was akin to spreading the plague upon the inhabitants.

Still, he had a responsibility—as the eldest brother—to fulfill the promises he'd made to his dying mother. Keeping the family together meant something else now that the boys had grown up and lived separately, and it was up to him to figure out what that was. He parked on the street in front of Terry's house and automatically reached for the sheaf of papers he'd printed off on his computer at work and spent the day reading. Some of the information contained in these pages about childbirth and pregnancy terrified him. Three steps toward the front door, information in hand, he thought about Trick's hypersensitivity. Maybe giving Terry this information wouldn't be such a good idea. He stood considering the pages thoughtfully, turned, and walked back to his car. He'd opened the door and leaned forward to throw the papers back on the seat when he reconsidered again.

The information could make a difference in the health of Terry's child. Surely that was more important than not stressing Trick out? Considering the smooth Italian leather of his favorite pair of shoes, Brandon's stomach churned, acid burning. Stressing Trick out could result in the loss of his favorite loafers, a bout of tears, a punch in the jaw from Dex, and the further erosion of his relationship with Terry. His invitation to visit might be revoked permanently. Cursing, he snatched the pages up and folded them in half. He'd sneak them to Terry, and Trick wouldn't have to read about the odds of birth defects, the importance of the proper diet, and all the things that could go wrong even when a mother did everything right during a pregnancy. Slipping the papers under his arm, he made his way back up the sidewalk to the front door.

He reached in his pocket to touch his cell phone. *Maybe I should call Arden and ask what she thinks.* It wasn't controlling or interfering to provide important health information, was it? He turned back down the path toward his car, dialing as he went. He needed to put Arden on speed dial. The phone rang a few times then her cool voice picked up. Just a recording though. Damn it. What to do?

The door opened behind him, and Dex's mocking voice rang out. "I got tired of watching you dance around. Are you coming in or not?"

Making a snap decision, Brandon whirled back up the walkway. Dex was strong. He could handle it. "I'm coming in. Here, I downloaded some information on pregnancy. Can you give it to Terry later?"

Dex's brow shot up in a gesture that Brandon recognized as his own, copied from Mischa, no doubt. "Thank you? But why don't you give it to him yourself?"

Confusion and admittedly a little pain that Arden hadn't been available to take his call—after all she'd told him to call her—made Brandon's voice terse. "I don't want to be accused of interfering or being controlling."

Dex laughed. Brandon felt a lick of anger flaring through his body, but swallowed it down. Terry loved this man. He was a part of the family. He could *not* knock the guy on his ass just because his feelings were hurt. Deep breathing exercises. In… out…in…out. Dex reached for his arm and tugged him toward the front door.

"I'm sorry, Brandon. Terry's been Googling this shit for months. He's got a stack of books on pregnancy, another on parenting, and I couldn't even tell you how many websites we've looked at already on designing a baby's room, choosing the right car seat, and what toys are good for what age. He'll love it."

Relieved that his meddling had been well-received by at least one of the baby's fathers, Brandon smiled and allowed himself to be led into the family room of Terry's home. Terry sat in the corner of a broad, green, suede sofa, Trick's pale head in his lap. Both men were reading, and it amused Brandon to note that Terry's book was indeed on pregnancy, while Trick seemed to be absorbed in a novel.

"Look who I found when I went out for the mail." Dex's cheerful voice brought both heads out of their books, and all eyes focused on Brandon. He smiled weakly. Dex waved the folded sheaf of papers in his hand and handed them off to Terry with a brief kiss. "He brought you this stuff from the Internet. Looks like you've got someone to share all your research with after all."

Dex flopped at the other end of the sofa and dragged Trick's bare feet into his lap. He absently stroked and rubbed while using the universal remote to turn off the television and surround sound system that he had evidently been watching.

"What brings you out tonight other than the delivery of information, Brandon?" Terry had put his book down on the mahogany end table and waved Brandon to the adjacent chair. He looked over the downloads Brandon had brought and then set them aside on his book.

Trick shifted upright, and as he did a strange waft of odor that Brandon recognized from years of working with actors, writers, and groupies reached him. His gaze jerked automatically to Trick, and before he could even consider what he was going to say, he blurted, "Have you been smoking pot? That can't be good for the baby!"

Trick's face took on an instant green tinge, and his lips tightened as he visibly strove to hold back his nausea. Dex instantly went to his brother's aid, scowling at Brandon as he did so. "Damn it! When will you ever learn?"

The sense of camaraderie he'd felt toward Dex on the sidewalk earlier vanished. "What? It smells like pot in here, and the studies are quite adamant that smoking, drinking, and doing drugs are detrimental to the baby!"

Terry placed one hand on Trick's thigh, concern evident, then turned to Brandon with a sigh. "We know that, Brandon. We're not stupid, however—"

"It's especially important that the mother not indulge during the first months of pregnancy!"

Dex led the obviously ill Trick from the room, casting scowls over his shoulder at Brandon as he did so.

"Fuck you, Brandon. In case it has escaped your notice, Trick is not the one who's pregnant, here. Bella is. The doctor prescribed the marijuana to help with the nausea because Trick is allergic to the usual stuff. It's just for a few weeks. I was going to invite you to stay for dinner, but since you've just incapacitated the chef, I guess you'd better go."

Stunned, Brandon rose to his feet and headed blindly for the door. Why did that always happen? One little innocuous comment and the whole night, fuck, the whole past month, all the effort he'd put into rebuilding his family relationships, shot to hell.

He sat, head on the steering wheel of the car, and struggled to calm his breathing and his stomach. Damn. He knew just how Trick felt right now. Slowly pulling himself upright, he reached into the glove box and pulled out the chalky-tasting antacid tablets that he never went anywhere without these days. He tossed a few of those down and chased them with some water from the bottle in the cup holder.

He couldn't drive yet. Driving required all his concentration, and he just couldn't get that focus back. He watched the lights in the house flicker on in one room, off in another, and then turned to see the same thing happening across the street at Mischa's. He'd planned to visit over there this evening as well, but now? Couldn't take the chance. Matt, Mischa, and even Donovan were too important to him. He couldn't risk fucking up another family relationship this evening.

He turned on the car and drove slowly down the block. Around the corner, there was a little coffee shop. He could make it that far. He pulled slowly into a parking space in front of the shop and contemplated going in. There wasn't anything in there that he could eat right now, not without risking his shoes, and just the thought of coffee made his stomach protest again. He pulled out his phone and absently dialed Arden again. It went to voice mail again, but this time he waited for the tone and left a message.

Disconnecting the call, he stared at his phone. His stomach had calmed a lot. His mind cleared rapidly. Arden would get his message, and she'd help him. She would take control of the situation for him. He wouldn't have to make any more decisions. His one decision in the whole affair had just been made. Strangely, just that fact made him feel better, stronger, and more capable. He'd go home and call Terry to check on Trick and apologize from the house phone. He wanted to keep this line clear for Arden's return call, whenever it came.

CHAPTER SEVEN

Arden listened to her messages outside the New Hope Building while waiting for Rick to bring her car around again. No doubt he'd picked Bastian up as well. Brandon Blake had called not once, but twice while she'd been counseling the women of New Hope about the importance of self-image. The first time he hadn't left a message, but the second call indicated he had. A warm tingle of pleasure melted through her. She was retrieving that message when once again she felt the harsh grasp of a masculine hand on her shoulder. Turning to the side, she noted that the large, brutish hand belonged to the same jerk who'd accosted her outside the center the week before.

She pursed her lips in a ladylike scowl before flipping the phone shut and sliding it into her pocket as she straightened to her vastly intimidating five-foot-nothing status. She could defend herself physically if she had to, but didn't look forward to doing so. In the past twenty years since she'd first mastered the basics of self-defense, not once had she been called upon to actually knee some guy in the family jewels or gouge out an eye. Calm, reason, and logic had always provided the out to any situation, and it would do so tonight as well. Unless Rick and Bastian pulled into the parking lot to create a distraction once again.

"Look, I just want Mary back. Tell me where she is!" The man's eyes glittered with fury, and once again, his voice drowned her in alcoholic fumes. "She's here, isn't she?"

"I'm sorry. I can't help you. I don't know anyone by that name." And a very good thing that group participants took the precaution of not using their real names. If this man was after one of her women, then it couldn't be for anything good. He stank of alcohol and appeared to believe that brute force would get him what he wanted.

Ahh, there they are. Rick's exit from the automobile once again coincided with the behemoth's departure into the shadows, but this time Rick stood and watched him go for longer. "Who is that guy? He was here last week harassing you as well, wasn't he?"

"Yes, Rick, it's the same guy. He's looking for someone else, though. Not me. My keys?" She wanted to listen to Brandon's message, but definitely not with an audience.

"Would you consider letting me drive?" Rick's gaze pleaded as he reluctantly handed over the keys.

Shaking her head, she laughed softly. "Now Rick, you know better. No Bastian tonight? Aren't we having dinner with him?"

Rick's smile faded, and he shook his head. "He had a date. Couldn't come with."

Now that surprised her. She could have sworn that Bastian was as into Rick as the other man was into her little brother.

Since neither of them really wanted dinner, she dropped Rick off at his apartment and continued on to her own home. Not listening to Brandon's message until she got inside her own apartment became a test of her self-control. She hung up her jacket, made a pot of tea, and carefully ignored her phone. When the teakettle whistled, she sat at her kitchen table and sipped the cup before listening to the message. Concerned, she heard the stress in Brandon's voice as he rambled about some snafu with his brother's boyfriend and pot? That stress was gone when he concluded his message with a more confident sounding, "Yes, I'd like to see where this thing between us leads."

She was tempted to do a little happy dance in her kitchen. *What the heck? Why not?* She did the dance, a few graceful twirls, and a light humming accompaniment. Plans she'd made weeks ago could now be put into play.

She should really wait to call until the morning, but Brandon might want to talk about this incident with his family. She dialed, pleased when he answered straight away.

"Arden, you got my message." It was a statement, not a question, but she felt compelled to answer it anyway.

"Yes, I just got in and got your message." She absently rubbed the spot on her arm where the jerk had gripped her earlier. There was no bruise, but the imprint of his touch lingered on her still. "Would you like to tell me about what happened with your brother's boyfriend?" She'd rather jump right into their personal issue, but Brandon needed more than that from her.

"No, not really. I already called and apologized to both of them." His voice changed when he spoke of his family, as it always did. He was tense again and unsure of himself.

"You know, Brandon, I can help you with your familial relations; I told you that. Tell me what happened so we can see what went wrong." *Poor baby.* His brothers really were his world.

"I took some information on childbirth over to Terry." Hesitation told her there was more to it than that.

"He didn't appreciate the information?"

"No. I mean, yes. He did. He was fine with me giving him information about pregnancy. They all were." Ahh. The boyfriends were present. They always seemed to trigger Brandon's foot-in-mouth disease.

"Then I smelled it, and I couldn't not say something!" A moment of brief silence descended. "Could I?"

"That depends, Brandon, on what you smelled. Was the house on fire? Then you'd have to say something. Someone forget to shower? No, you don't have to point that out."

"Pot. I smelled pot. It's bad for the baby if the mother smokes pot."

"I see. You didn't say that Bella was present for this gathering. And they took offence to that?"

"She wasn't. This is going to seem strange, but Bella and Trick keep merging in my mind. I kind of think of them both as the baby's mother. That's weird, I know. Anyway, my comments made Trick sick again. Terry told me that the doctor prescribed the marijuana to treat the nausea Trick's been having. Do doctors really do that these days?"

"Some do, under certain circumstances. That doesn't actually sound so bad, Brandon. Why were you so upset?"

"Then he threw me out. I was afraid I'd done it again, alienated my family by being too controlling."

"So, you called and apologized because you knew they were upset with you? And what did they say?"

"Terry told me to shut the fuck up and come back some other time instead, and Dex said to suck it up and quit whining. So, it's all good." His deep voice was back to confidence now, pouring over her like warm honey, nearly a physical sensation in itself.

"Wonderful. Then I'd like to pick you up after work tomorrow for dinner." She purred a little under her breath, imagining the sexy man's green eyes widening at that statement. His sudden indrawn breath on the other end of the line was audible, and she felt a twinge of unease. Had she been overconfident? Maybe he hadn't really understood what she'd tried to tell him at lunch the other day?

"No." That tone went beyond uncertain. Brandon seemed downright frightened of something.

"No? Do you already have dinner plans for that day?" She tapped her lower lip with the slender tip of one finger. Other plans she could deal with. An outright refusal to the first request she made? That was a different matter entirely.

"No. I don't have plans. Yes, I'll have dinner with you. But you can't pick me up."

"I can't pick you up? Brandon, did I not specifically tell you that I would need to be in control of this relationship?" Her temper began to fray ever so slightly as she felt a sense of disappointment. She'd never had quite such a brief relationship with anyone before.

"Yes. I understand that, but I can't be a passenger in a car with you. Can I just meet you somewhere? I promise, everything else is all you, but I need to drive myself. You can order the food, choose the wine, whatever." The pleading was a nice touch, and his voice rang with sincerity, so Arden gave in as gracefully as she could.

"I'll email you directions to my place." She hung up, unwilling to talk further with her emotions so close to the surface. She couldn't help Brandon maintain his calm and let go of his need to control the world if she couldn't present an image of herself as a responsible, reliable adult who could be trusted to take over for him in some aspects of his life.

CHAPTER EIGHT

If he'd known what she would take "everything else is all you" to mean, Brandon wondered, would he have made the same rash statement? He tugged his hands lightly where they were bound by the tie of her slinky, ivory and rose-printed robe to the brass headboard of the bed. His feet were likewise restrained, and a delicate scarf prevented him from speaking.

Arden had discarded the silky robe she'd worn for dinner in favor of the absolute nothing she'd worn under it. She perched between his widespread legs and assiduously tortured him by completely ignoring his presence. She didn't touch him. She didn't speak to him. She didn't so much as make eye contact. He was left to watch as her hands made slow trails over her smooth ivory skin, stroking flesh he wanted to touch, teasing the tiny pink nipples he wanted to suck, and spreading the bright red curls that guarded the treasure he wanted to plunder.

His cock stood in front of her, proudly begging for the opportunity to take over, to show her what pleasure his body was capable of providing. His pulse thrummed loudly in his ears, and his gaze raced avidly over her, anxious not to miss a single detail of the display in front of him.

Her slick pink tongue traced her pouting lower lip, leaving a delicate trail of moisture behind that he wanted to lick and suck away. For all the intimacy of their current position, he hadn't even been gifted with the opportunity to kiss those soft rose-tinted lips. Suddenly he realized that he wanted, more than anything else this evening, to taste the essence of Arden. Her mouth opened in a gasp of pleasure. His gaze darted down to see that her fingers had parted the sleek bright curls, and this matching rose flesh gleamed with moisture as well.

Twist and struggle as he might, he could do nothing but watch as delicate fingers toyed with slick flesh, showing him plump little curves and enticing dips, teasing him with the hint of a darker destination. Her fingers stroked over her stiff clit again, and she repeated the gasp of pleasure. Realizing there was nothing else to do, he ceased struggling against the bonds and leaned back to enjoy the visual feast. In that moment, he realized her focus had switched, and her eyes locked on him. She leaned forward and reached across him to the bedside table. She was poised inches from his body, but still making no contact with his aching flesh, no concession to his presence in her bed except the avoidance of physical contact. He strained his neck to the side to see that she rifled through a white wicker basket that sat on the floor under the ridiculously frivolous little ironwork table that held the lamp. His eyes widened in surprise as she drew back clasping a translucent pink dildo in one hand and a smaller flesh-colored one in the other. The small one she dropped between his legs, and he winced in anticipation of its coldness rolling against his heated body.

Still staring directly into his face, she brought the other one to her lips and held it there. He groaned behind his gag. She licked it. He felt as if the swipe of her tongue had actually stroked across the tip of his cock, and his hips jerked in response. He watched in avid fascination as the pink object slipped past open lips, and she sucked it lightly, thrusting it gently, never more than a few inches at time before drawing it back, glistening with saliva.

She shifted into a more upright position, and he jerked his gaze immediately to the juncture of her thighs, where gleaming moisture waited. Seconds later the dildo entered his line of sight and stroked over the flesh he wanted to feel melting around his dick. The hot liquid he knew would scald him with her passion adorned the plastic toy as it slid over her clitoris, down into the hidden shadows, and back. Her breathing was rapid and shallow, he knew she was turned on by this, but still no sounds that weren't simply an exhalation or inhalation of air escaped her parted lips. No whimpers, no moans, no cries. He could make her give him those sounds. He wanted to hear them. *If only…*his hands jerked, and the bed frame rattled. Breathing deeply at the reminder that there would be no *if only*, he settled back again, unable to look away as the toy disappeared into the cavern he wanted to explore by slow inches.

"Brandon."

He pulled his gaze from the red curls between her legs to see the tiny white teeth bite into her plump lower lip.

"Oh, Brandon, watch me come."

Frantically he nodded, eyes drawn back like a magnet to that swollen honeyed flesh. Her thighs strained as she moved with her toy, riding the leisurely thrusts until at last she froze and threw back her head, releasing a long slow breath. "Ahh." She rose up, withdrawing the little toy from her throbbing flesh with another soft murmur of pleasure. Knees splayed, she sat back on her heels between his legs again. She played with the dildo, at last reaching forward and touching it to the tip of his cock. He shuddered. He couldn't help it. The scent of her was thick in the air; he ached to feel her hot flesh around him, and though it cooled rapidly, the toy was still slick with the juices of her lust.

"I'd much rather have had you inside me," she whispered softly. "But you must learn that you cannot override my wishes. I can take care of myself, and of you."

She tossed the toy to the side and leaned forward, breathing softly against his cock. Her breath was a torturous caress all its own, and he wondered briefly if it would be enough to make him come. "Would you like me to take care of you now, Brandon?"

Frantically he nodded. He didn't know what she had in mind, but he definitely needed taking care of right now. His erection was painful, and his body tense with the need that raced through him. She picked up the little vibrator she'd dropped between his legs, and he groaned as it went straight to her mouth.

She laughed, licking it delicately. "Do you think I have an oral fixation, Brandon? That would be good for you wouldn't it? You're so sexy, such a beautiful body. Do you mind if I touch you? I don't want you to come yet, but I really want to touch you."

He shook his head, nodded, shook it again, and groaned in frustration at his inability to communicate. He tried to beg with his eyes to be released, to be allowed to speak.

Sucking the little vibrator like a lollipop, Arden leaned over him, this time allowing her soft belly to press directly against his cock. She pulled the scarf away from his mouth as she sat back, but a delicate finger, scented with the essence of her womanhood pressed against his lips. She pulled the vibrator from her mouth with an audible pop.

"You can speak only to answer a direct question, Brandon. Learning when to be quiet is a big part of your control issue, isn't it?" Her expression was solemn as she stared deeply into his eyes.

"Yes. Touch me. I won't come. But I need you to touch me." Speaking was nearly impossible anyway.

Arden smiled and stroked her hand down his chest. He drew in a harsh breath, biting back a moan as she brushed his nipple. Her action reassured him, and he breathed again slowly through his nose. More delicate feminine scent wafted to him. Her hand explored farther, the taut abdominal muscles twitched under her fingers. His cock leaked onto his belly, and he shivered as her fingers drew a tiny pattern in the liquid. He couldn't concentrate enough to tell what it was; her hand was too close to where he needed it most.

He nearly burst into speech as she carefully avoided his hungry cock and cupped his balls instead. She cradled them, squeezed gently, then rolled them together, studying his face, his body, his every reaction as she did so. She moved on, pressing against his perineum, rubbing gently, then lower. His eyes widened. She brought the vibrator back to her mouth, licking and sucking at it as her fingers toyed with his anus in the same manner they had played with her cunt.

He wanted to protest. She couldn't be planning to do what he thought she planned. No way was he letting anyone... The tip of a wet finger dipped just barely inside him, and he squirmed wanting to jerk away. He forced himself to stillness, remembering his promise.

Her fingertip pressed gently inward, and he breathed deeply. Her voice came to his ears in a soft whisper. "Breathe in, Brandon, and when you exhale, push out to meet me."

He obeyed, and the finger slid deeper. Gasping, he stilled, and so did Arden. She smiled encouragingly again, and he breathed more easily. The probing finger slipped a bit deeper and brushed against something inside that sent a flare of sensation rocketing through his cock.

He clenched his teeth to keep the moan inside, and Arden brushed over that spot again. "Hmm," she purred again. He was so lost in the surprising pleasure of that stimulation that he nearly missed her intent as she bent across him again, this time trailing the saliva slick vibrator over his balls and up to the tip of his cock before twisting the base to ignite a tiny hum.

She repeated the trail of the vibrator in reverse, and he was adjusting to that little tingle when her finger pulled from his ass, and she carefully pressed the little toy against him, then inserted it slowly. He jolted in shock when it pressed into the same place her finger had caressed at the exact moment that her mouth opened over his cock and she flicked him with the tip of her tongue.

His hips thrust instinctively upward as her hot mouth closed around him. He wouldn't last—couldn't last—as she sucked and licked him with abandon. Jesus, who would have believed the suit-clad Dr. Grey held such hidden depths? He nearly cried out in protest when she pulled away from his cock, but eagerly accepted the kiss she bestowed on his mouth in its stead. The kiss was deep, ardent, and over too quickly.

"You can talk now, Brandon. You can come now."

The words had scarcely registered in his mind before her mouth closed around him once again, and he exploded in an intense orgasm, words of pleasure, ecstasy, lust, and foolishness spilling from his mouth unheeded.

When he returned to his senses, Arden was busily untying his hands and his feet had already been freed. She curled up next to him at the head of the bed, and he lifted his head to rest it on her lap. Her hands ran through his blond hair, rubbing tiny circles at his temples, and he sighed in pleasure.

Comfortable silence reigned for a while; Brandon mulled over the sense of peace he felt, the rightness of the moment, contentment with his situation. Normally after hooking up with a woman, he would be looking for his pants and heading out the door right now, but Arden's presence comforted him, and if he remembered right, his pants were safely folded on the sofa, his favorite shoes tucked underneath. Drifting, he nearly missed Arden's soft voice.

"Brandon, why wouldn't you let me pick you up?"

He tried to pull away, to right himself; his pants were calling from the other room after all, but she refused to release him, and he couldn't bring himself to treat her roughly. "I don't like to be driven."

"You told me Terry drove you to his house the other day."

He covered his face with a trembling hand. "Terry's different."

"He's family." Concern etched her voice. "Is that what makes it different?"

"No." Could he admit it? What would she think of him? Did it make him a jerk? "He's a man. I don't let women drive me anywhere."

Silence. She didn't react, just stroked his hair, and then a gentle kiss pressed into his forehead. "It's because of the accident you told me about, isn't it? The one you dream about?"

He shuddered. Her grip tightened. "Yeah. I guess. I shouldn't have let her drive. I knew she'd been drinking and other stuff. I had just gotten my license; I could have driven us home, but she wanted to."

"Shh." Arden's soft voice with its calming effect washed over him, the hypnotic effect of her stroking fingers, and the exhaustion of his day caught up with him all at once. The peaceful lure of sleep that had enticed him earlier teased him again, and he began his nightly ritual, letting all his problems go, one by one, person by person, putting trouble to bed until the next day.

Terry, Trick, Dex, and Bella, baby Blake-to-be, all settle down for a night of sleep. Sleep. Wait. His eyes popped open. Was he actually sleeping here? He never spent the night. Regardless of the intimacy of the situation, he was still prone to random nightmares. "Am I sleeping here?" He knew it wasn't his choice to make. Arden would tell him if he needed to get dressed and go home.

"Of course you are." Arden wriggled down in the bed until his head rested on her chest instead of her lap, and continued her soothing petting motions. "Now put your concerns to bed, and I'll make sure you get to work on time in the morning."

CHAPTER NINE

"Why am I driving you and Blake around again?" Even through the phone, Rick's impatience with the situation was clear.

"You are driving, Rick, because driving is symbolic in a relationship. The person who drives the car drives the relationship."

"So, by that logic, I'm in charge of my relationship with Bastian since I'm driving him around in your car all the time. And that's just not the way it is."

"Isn't it? Bastian's been eyeing your ass since you first started working for me five years ago. If he were driving your relationship, you'd be Indy 500 winners by now."

"Never mind me. How does driving affect you and Blake?"

"We both want to drive; neither of us wants to be the passenger. The fastest, easiest way for us to be together while we work it out is for neither of us to drive. Simple."

"Right, well, Bastian's lost something, so I'm going to be late to pick you up. I'm getting Brandon now and then we're five minutes out from Bastian and ten from you. Will you be okay until then?"

"I'll be fine. It's not that bad a neighborhood."

"Yeah, but I don't like the look of that guy that's been hanging around the last few times I picked you up." Rick's concern was clear in his voice. "Stay close to the building and that street light, okay?"

"Rick, really. I can take care of myself. I'm hardly naive and stupid anymore."

Exasperation crackled through the phone line. "I know that. But those of us who love you are entitled to worry about you. Our concern doesn't take anything away from you Arden; you should know that. Do you worry less about Bastian when he's jumping out of airplanes or bungee jumping off skyscrapers than I do?"

"Right. I'll be out front." She disconnected the call and leaned back against the rough stone in her usual position.

Arden felt almost tempted to borrow Brandon's favorite curse, but instead she took a deep breath and turned to face the inebriated man who grasped her arm just below the shoulder, yet again. *This was getting really old.* She pressed the speed dial for 911 on her cell phone and hoped that they would pick up enough of her voice to get the general idea.

"Hello, again." She smiled calmly. "This is becoming quite a regular meeting for us."

"Where's Mary? I want Mary back." Something struck her as different about the man this time; he seemed not just angry, but on edge. Then the glint of light on metal flickered in the darkness at his side, and she couldn't control the sudden stiffening and lurch backward. He had a knife, or a gun, or a lead pipe, or something.

"Fuck." The word slipped out.

Her brain scrambled quickly for the best course of action. *Make it personal. Be real, not a victim.* "I'm Arden. I come for a meeting here on Wednesdays. My ride is a few minutes late. I'm glad to see a familiar face to wait with me."

He seemed taken aback by her speech and answered automatically. "I'm Donny. I want Mary back. She went in there a while back. Now I can't find her. Did you see her in there?"

"Hmm, no. I don't believe I did. What does Mary look like?" *Try to seem like you're going to help him.* "What color hair does she have?"

The ire in his eyes faded, and she felt he really saw her as a person. "She's got gray hair and blue eyes. Was she in there? They took her in there."

"No, I didn't see anyone in there with gray hair and blue eyes." And that was the truth, so sincerity wasn't hard to achieve in her answer.

Lights sweeping across the parking lot sent a wave of relief through Arden. Thank God. She had no wish to defend herself, but if that glint of metal had turned out to be a weapon of some kind, she'd have been forced to do something she definitely didn't want to do.

She turned to Donny. "Have you tried asking the police?"

Donny had opened his mouth to answer when the slam of a car door caused him to whirl around. Seconds later he was stretched out at her feet with Brandon looming over him in menace. The flashing red and blue of police lights as a cruiser pulled into the parking lot behind Arden's Mercedes painted the whole scene in blood and shadow.

"Brandon?" Stunned, she melted into the arms he wrapped around her before she realized what had happened. Policemen helped Donny up and cuffed him, pushing him against the patrol car as he protested that he just wanted Mary.

"Are you all right?" Brandon ran his hands over her, peering intently into her face searching for nonexistent injuries. He led her to the car and practically shoved her into the back seat before turning back to the cops.

While Brandon spoke to the police behind the car, she met Rick's eyes as he turned around in the front seat. "You picked up Brandon?" Dumb maybe, but it was the only thing she could think to ask.

"Ahh, yes? I thought we talked about this earlier." Rick tilted his chin toward her younger brother, who had his head out the window studying Brandon intently.

Sighing, she slid into the back seat of the car as gracefully as she could, "Yes, I remember."

Brandon seated himself beside her in the back seat and took her hand in his again. "I don't know that I approve of you working here this late. This is obviously not a good neighborhood."

"I'm fine, Brandon; I can take care of myself."

Rick added from the front seat, "She can. She's been studying kickboxing since I met her five years ago."

Brandon's dubious expression annoyed her more than a little, and the tension of the incident made her a little snappy as she responded, "I can defend myself, Brandon. I just prefer to use logic and reason as a first resort and violence as a last resort."

"How often have you ever had to use these kickboxing skills on a real person?"

She pulled her hand away and clenched it in her lap. *Patience. Deep breathing. This relationship is still in the getting-to-know-you phase, don't freak out on him now or he'll never trust you.* "I spar with Bastian there every week, and have for the last five years. You have little brothers. Would Terry or Mischa pass up a chance to knock you to your ass on the mat every week?"

"No, they wouldn't, but I'm not five-foot-nothing and a girl to boot." Brandon's scowl told her he caught her sarcasm. "Are you telling me he doesn't go easy on you at practice?"

He'd transferred the scowl to Bastian, who rubbed his jaw in reminiscence. "Dude, I did. The first time we sparred, she broke my jaw."

"I broke your jaw by accident because you were too busy looking at Rick's ass to defend yourself!" she asserted. Bastian grinned, Rick blushed, and Brandon snorted. "Thank you, Brandon. Even if I didn't need rescuing, it's nice to know that you care enough to rescue me."

Brandon's smile made the sacrifice worthwhile, and she melted into a hot kiss, grateful for the distraction so she didn't have to worry about Rick scratching her paint job.

A momentary dilemma arose as Rick pulled into his parking space outside the complex he lived in. He and Bastian turned to the back seat, and Arden pulled away from Brandon's devouring mouth. "Ahh…" She looked around dazed; then, realizing where they were, turned considering eyes on Brandon. Now would probably not be a good time to push the driving issue. "Can you take us to my place?"

Without words exchanged, Bastian and Rick turned back to the front, and in moments, they pulled into her complex instead. Brandon had the door open and tugged her toward the entrance to the building while she still tried to decide if her clothes were all adequately fastened.

Not able to resist, she flung over her shoulder to Rick and Bastian, "Be here at seven!"

"Six thirty!" Brandon bellowed. "I have a meeting." He added in response to her quirked brow.

They rushed forward, disregarding Bastian's laughter as the Mercedes reversed out of her assigned parking space.

CHAPTER TEN

When Arden left him in the frilly, white bedroom, Brandon felt a momentary unease. What the fuck was he doing? Six weeks he'd known the woman, and he'd just given her permission to "get the cuffs." Was he really contemplating letting a pretty little thing like Arden cuff him to the bed? What if there was a fire?

Absently, he flicked open the buttons on his shirt as he studied the room and racked his brain to recall the layout of the apartment and the best emergency escape route. It was too many floors up for the windows to do any good. He tossed the shirt onto the white velvet armchair in the corner and slipped open the fastenings of his trousers. It was an expensive, obviously well-maintained complex. Surely the management had well-thought-out emergency plans. He sat on the bed to remove his shoes. He passed a careful hand over the handcrafted Italian leather. Love of good shoes was a trait he shared with his dearly departed mother, a legacy she'd left him as surely as the nightmares and his abhorrence of drugs and Hollywood actresses. He placed the shoes under the chair and rolled his socks together in a sock bunny. He smiled. He'd forgotten about sock bunnies. His mother had shown him as a child how to make one, and he'd shared the little trick with Mischa when he was a toddler.

His pants quickly joined the dress shirt on the chair. Brandon peeled off his boxer briefs and tossed them on the floor near the chair, reclining on the white bedspread, resting his head on his crossed arms. Where had all the good memories been hiding all these years? Sock bunnies and nice shoes were just the beginning. He'd been his mom's first child, her confidant, her "date" when his dad was out of town. They'd spent a lot of time together, and before he'd turned sixteen, it had been good time.

The faint clink of the metal cuffs signaled Arden's approach, and he opened his eyes. He smiled at her. Her little face was intent and solemn, her movements slightly hesitant.

"Brandon."

He'd never heard her voice so hesitant, so uncertain.

"We don't have to do this if it's not what you want."

And just then, he knew. More than anything, he wanted to be what Arden needed him to be. He didn't want to choose, to make any decisions, to be responsible for anything. He just wanted to give her the same safety, security, and happiness she'd brought to him, and if cuffing him to the bed and driving him crazy with her hands and mouth would do that, then who was he to complain?

He smiled, pulled his hands from behind his head, and stretched them out toward the bedposts. The resurgence of confidence and Arden's rapid approach made his pulse leap and his heart pound.

One knee on the bed, she grasped his wrist and leaned over him, putting his hand around the rail of the headboard. Her breasts brushed his chest, sending shivers up his spine as cool metal circled his wrist. The metallic click caught the breath in his throat. The rush of blood pooled in his groin, sending an aching throb through his cock. Knowing she'd pull away if he demanded, he tilted his head to entice a kiss.

Soft warm lips settled against his, parting moistly to allow a sleek tongue to probe between his lips. He eagerly opened wider and met her tongue, stroke for hungry stroke. The fire caught, the flames burned, and they moaned and writhed against each other. Arden pulled back, panting. He arched his neck, reaching for more.

"Brandon." The tentative whisper, so unlike Arden's usual brash confidence, grabbed his attention. "I don't want to use this." She held up a foil packet.

Brandon struggled to comprehend. "You don't want to use a condom?"

"I can't have children. I'm past that stage of my life. I'm healthy." Tiny white teeth sank into the slick red lower lip. "I trust you are too."

He was. But did he have that level of trust? What if she was wrong? What if she did get pregnant? Deciding that wouldn't be a bad thing, he nodded his consent. With a wicked little smile, Arden tossed the packet to the floor.

She slung one sleek, creamy thigh across his flat belly and sat astride him. His cock nestled in the cleft of her petite ass, and he thrust gently against her. Anal sex wasn't ever something that had interested him before, but after her play with the toys, his curiosity and desire to try it with Arden had grown steadily. He wouldn't suggest it though. If Arden wanted him to take her that way, she'd let him know it. He couldn't help the suggestive thrusting though; that smooth skin felt so damn good on his cock.

Arden shifted slowly upward, and Brandon gasped in pleasure as he felt the hot, wet kiss of her swollen lips against the head of his cock. She stayed there, poised to take him in, blue eyes gleaming as they locked with his own. Then slowly, she lowered herself, immersing him in tight wet heat until his full length felt the clasp of her body.

Strong inner muscles clamped around him, drawing him deeper as she slid lower, enfolding his entire length deep inside her. The pleasure spread, rippling all the way to his fingertips and toes, and he bucked upward, driving deeper and deeper, scorching heat urging him to pull against the restraints, hands eager to touch. She wrapped her hands around his bound wrists, silently admonishing him not to move. "Just feel," she whispered. "Feel what I can do for you."

He felt all right, felt the tingling in the base of his spine as she began a rapid, hard rhythm that had him groaning in ecstasy. The end came all too fast, but her sweet gasp and clenching walls told him the timing was perfect. Arden stilled as he jerked upward, grinding as deeply inside as he could, while the hot liquid spurted from his cock.

He drank in the look of sheer ecstasy on her face as her slick walls pulsed around him and welcomed the sweet, slight weight of her body as she fell forward onto his chest. She tucked her bright red curls beneath his chin and breathed deeply. Her tiny tongue licked delicately at his throbbing pulse, and she released a sigh of contentment. They lay like that for a few moments before she shifted and released the metal cuffs from his ankles. She moved up his body and released the cuff on his right wrist, leaving it attached to the bedstead for future use. When she reached to undo the cuff on the left, he guided her fingers to the bed frame, and she obligingly released the cuff from the metal frame, quirking a brow in question.

He snapped the cuff around her delicate wrist. "Can we sleep like this?" His heart stalled a bit as he waited for her answer. Was he being too demanding, too needy? Asking for too much?

Arden studied the metal cuff where it rested, much too bulky and large against her fragile skin. She raised her eyes to Brandon's face, and he quailed at the intense concentration he saw there. She gently unclasped the cuff from her wrist and then reached to undo his. He watched in stunned silence, heart sinking. Had he gone too far? Had he pushed her into cutting him lose by demanding too much? *Shit. Fuck.* Bewildered by her continued silence, he watched Arden reach into the basket below the bedside table and come back with a length of black silk in her hand.

"Give me your hand," she commanded huskily. Obligingly, he held it out, and she put one end of the silk in his hand. He automatically clasped it. She wrapped the silk around his wrist and her own, binding them together. When she came to the end of the silk, she used her teeth and free hand to form a simple knot. "Will that do, love?"

Swallowing hard, he nodded, gaze locked to the place where they were connected. Together, they lay back onto the soft white sheets, her head resting on his chest, their clasped hands lying next to her face. Contentment, a sense of rightness spread, and for the first time in a long time, Brandon drifted into sleep without worrying about any of his brothers, his business, or problems that might occur.

CHAPTER ELEVEN

Waking up in the same position—with her head on Brandon's chest, their bound hands the first thing she saw—felt right to Arden. She could easily imagine waking up like this for the rest of her life. She stealthily shifted upright, taking in the beauty of the man in front of her. She traced his golden brows with her fingers, admiring the perfect clarity of his skin, and then trailed her hand over the rougher texture of his jaw, enjoying the tingle of sensation in her fingertips as the stubble of his golden beard prickled her sensitive flesh.

Cupping his jaw in her hand, she bent forward and pressed her closed lips to his, wishing they had time for more, but Brandon had said he had an early meeting and she wanted to go to the police station and see about getting the charges dropped against Donny. She felt certain that despite the gleam of the weapon, he hadn't meant to hurt her. Maybe she could find out about this Mary and see what had happened to her. Donny clearly needed help, and he really hadn't hurt her.

When Brandon's lips parted and the kiss slipped into a deeper intimacy, she pulled back. Brandon stared intently at the way their hands were bound, and flushed slightly. At what she thought might be a rebuke, or even an urge to hurry and release him, Arden reached to pull the silk. A single tug and the knot came undone. She carefully unwound the fabric, not looking at Brandon's face as she did so. Brandon's ongoing silence unnerved her. What was he thinking? Had she somehow misinterpreted his meaning the night before? She'd thought he wanted, needed, the feeling of connection between them, just as she did.

The silk fell to the bed, and Arden forced a shallow breath, just then realizing she had been holding it in. She stared at the strip of black lying on the pure white, and then turned her gaze to Brandon, to find him staring at the silk. As though sensing her gaze, he met her eyes, the uncertainty, the question in those green depths went straight to her heart, and she reached out to him, going eagerly into his arms.

"I love you." Their voices mingled. The same sense of wonder reflected in both. Their lips met in a kiss of sweet understanding, and they pulled reluctantly apart.

"Meeting," Brandon whispered, leaning his forehead against hers. "I have a meeting. You have a meeting. We need to get up. Rick will be here at six thirty." He gently fingered the black silk. "Don't put this away. Arden." He gently guided her mouth to his again, and to her surprise, she let him.

"Brandon?" She urged him to go on, wondering what brought the solemn tone to his voice again.

"Don't put this away, okay? I like it. I really like it." He pushed away from the bed, and she watched his taut buttocks flex as he strolled into the bathroom, leaving the door open behind him as he started the shower.

Smiling foolishly, Arden rolled the silk into a ball and dropped it on the side table. She rose, pulled on a robe, and went to make coffee, contemplating the changes Brandon was sure to bring to her life. Brandon had just issued a clear order, in a pleasant tone of voice, no doubt, but an order just the same. Had any of her past lovers had the temerity to command her to do something, no matter how much it was something she wished to do, she'd have shown them the door. She had never been an indulgent woman. Beyond delivering a satisfactory conclusion to a night of sex, she always insisted on mapping the journey to that conclusion her own way. Yet, last night and this morning, that Brandon had guided her choices.

The idea still occupied her thoughts when Rick picked them up in her car. Another concession she had made to Brandon's control.

"Where to?" Rick demanded in a surly tone. Rick's obvious temper drew Arden's attention from her self-absorption. Things must not have gone well with Bastian the night before. She would have to look into that later.

She placed her hand on Brandon's strong thigh, slightly distracted by the heat and tautness she found there. "Take Brandon to his office first so he doesn't miss his meeting; then I want to go over to the police station."

Brandon covered her hand with his, grip tightening when she tried to pull away. "No." His voice overrode hers. "I was going to the police station too. I feel like I may have overreacted last night to the situation, and I want to make sure that Donny is going to be okay."

Arden couldn't help the smile. "You mean, you found someone whose life could use a little prime Brandon Blake interference, and you can't resist the temptation to meddle on Donny's behalf."

Rick's scowl turned to a grin, and his chuckles filled the car. "And you, boss lady? Your intentions are pure and lack any quality of meddlesomeness?"

Arden shook her head. "Of course. I'm going to go make sure that no charges are pressed against Donny on my behalf. He's harmless."

"He could use a stint in rehab." Brandon asserted.

"Do you think he'll go?" Arden asked curiously.

"I'll gladly pay for rehab and give him a job at the studio when he gets out." Brandon seemed eager to help with the situation, which pleased Arden greatly.

"We need to resolve this situation with Mary, though. The center is for the protection of women and children who have escaped abusive situations. If his Mary went in there, then the chances are that she did it to get away from him. We can't break that barrier of silence."

"What if she's not his wife? What if she's his daughter or neighbor or something?"

"We can figure it out. Maybe if he gets clean and sober and has a job, we can find out if Mary is willing to meet with him in a protected setting."

As the car pulled into the visitor's lot at the police station, Arden's admiration for Brandon grew as she listened to his willingness to solve the problem with practical means, taking into consideration Mary's needs as well as Donny's.

Two hours later they exited the police station hand in hand to climb back into her car.

"I cannot believe that Mary is a cat." Arden chuckled as she fastened her seat belt.

"It's funny, isn't it? The people at that center of yours took in a stray cat thinking they were doing a good deed. How were they to know that cat belonged to a homeless man who loved it?"

"Well, at least we know getting Mary back together with Donny is going to be easy enough when he gets out of rehab." Brandon nodded. He seemed reluctant to let go of her hand.

"We'll have to get some shelter cats to replace Mary at the center though. The kids probably really like playing with her." Arden narrowed her eyes at Brandon. First he was telling her what to do, and she let him, and now he was going to get involved in the center where she volunteered? This bore thinking about. Brandon's control issues were far from resolved. *So are yours.* She waved an impatient hand.

"You're right. The cats are important to the kids." It really didn't matter, after all, did it? She knew well enough that Brandon would allow her to control their relationship when she needed to; she could certainly allow him access to all facets of her life without fearing that he would use them against her.

CHAPTER TWELVE

There were a lot of wandering gazes and nervous movements at the Blake brothers' poker game. The only one who seemed capable of concentrating on the cards was Dan, who raked in pot after pot with campy cackles of glee.

Brandon watched his brothers watching the door and fought a grin. Arden had declared that if Wednesday night was poker night for the Blake boys, then it was "girls' night" for the rest of the family. Dex, Trick, and Donovan had objected to being called girls, but eagerly accepted the idea of a spousal support night for Blake brothers.

Now, Mischa and Terry, aware their loved ones were in the media room with Arden, couldn't seem to keep their eyes off the door.

"What are they talking about out there? They have nothing in common." Mischa shuffled his cards, lay them face down on the green baize tabletop, and reached for his glass.

"They have one thing in common," Dan inserted, before swallowing a mouthful of whiskey.

"How so? Dex and Trick are absorbed in baby stuff,

Donovan is a fount of information on advertising, and Arden's a psychologist. What are they going to talk about?"

"You guys. They're in there, comparing the trials and tribulations of couplehood with a Blake. What do you think they're doing? Exchanging recipes?" Dan smirked laying out a full house. "Read 'em and weep, boys."

Brandon grasped Dan's wrist as he reached forward to scoop up the pot. Terry and Mischa were communicating in silent alarm over the prospect of their spouses sharing family secrets. "Not so fast, there, Dan. I'm calling this a Truth or Dare hand."

Three pairs of green eyes turned to Brandon, and he met each one with a smile. "I thought we quit that game." Terry picked up the hand of cards he'd barely glanced at previously with renewed interest. He shook his head. "I got nothing."

Mischa didn't even look at his cards. "Nothing. And no, I don't recall that we did. So this is between you and Dan, Brandon."

"Okay. Fine." The trickster tricked, Dan pouted. "Truth or Dare it is. What have you got?"

Brandon laid out four of a kind on the table. Terry and Dan's laughter drowned out Dan's lame protest. "My win. Dan, you've had a blast manipulating us in your little game these past months, and now it's your turn."

"Nice haircut, Mischa." Dan's jibe about Mischa's gleaming bald head was a tempting distraction, but Brandon had learned not to fall for Dan's red herrings.

Brandon paused dramatically, savoring the inside edge he had over his crafty brother. "I've had more leisure time of late, and thank you," he nodded graciously to Terry and then Dan, "for taking over so much of the workload. Anyway, it's given me time to be more observant and less reactive. Do you see where I'm going with this, Dan?"

Dan paled. "I do. Don't do this, Brandon. You've turned over a new leaf, remember? No interference in your brothers' lives? What would Arden say?" Desperation colored Dan's outburst.

"She'd say you need to bring the person you're seeing to meet your family, Dan. I'd especially like it if you brought this special someone to my wedding."

"You're daring me to bring a date to your wedding?" Dan's hopeful tone was buried under the startled exclamations of Terry and Mischa.

"You're getting married? When? Where?" Their voices mingled, and Brandon smiled broadly.

"I am. As soon as possible, and… in your backyard?" He directed an inquiring gaze at Mischa, who nodded his consent with a proud smile.

"Did you ask her or tell her?" Dan demanded snidely, gathering cards from around the table and snapping the deck together.

"I'm *asking* her in about ten minutes."

"And that's why it was so important for everyone to be here tonight? Mischa asserted with satisfaction.

Nodding, Brandon refused to break eye contact with Dan. He'd given up interfering in his brothers' lives for the most part. But the master of manipulation deserved a dose of his own medicine. "Let me be as clear as possible here, Dan. I know you're seeing someone special. I want you to bring that person, not just a date, but that person, to my wedding, assuming Arden says yes to my proposal."

"She'll say yes. Why wouldn't she?" Ever optimistic, Mischa eyed the door, clearly in a hurry to get to his own life partner.

"Because of who I am, the way I am." He'd become certain that Arden loved him, but he also knew about her harrowing experiences with her first husband.

Terry bridled in indignation. "What's wrong with who you are? You're a Blake. You have wealth, position, and good looks."

"Thanks, Terry. I meant because of this control issue I have."

"Why would that bother her? Clearly she has control issues of her own," Dan mumbled, then sipped from his tumbler of whiskey again.

Brandon nodded. "She does. We both do. Control issues related to specific incidents in our pasts. We're working on them, but we've discovered we work well together. I love her." He coughed into his hand. "I love you guys and the studio too. I've decided to keep the lighter work load, though."

"Oh, for fuck's sake. He's getting maudlin now. I'm the only sane one left," Dan grumbled into his glass.

Brandon eyed him meaningfully. "I'm going to stick to my promise to try not to interfere in your lives too much. I'm holding you all to your commitment to let me know when I cross any lines."

"Fine." Dan slammed the glass on the table. "You're crossing a fucking line tonight with me."

"It's a simple dare, Danny. And I consider it more along the lines of returning the favor you did me when you forced me to ask Arden out."

Dan looked away. He hid everything behind a devil-may-care attitude, but Brandon knew well that Dan had been torn apart by the emotions that followed their mother's death years ago. He sensed this relationship Dan concealed from everyone could bring his brother the happiness the rest of them had found. If, that was he could let go of his screw 'em and leave 'em methodology.

Mischa and Terry looked on, mouths agape. Dan defensive was a novelty.

"Catching flies?" Dan dropped the deck of cards on the table. "Let's get this show on the road."

Mischa and Terry hurried ahead out the door, each anxious to meet up with their lover, or lovers as the case may be. Brandon put a soothing hand on Dan's shoulder. "You don't have to. I just want you to be happy like the rest of us are happy."

Dan shrugged the hand off and pasted on a forced-looking smile. "Screwing around makes me happy. Seeing you get married makes me happy. Being stuck with one person 24-7, three hundred sixty-five days a year wouldn't make me happy. Leave it alone, Brandon. I'm too much like Mom for the one-woman one-man scenario to fit. Now, let's go get you engaged so you and Arden can micromanage each other."

CHAPTER THIRTEEN

Arden smiled down at the cooing baby on her lap. He was sweet and adorable, and best of all, she could hand him off to either one of his fathers if he showed any signs of fussiness or stinky diapers. The baby had mastered the art of bubble blowing, and both Dex and Trick smiled with pride in his accomplishment.

Arden glanced surreptitiously at a mantle clock as Michael, named for his Uncle Mischa, began to fuss a bit. Brandon had sworn the poker games ended by eleven, and that they would join the spouses in the media room by quarter after. She resisted the desire to go seek them out. It was five minutes after eleven. Neither Dex, Trick, nor Donovan seemed concerned about their partners. In fact, all three of the other men were absorbed in the antics of Matt, Donovan, and Mischa's eight-year-old son.

She'd felt positively foolish when the three men and their children had wandered into the media room together, eyeing her with interest, but this was her family now, and she had immediately set about getting to know everyone.

"Ah, Trick?" She hoped she'd gotten the name of the baby's father right. The man she was looking at smiled and rose to come to her side. "He's making a rather strange face. Maybe you'd like to uh…"

"Oh sure. But I'm Dex. I'll change him."

She'd scarcely handed the baby over when the media room doorway was flung open. Brandon strode in, a commanding presence that made her weakening knees grateful she was already seated. Her golden-haired, green-eyed lover was flanked by his brothers, two slightly smaller, but just as masculine green-eyed, blond gods, and the perky smiling Mischa.

The other men scattered about the room rapidly as Brandon strode directly toward her with seeming intent. She was vaguely aware of whispers and a few gasps in the background, but couldn't take her eyes from Brandon's determined countenance long enough to search out the source.

Brandon dropped to his knees on the floor in front of the sofa, and she drew in a deep unsteady breath. He couldn't, he wouldn't.

"Arden, I love you. Will you do me the very great honor of becoming my wife?" That voice was no whisper. He fully intended everyone in the room to hear him. Frantic noes and other protests chased themselves around in her head, and he took her hand in his.

Was he trying to manipulate her? To control her response? Did he think she wouldn't say no if he proposed in front of his brothers? The temptation to do just that warred with the knowledge that beneath the commanding exterior was the heart of a man who'd shown himself willing to acquiesce to her every desire. He had taken charge when needed, but he'd given her the opportunity to be in control of herself and even in control of him, at all other times.

But there were other things that had to be considered. She'd seen Brandon's face when he looked at baby Michael, seen his joy in playing with little Matt, and the tenderness with which he interacted with the children at the shelter.

"Brandon." She leaned forward to whisper close to his ear, not wanting the brothers to hear this. "I would like to say yes."

Wise man. He didn't leap on the statement as an acceptance. "I hear the 'but,' Arden."

"But… I'm afraid we're both too controlling."

His face whitened. "That's not the truth. We're perfect together. We'll fight for control some; I'm sure of it. But we'll learn to compromise or we'll find ways around things, like having Rick drive when we go out. Just like we do now. That wouldn't change if we married. So, what the fuck is telling you to say no?"

For the first time in a long time, she couldn't control her physical reaction. Her gaze turned unerringly to where Dex deftly changed the baby's diaper.

Brandon snorted. He lowered his voice as the others seemed to raise theirs, creating a cover of jovial chat. "You don't like Dex and Trick and Terry? No. That's not it. You're not judgmental. The baby bothers you. Why?"

With a shaking hand she brushed the tears from her eyes, her voice so soft he had to lean even closer to hear. "I meant it when I said I couldn't have children. And if anyone was meant to father children, Brandon, it's you. Do you think I don't see the way you look at them? Babies, young children like Matt, even the teens at the shelter. You were meant to have children, Brandon."

"That's it?"

"They're adorable, and I love them, but if you want babies…" She hated the feeling of inadequacy that swamped her, hated feeling less than confident in her ability to provide whatever Brandon needed.

"Shush, woman. I raised three brothers! I am not marrying you to turn you into a baby machine. I thought we could actually volunteer to be foster parents, but we can talk about that later."

"But you love kids."

He wrapped an arm around her shaking shoulders. "I do. I especially love when their parents take them home. But not as much as I love you. I'm thirty-nine-years old. If I wanted to have kids at any time in the past twenty years, I would have. I did my part with babies when Mischa was born. I played father to Dan as a rebellious teen and Terry as an adolescent who was eager to fit in. Now, I want to do something just for me. I want to spend the rest of my life with you, spoiling our nieces and nephews and sending them home high on sugar to torment their parents. Will you?"

Shivering, she smiled, and brushed her lips along his jaw. "One more thing. Did you propose to me here and now to manipulate me into saying yes?" She was sure he hadn't now.

"No. I proposed to you here and now because it was the least likely scenario. I'm not an exhibitionist as a rule. I just wanted to surprise you, and... um," He ducked his head shyly. "I wanted to prove I could change, could act out of character."

Arden laughed. "Well, surprise certainly covers it."

"Are you going to put him out of his misery anytime soon, Doctor?" Dan's harsh voice broke into the intimate hush of their conversation. She hadn't had much contact with Dan, but sensed the secrets that guided his behavior were as deeply hidden as Brandon's had been.

"Yes. Yes, I am, and yes, yes, I will marry you."

Brandon continued to study her expectantly. He raised her hand to his lips and kissed each knuckle lightly. "And?"

"And I love you." Her voice rang in the sudden moment of silence before congratulations spilled out from all corners of the room.

EPILOGUE

It was a glorious sunny day in Southern California, and once again, the outdoor entertainment area at Donovan and Mischa's house was pressed into use by the Blake brothers and their friends. An enticing array of food created by Mischa and the twins made a lovely buffet. A tuxedo-clad bartender served beverages to the guests, and garlands of white and pink flowers draped over every available surface.

Everything had been arranged for a traditional wedding ceremony. Rows of folding chairs stood in neat lines along the green grass; a makeshift altar waited in front of the trees. Guests were seated and lilting music drifted in the air from hidden speakers.

Brandon and Arden stood, hands clasped together in front of the altar, waiting to speak the vows they had written. Brandon's brothers looked on. Terry smiled widely, holding baby Michael in his lap. Trick and Dex sat beside him in the first row of chairs, smiling genuinely at Brandon as they cooed at the baby and rested their heads on Terry's shoulders. Mischa, Donovan, and Matthew sat on the opposite side, Donovan with his arm around the weeping Mischa's shoulders. Matthew awkwardly patted his father's arm and cast longing eyes at the buffet tables. Dan, mischief maker extraordinaire, sat next to Matthew, looking a bit astonished. Occasionally his gaze roved the crowd of studio employees, actors, actresses, and family friends. From being one of a band of unmarried brothers, he had become, within a relatively short time, the odd man out, the bachelor uncle to a growing family.

At the altar, Brandon patted his pocket nervously. He and Arden had decided not to exchange rings, but he'd gotten her one anyway. He hoped she liked it enough and understood the message he wanted to convey enough that she forgave him for it. When the judge indicated that they should exchange rings, Brandon saw Arden reach into the bodice of her white suit and pull something out.

She'd bought him a ring too? They held their hands out toward one another, hands clenched in identical fists. As their friends and family watched, each turned their hands over and slowly uncurled their fingers.

It was obvious to all the viewers that rings were not being exchanged, and Brandon laughed as Arden gasped. He looked into her sparkling blue eyes, and then back again to their hands. Arden held a tiny silver keychain, and on the chain were the keys to her car. Overwhelmed with pleasure, he picked up the key chain from her palm and replaced it with the diamond heart keychain that held his car keys.

"Arden, baby, you can drive my car whenever you like."

Arden laughed and threw her arms around his neck, whispering the same into his ear just before their lips met in a scorching kiss. Dan's catcalls at last penetrated the fog of lust, and Brandon raised his head to find his family smiling broadly, and Matthew blushing fiercely. He turned back to Arden to see her staring at baby Michael in concern.

"We're not going to worry about that, anymore. You're all I

need. I love you." Pleased to see his bride smiling and happy again, Brandon looped her hand through his arm and led her through the crowd, stopping to chat with people along the way. He kept his eye out for the elusive Dan and finally spied his errant brother slipping out the door of the house about a half hour later.

"I'll just be a moment, my dear," he murmured, handing Arden off to her behemoth of a brother.

He caught up to Dan at the refreshment table, aware that Arden and Bastian followed closely behind. "Danny. Did you bring a special guest to my wedding?"

Dan's slight flush was as novel as it was amusing. "The person we talked about is here."

"But you aren't going to introduce us to *him*?"

"Fuck. If you know it's a him, then you know there's no need for that." Dan strode off as Arden and Bastian caught up with him. Arden gave him a curious glance.

"Nothing." He dismissed, watching Dan stop to flirt with a buxom brunette. "Just making sure Dan understood what needs to be done while we're away on our honeymoon."

He ignored Arden's unconvinced smile, and took her hand in his again.

They ambled through the crowds of guests, chatting, laughing, and enjoying the company of their family and friends.

Author Biography

I wish I had some dramatic tale of daring do and adventure to share, but at the same time, I can promise you that I write about love because it's been the greatest adventure of my life. That's what you'll find in the fiction I write, real people who lead real lives and find real love. I spent a lot of time writing during my college years, and fourteen years teaching grammar and composition to junior high school students exposed me to more forms of writing, editing, and proofreading than I thought possible. I have taught creative writing, served as faculty editor of the school newspaper, even took a turn or three at being yearbook advisor, and had the privilege of guiding some truly gifted children into the writing world. Somehow, though, I found myself writing more for the classroom, and not writing the romantic poetry and stories that inspired me to major in English in the first place. With my retirement from the teaching profession, I have rediscovered the joy of storytelling, and the essential urge to put the stories on paper.

Relocating from the crazy pace of life in Southern California's Orange County to the beautiful and leisurely atmosphere of the

Illinois countryside has given me the time to indulge my desire to write. Readers can find out more about me and my writing by visiting me at my blog, http://leebrazilauthor.blogspot.com/ or finding me on Face Book at http://www.facebook.com/ profile.php?id=100001551666797 or feel free to drop me a line at lee.brazil@ymail.com.

CPSIA information can be obtained at www.ICGtesting.com
Printed in the USA
LVOW11s2051031114

411809LV00001B/162/P